THE
CONFESSION

THE
CONFESSION

CHARLOTTE BIGLAND

First published in Great Britain in 2023 by

 embla books

Bonnier Books UK Limited
4th Floor, Victoria House, Bloomsbury Square, London, WC1B 4DA
Owned by Bonnier Books
Sveavägen 56, Stockholm, Sweden

A CIP catalogue record for this book is available from the British Library.

ISBN: 9781471415678

This book is typeset using Atomik ePublisher

Embla Books is an imprint of Bonnier Books UK
www.bonnierbooks.co.uk

For Harry and Matthew.

Chapter One

At the start of the evening, I hugged Joe's warm, whole body. Now I'm dragging it – cold and broken – from the river.

We're damp, from the water and from the sticky red . . . from the slick crimson . . . from the blood that seeps from his head. Rocks are hard against my back and my feet scramble as I try to drag him up and onto the shore. Tears are streaming from my eyes, which is simultaneously helpful and not; further hindering my rescue attempt, but at least obscuring my view of his . . . his protruding bones, raw gash, flesh and blood . . . blood . . .

I scream into the night. My scream chases away other sounds: the distant shrieking of Courtney and Devlin, the rush of water as I finally haul him from it. The gasping of some middle-aged woman, gawping at us and filming the whole sorry episode.

'HELP!' I yell at her. 'I think he's . . . I think he's . . .'

He's still alive. Please. My younger brother. Eighteen today. Eighteen, not out, not gone, not over. My head lolls against the muddy shore as exhaustion seizes me. Above us is the bridge from which he fell.

Fell?

The dark sky flashes red, for an instant. I recall hands on Joe's back, recall seeing Callum up there with him, a brief scuffle before Joe dropped fifty metres into shallow water.

Fell?

No.

Pushed.

And Callum? My other brother is human fog: intangible and unreal somehow. I look for him; can't see him. I push myself up onto my elbows, and twist my head from side to side, scanning Middlesbrough's industrial skyline, trying to spot my murderous brother through the dark, through my tears.

1

He's gone. The woman with the phone has disappeared too. I squeeze Joe's damp jacket and drag him further up, not daring to move my fingers from under his armpits, incapable of allowing them to shift further round, to check for a heartbeat I'm not sure is there.

I need to administer CPR. I need to administer CPR to a broken, bloody face I can't bear to look at.

There are footsteps from the path which runs along the river, and I look towards the noise as a man and his dog appear a couple of dozen metres from us. Relief floods my body. Help. Finally, someone I can rely on to help.

'It's Joe! Please, need an ambulance or help me and he's all . . . he's so cold and so wet and . . .' and so broken and so heavy and so . . . empty and heavy all at once.

'PLEASE!' I scream. The dog barks. The man's face is in shadow but I imagine it hardening, until it becomes reminiscent not of flesh and familiarity, but of stone, or ice. Impenetrable. I thought I knew him. I thought he would help. 'PLEASE! PLEASE! Please! Please. Please . . . please . . . please . . .'

He leaves and it's just me and Joe. Joe's blood on my palms, palms which grow brave and travel to the shattered parts of him I don't want to acknowledge now exist. I try in vain to hold my broken brother together.

Chapter Two

There's blood under my nails, in the cracks of my knuckles and across my left cheek: a streak which is now dark and crusty, more reminiscent of mud. My shoulder-length curly hair has become slick with grease, so that whenever I catch sight of myself in a mirror, I'm reminded of a seagull dipped in oil. I'm still wearing the same clothes. Denim dungarees. A check shirt which has served me well, for it seems to be concealing grime in the way that bus or Tube seats are designed to. Or at least, that's what I think. The police officer opposite me crumples her nose in what must be disgust.

Two days and ten hours ago I'd have been embarrassed. Now I couldn't give a shit.

'Thank you for joining us today, Elizabeth. I appreciate this must be very hard for you,' says the other police officer, the one proving slightly better at concealing the fact I smell like a long-abandoned fish supper. Salty. Rancid. 'Please can you state your full name and occupation?'

My gaze flickers between the two of them: generic middle-aged woman, generic slightly younger woman. I wonder whether the younger one sees her future in the older one, whether she's happy about the direction in which her life is heading, whether she might be pushed to her death before getting the chance to follow the mundane projection of her life into reality.

'You already know my name,' I say, looking at the spot between their two heads. Grey bit of wall. Nothing.

'It's for the witness statement.'

'Right. Elizabeth. Elizabeth Mandeville. What was the second bit? Occupation? Don't . . . I don't . . . just finished uni. Used to work at a pub. Nothing at the moment.'

Nothing. The grey wall of nothing blurs.

'And please can you confirm your relationship with Joseph Karev?' asks one of the police officers. I'm not sure which. I'm not sure it matters.

'Half-brother.'

'OK. We are going to make this as pain free as possible, Elizabeth, I promise. Please can you start by telling me what you saw on the evening of the 18th of August?'

I nod. 'Yes. I saw my brother Joe being murdered.'

The officers exchange a glance so fleeting I might have missed it if I didn't feel I was floating, detached from my flesh – a blank, omnipresent being within these four grey walls. The look is loaded with cynicism.

'My witness statement is that Joe was murdered,' I repeat.

'OK, I'm listening, Elizabeth,' says the old one or maybe the young one. 'Can you tell us about that in more detail?'

'Mmm. Yes. Of course. Courtney and Devlin, his . . . well I'm not sure you could call them his friends . . . had been . . .' I pause. My memory sloshes. Sticky and impenetrable. I frown in concentration. 'They'd been horrible to Joe all night. And it was his birthday but they'd still . . . they'd still been so mean.'

My memories from the early evening are clearest. I bite my bottom lip as I think back to a couple of days ago. It couldn't have been described as a birthday party. The atmosphere was too sour, too tense, and even if it hadn't been – five people probably can't be classed as anything more than a gathering. Still, it had felt so good to see Joe. It had been hard to pinpoint the changes in him. He'd grown taller and smaller simultaneously, limbs stretched long but torso like dough, not yet strong enough to hold him all together. There was a new wiriness to him, though. A slender brawniness which I imagined made him even faster than he already was. His face was still boyish, cheeks still chubby, still ruddy, but his eyes seemed deeper set: currants pushed into the flesh of his face – more observant, more nervous. He'd hugged me, squeezed some life back into my aching muscles.

'After a few hours, Courtney and Devlin told him to climb to the top of the Transporter Bridge,' I say. The bridge was just minutes from where we were drinking. It's Middlesbrough's landmark – a large blue structure that stretches from the north bank of the Tees to the south. It reaches high into the sky, and the criss-cross pattern of the metal has always made it a tantalising prospect for daredevils.

'And then . . .' I continue to thumb through my recollection of the evening, but it's like reading a book laminated with syrup; I keep getting stuck on the same page. 'And then Callum . . . Callum was up there with him and pushed him from the bridge. I know that bit. That's the bit I know for sure. And I know I tried to save Joe. Alone.'

The police officers nod.

'That must have been traumatic for you, Elizabeth.'

I seem to come back to myself, focusing on the older police officer for the first time. Her eyes are a rusty brown colour, bloodshot and slightly droopy, like a bloodhound's.

'No,' I say. 'No. It was traumatic for Joe.'

'Yes. Of course.'

'Could you estimate the distance between the top of the bridge and where you were standing?' asks the younger police officer.

'Mmm.' I draw a diagonal line in the air with one finger, as if that has any chance of helping. Blood has seeped so far beneath my nail, I'm not sure it will ever wash out. My finger shakes. 'I was maybe fifty metres from the bridge. And the bridge is maybe fifty metres tall. And Joe and Callum were at the top of it. Pythagoras did something to help you figure out the other bit. I can't remember it.'

'OK, so it would be fair to say you were quite a distance away?'

I bristle, once again feeling more connected to my physical being than I have since the fall. 'No. That wouldn't be fair to say.'

'Tell me,' says the older officer, sounding disconcertingly similar to the younger officer, 'what was visibility like at the time of the incident?'

'It was dark,' I say. 'But it's not like we all stumble around blindly as soon as night sets in, is it? I could see fine.'

'It's not a well-lit area though.'

She's right. But honestly, fuck the holes they're trying to poke in my account, so I say, 'I've always found it very well lit.'

They exchange another cynical glance. I try to fix my gaze on the nothing grey wall, but the police officers seem to be merging, the fibres of their flesh stretching out across the air between them, knitting together to become one inquisitive beast.

'Do you wear glasses, Elizabeth?'

'No. I'm renowned for my excellent vision.'

The officer nods slowly, as if she thinks what I've just said is ridiculous.

'People are renowned for having excellent singing voices. Why shouldn't I be renowned for hawk-like vision?' I ask.

I'm being an arsehole. I'm being an arsehole to two people who are trying to help me. But the truth is, they'll never be able to help me enough. Regardless of the questions I answer, the details I give them, they will never bring Joe back.

I clear my throat, as if challenging them to argue, but they don't. They merely look solemn and hand me a tissue.

'What's this for?' I ask, gazing at it.

'For your . . . for your eyes, Elizabeth.'

I push it in the general direction of my eye sockets. The bodies of the police officers separate.

'We haven't been able to find Joe's phone. Did you see it on the night he died?' asks the officer who just handed me the tissue.

I pause for a second before saying, 'No. Maybe it fell into the water.'

She nods and makes a note while I run my fingers across the desk. They leave a couple of flakes of dried blood in their wake.

'I'm sorry if this is uncomfortable,' says the older officer, her bloodhound eyes fixed on my face. 'But you were drunk when you were picked up by the ambulance. Do you remember how many drinks you'd had?'

The flesh of my cheeks heats up, until they're so hot that any wayward tears will surely evaporate.

'Two drinks. Perhaps three,' I say, leaving out an extra zero and a number of other details. The fact I numbed myself with cider on the train journey from Newcastle to Middlesbrough, terrified at the prospect of seeing Callum for the first time in years, even more terrified by the prospect of bumping into Mam and my stepdad, Liev. That my insides felt scrambled from being dumped by my ex, that my hands were shaking even more than they are currently, so that I spilt sticky liquid down my jacket every time I went to take a drink.

'You know, we're not trying to blame you, Elizabeth,' says the younger officer. 'We just want to know as much about the incident as possible.'

'I know you're not blaming me,' I say. 'You're blaming Callum, I hope?'

Neither officer answers. Their uniform starts to knit itself back together, back into a single organism that can't be reasoned with.

'Have you interviewed Callum?' I press. 'Have you interviewed Courtney, Devlin?'

'We're interviewing everyone we think might be able to help.'

'Help? *Help*? What do you . . . what you're . . . ?' I search the organism for clues. A single set of lips, stretched into a hard line. Two eyes: one brown, one blue. 'You can't go to Callum for help. You have to go to Callum to arrest him.'

'We're gathering as much information about Joe's accident as we can.'

My heart pounds at that word. *Accident.* 'You've already interviewed them, haven't you?' I ask. 'And that's what they say? That it was an accident?'

'I'm afraid we can't give that sort of information away.'

'And you *believe* them?' I writhe in my seat, gripped by the sudden terror that the truth is going to be discarded. Callum Mandeville, my charming older brother, has already pulled the wool over the eyes of the officers. Two blue, two bloodshot brown. No, one blue, one bloodshot brown. No, just one . . . just the one eye.

I blink.

'But you need to interview other people. Other people who won't lie about Joe's death being accidental. There was a woman with a phone, have you interviewed her? And a dog walker, he'll have contacted you? He must have contacted you?'

'Elizabeth, we know this is very hard for you. You've suffered a terrible loss. Have you got somewhere safe to stay tonight?'

I shake my head. 'What does that matter? We're not done here? We can't be done here?'

They close their notepads and put the lids back on their pens.

'We'll be in touch if we need anything further from you. You've done a great job. Joseph would be proud.'

I'm overcome by the same helplessness I felt on the banks of the river. My fingers have curled, as if they're holding on to Joe's soaking jacket. I flinch, feeling slippery rocks press into my back.

'Please,' I say. 'Please.'

The officer in front of me morphs further, until it's just a black uniform, which becomes a black sky, a blue bridge and Callum staring down at me.

Chapter Three

Kayin works nights, so this is when I return to Newcastle, to throw some of my things into a suitcase, safe in the knowledge I won't bump into my flatmate. I check into the cheapest hotel I can find in Middlesbrough, not wanting to give myself any extra enjoyment at a time like this. Still, for the sake of others, I give myself a thorough wash, squirting shower gel onto my fingertips and trying to rub it beneath my nails.

I bin the denim dungarees and the check shirt. Today is Joe's . . . it's Joe's . . . today is the day I'm going to be in the same space as Callum and Courtney and Devlin. Today is the day that the guilty will be held accountable.

I slink into a pew at the back of the church, and scan the pitiful cluster of people who've gathered for Joe's thing. Mam and Liev, of course, sitting front and centre, Mam's hair freshly bleached for the occasion, her sobs coming at oddly consistent intervals. A couple of teachers, the sad, grey-looking ones who evidently have nothing better to do. A handful of Joe's classmates, whispering about football scores and where they'll be drinking after. Courtney's long, dark ponytail is among them. So is Devlin's shaved skull.

No Callum, though. I'd been certain he'd come, certain I might finally get a chance to talk to him. My body tenses as I recall the eight and a half years since he left home, left Joe, left me, and never looked back. The lengths I'd gone to try to find him. An address, a phone number, a job, something, *anything* that might reunite me with my older brother.

I glance around the church again, eyes lingering on the shadowy corners. What the police officers said – about my being drunk, it being dark, Joe and Callum being distant – has been playing on my mind. For, despite Callum being a stranger to me now, I'm still finding it hard to truly believe he pushed Joe.

I need to talk to him. I'd been certain that this would be my chance. But nothing. He's not here. He's left me and Joe alone again. What kind of person doesn't come to his own brother's funeral?

'The kind of person who could push their brother to his death,' I whisper.

Insults I might use to puncture Callum's impenetrable wall of indifference start to bubble up inside me instead, threatening to turn on me, as I feel more and more stupid for believing he'd show.

The saffron smell of incense adds an extra push to my already turbulent stomach, and I dash from the church, vomiting into a pot of magnolias just outside the large oak doors. I move away a little and vomit again, this time next to a black Ford I think might belong to Mam and Liev. And a final, pathetic puke against the red brick of the church. A sinful action, probably. Ensuring that hell is where I go, whenever my own time runs out.

There's a board to the side of the church, and it's been decorated with pictures of Joe. An object I was incapable of looking at when I first arrived, but one I'm drawn to now. I stretch my hand out to the shiny film of an old picture showing me holding baby Joe, all wrapped up in white blankets. My lips are brushing his forehead, as if I'm making a promise to protect him.

My fingers trail the different Joes in the pictures: chubby toddler, adventurous child, thoughtful adolescent. The changes in his body but the sense that his character remained the same: sweet and curious and caring. I might have vowed to look after him, but he did his fair share of looking after me.

More. More than his fair share. The love between us feels suddenly skewed; he's dead and I'm alive. I didn't look after the bundle in the white blankets. I didn't look after him at all.

I turn away from the board and breathe deeply, in the hope doing so might calm me. If I can't speak to Callum, I need to speak to Courtney and Devlin. Ideally, I need to approach them in a cool, collected manner, but already I can feel the first beats of hysteria fluttering in my chest. They lied to the police. I'm almost certain of it.

There's a clack as the church doors open. I turn in their direction, readying myself to follow Courtney and Devlin. But they're not among Joe's classmates, who are louder now, talking about happy hour at Macy Brown's and how many goals Akpom scored that weekend. Mam and Liev follow them out. I got their car right; they start heading towards the sick-splattered Ford, and the first genuine smile of the day (scrap that – week, scrap that – month) crosses my lips.

It disappears as quickly as it emerged. Mam has spotted me. I tug a dark curl across my forehead, as if to conceal my identity. It's hard to read her expression, the result of a face artificially pulled in a dozen different directions – wrinkled by age and excessive sunbed use, tightened by questionable Botox. She strides across the car park, Liev a few paces behind.

'Elizabeth . . .' she says slowly, making my nine-letter name sound even longer than it already is. 'I didn't think you were here.'

'Of course I'm here.'

We're both wearing leather jackets. But where mine is oversized and most likely belonged to a man at some point, hers is cropped and rhinestone encrusted. I wait for a cutting remark, but nothing arrives. Instead, she takes me into her arms and hugs me tight. And she smells of Joe. Predominantly, she smells of Juicy Couture and watermelon vape, but under that she smells of Joe. The sour cream that my step-nan would lather over everyone's syrniki, and the peach house spray Mam would subsequently use to try to cover it up. The vanilla smell of the detergent she uses on his clothes. *Used* on his clothes. The remaining mourners blur into one ominous shape as tears form.

We unstick from one another, and I wipe my cheeks, desperate not to let Liev see signs of weakness. He steps forward and rests his hand on Mam's waist. I step back in time with him, towards the photographs of Joe, hoping to draw a little strength from them, perhaps.

'Alright?' he asks. He smiles, and I'm sure he means it to be comforting, but there's something off about his teeth: they're too small, too far apart, perhaps. His smile always sets me on edge.

'I . . . I don't know.'

He nods. Years of sedentary bus driving have taken a toll on his body. He always had a thick chest, broad shoulders, but now he has the belly to go with them, making his legs seem ridiculous in comparison, hardly thick enough to hold him up. The right side of his face is more weathered than the left, and his eyes have a glazed quality, as if he's waved one too many pensioners onto the 297. His brown hair has been in retreat since the day we met him (something Callum and I would mock relentlessly, silently) and yet – unbelievably – it's still not embarrassing enough to justify shaving off.

'Heading back up to Newcastle?' he asks.

'I'm at Haverton Hill Hotel, actually. Just for one more night, I think.'

His smile stretches wider, and I'm treated to a view of yet more of his small teeth. 'What, you and all the contractors?'

It's a joke, I think, a joke about my working men's choice of hotel. And yet the concept of Liev making a joke is so alien, it's hard not to read it as a threat.

'Yeah. Going to head back there now.'

'What? To have a pint and natter about the price of timber?'

I look past Liev, to his car, wishing I'd done a more thorough job with my sick. All the mourners have disappeared. I've missed Courtney and Devlin. I turn to leave, to try to find them, but Mam's hand grips my wrist. For a few seconds, she doesn't say anything, and it takes me a moment to realise that she's staring past me, transfixed by the photos of Joe. There's something lost and frozen in her expression, an emotion I recognise not as being caused by Botox but by grief. A longing to exist anywhere but our current reality. A need to immerse herself in the pictures, in a time when Joe wasn't a body in a box. I recognise her expression because it's one I relate to on a soul-crushing level.

Mam blinks and then turns to me.

'Come back with us. Just for a cuppa,' she says. I look down. Three red acrylic nails are squeezing into my flesh. The other two nails are bare and chipped, and I know how much this must bother her. 'Please, Elizabeth. We lost Joe. I can't lose you, too.'

She lost me a while ago, I think. But her over-plump lips are set in a desperate smile, as though she's genuine, as though she wants me as much as I used to want her. I scan her face, resisting the urge to look into her eyes. Her eyes are big, brown. Her eyes are Joe's eyes. As soon as I look into them, I'm fucked, destined to do whatever she asks of me.

The road from the church to Mam and Liev's house isn't long, and I know every inch of it. I know each curl of barbed wire, each dust-covered bus shelter, each terraced house. I know where each pothole is, the depth of each one, the way water shimmers within them if you catch the sun at the right angle. I know the twist and slope of every cooling tower and chimney, the exact moment you'll smell the salt of the river, hear the cries of the sky rats swooping above it.

Liev parks outside their end-of-terrace house. It's between the train track and the river. A quiet spot, but for the ever-present hum of machinery from the industrial estate. Industry is quieter than humans, I think. Industry doesn't have vocal cords for screaming, bones for cracking, organs for squelching. It doesn't—

'You getting out? You've gone dead white.'

I look up. Liev is holding the car door open, watching me with a renewed sharpness in his eyes. I'm reminded once more of Callum's departure, the way Liev's attention shifted from him to me. With a small shudder, I nod and clamber out of the car and into their house.

Enemy territory. A place I've entered only a handful of times since leaving for uni four years ago. Not much has changed since my last visit. It's still decorated in the style of the only book Mam's ever read: *Fifty Shades of Grey*. Not bondage and whips, thank God, but nearly every tone of charcoal – from the crushed velvet sofa to the mirrored coffee table to the heart-shaped photo frames to the mural on the wall that reads (what else?) *Live, Laugh, Love*.

'Shoes off,' says Mam. She's house-proud, in the way that people who don't have much often are. I don't begrudge her this, for trying to extend the life of décor which was once nice and is slowly ceasing to be so. I slide my trainers off and perch on the edge of the crushed velvet armchair. I wriggle my toes, fighting the urge to escape, the knowledge that I really don't want to be here. Not in this house. Not so close to where Joe . . .

I'm distracted by the cup of tea that Mam hands over. She sits next to Liev and I clutch the mug hard and make myself take a sip, though it's still too hot. Mam takes a puff of her vape. I read it as a nervous puff, though her expression doesn't change. Liev licks his lips and tilts his glass of cranberry juice back and forth, so that the red liquid shifts under light cast by the setting sun. Illuminating his sobriety. Lording it over us. Over me.

'I really fucking tried to save him,' I say, when I can bear the silence no longer.

'Aye. Shame you were pissed,' says Liev, tilting the glass again.

Coming back with them was a mistake. If it was just Mam and me, it might be OK. Without Liev watching us, perhaps we'd embrace once more, let our bodies fold heavy into one another, share our pain. But Liev is clutching her hand. A vice-like grip that I've never been able to crack.

I go to set down my mug, but Liev is quicker, bringing his glass down hard on the coffee table. If Mam could raise her eyebrows, I'm sure she would, as a drop of cranberry juice splashes onto the mirrored surface. It's not a violent action, but my heart flutters and my hands twitch.

'His death being recorded as an accident is bullshit,' says Liev.

'Yes. Yes, yes.' It's as though I've spent the past week banging against a locked door and someone has finally answered. 'It wasn't an accident.' I say it again, 'I'm almost certain it wasn't an accident.'

I look to Mam, half concealed by a cloud of her own creation. She bats it away and says, 'So what really happened? Because once we arrived, it was too late. And the police have been vague. Joe just fell. Joe just climbed up to the top and he fell, apparently.'

'Not what happened,' I say, once again finding myself angry that the police have dismissed Joe's death so easily. I shake away what they said about my vision and judgement being obscured and say, 'Me, Devlin, Courtney and Callum were on the riverbank. We ate sausage rolls and donuts. Drank. Did you . . . what did you think of Courtney and Devlin?'

'Devlin came round a bit. I'd met Courtney once or twice,' Mam says.

'Good kids,' adds Liev, and I almost laugh – of course, old bully likes young bullies.

'I don't think they were Joe's friends,' I say.

'No?'

'No.'

Joe had taken on a role he'd had since infancy in their presence: performing monkey. They'd dared him to do stupid, cruel things: eat grass, lick a slug, pour vodka into his nose. His reward would be Courtney's peals of laughter, Devlin's shouts that Joe was a 'mad man! Complete nutta, like!' It made me uncomfortable. Made me drink quicker. I should have said something. Should have stood up for my little brother, but I was four years out of practice, and my world had been wobbly for a couple of hours by that point.

'And what was Callum doing in all this?' Mam asks.

Callum was doing Callum. He was there, and he wasn't.

'He introduced himself to Courtney and Devlin – all charm and swagger, you know. He barely said two words to me,' I say, heart aching. I remember watching him, desperate for something: an apology for disappearing, his seal of approval, an explanation for why he hadn't kept in touch, some indication that he missed me. A hint that he'd loved me as fiercely as I'd loved him in childhood.

A small smile. The sensation that he was looking through me. That's all I got.

'Sounds normal enough,' says Liev, and I turn my attention back to him. 'Now, where's the big reveal? What's the real reason my son's dead?'

I take a shaking sip of tea. My memories of the night might be sticky and translucent, but they're also agonising. The syrup-smeared book is hot to the touch, burning off a little of my flesh each time I return to it.

'It . . .' I start and then stop. Mam sets her vape down. She reaches over the coffee table and takes my hand.

'What happened?' she asks.

I shake my head.

'What happened?' All five of the red acrylic nails on the hand gripping me are intact. I feel each squeeze into my flesh. I stare down at the blood-red daggers instead of answering.

'Fuck!' She releases me and bangs her fist on the table. 'Fuck. Fuck.'

15

There's a picture of Joe in school uniform next to her vape. She turns the star-shaped frame so it's facing down. Picks up her vape and takes a drag. Sets it down and grabs at the picture frame, squeezing the image of Joe into her chest.

I need to start talking.

'It got dark. Got a bit colder. I guess Courtney and Devlin got bored. They dared Joe to climb to the top of the Transporter Bridge. Joe was next to me and then he wasn't,' I say. 'He was suddenly at the top of the bridge. Courtney and Devlin were laughing and jeering. And . . .'

I take a breath. The sensation of wanting to turn back the clock is overwhelming. It's the only thing that occupies my mind. A sickening craving to jump back to the past and do things differently.

A month ago would do.

Three weeks ago. I could still have stopped things three weeks ago.

Less than two weeks ago. Ten days and fifteen hours ago. Looking up at Joe shaking at the top of the bridge. That was my last chance.

'And then I saw Callum up there with him.' I take another deep breath. 'And I know it was dark, and I know I was drunk, but I . . . I think Callum pushed Joe off.'

I expect outrage from the pair on the crushed velvet sofa. But they react in much the same way the police did. They look sceptical.

'Lord knows, Callum made my life hell, but he loved Joe,' says Mam, shaking her head.

I don't know how to reply to that, because I spent years of my life believing the same thing. Despite everything, my brothers loved one another. It had been a truth I'd never questioned. But Mam and Liev arrived too late – in a blur with an ambulance I'm not sure who called. They didn't see what I did.

'I can't believe it either,' I say, the pitch of my voice rising. 'But it's what I saw.'

'Doesn't seem unbelievable to me,' says Liev, his disposition shifting. Darkening. He rubs a small scar above his eyebrow. 'Knew he was a bad egg the day I met him. Remember how he'd bite me, Kim? Remember how hard I tried with him, how he'd burn my shirts and scratch the paintwork off our cars? Only ever tried to be a father to him. But he was a dangerous kid and he's become a dangerous man.'

Mam opens her mouth, and for a second, I think she might defend her eldest child. Not a chance; we've always played second fiddle to the man in her life. Instead, she says, 'But why the hell would he hurt Joe?'

It's the question I've been asking myself over and over since I saw it happen. The question which has prompted me to doubt my own eyes.

'I don't know . . .' I flounder, as my two overwhelming emotions in respect of Callum writhe within me: the love created by growing up with someone, enduring childhood and its various trials and tribulations with them, and the rejection and distrust which follows being abandoned without a second thought. 'But I've been thinking, since I can't get hold of Callum, maybe I can speak to Courtney and Devlin. See if they remember things the way I do. See if they were lying about Joe's fall being an accident. Or actually . . .'

I pause, remembering the way my face had felt as I'd watched Joe fall, stretched into a dozy smile of disbelief, even as he'd hit the shallow water. I recall the length of time it took for horror to flood my body, and I recall, too, the frustrating sensation of being watched but not helped.

I drink my tea in one continuous gulp, enjoying the pain of the hot liquid sliding down my throat. And then I say, 'A woman filmed it all. This is what we need. Concrete proof of what happened.'

A desperate, manic excitement grips me, emotions which evidently aren't felt by Liev, for he snorts and says, 'Like hell are we going to find this mysterious woman.'

My excitement ebbs. I don't reply. I can't reply; I've a vague recollection of her bobbed hair and sour face, I'm not sure I'd recognise her if she passed me in the street.

'You know where we might find her?' says Mam, picking her phone up from the coffee table. 'I'll have a look through the *Spotted: Middlesbrough* Facebook page. Always loads of busybodies posting on that. Some of them even go out looking for anti-social behaviour just so they have something to post.'

She stands up and then squats down beside me, and I can't help but focus on her hand, hoping it might find its way onto mine. This desire is fleeting, and wanes when we start the long process of scrolling through the Facebook page, past endless posts advertising sweet and bath bomb businesses, looking for lost kittens or moaning about litter.

We scroll for so long that my concentration falters, and I look to Liev with a question.

'Where's Step-Nan?' I ask. It's rare to be in this house for so long and not be struck by one of her withering put-downs.

'Sleeping, most likely,' replies Liev.

'She didn't fancy her own grandson's funeral, then? I know she hates me and Callum, didn't realise she didn't care for Joe, either,' I say, a satisfying amount of venom present in my voice.

'Now then,' says Liev. 'That's not true. She loved Joe. She liked you. Callum wasn't good to her. You're just regurgitating the shite he used to chat.'

'I really—'

Liev interrupts. 'I'll go get her. Sure she'd love to see you.'

He leaves, and I turn back to Mam, still scrolling through the Facebook page. I almost tell her to stop, losing hope as we pass our fifth illustrated PICK UP YOUR DOG SHIT IN STEWART'S PARK post, when she shrieks.

'There! There it is!'

A video posted by a woman called Janet Braithwaite. The still cover shows the Transporter Bridge shrouded in darkness.

'I can't watch it,' I say.

Mam dabs at her eyes. Her voice wobbles as she says, 'We need to know what really happened.'

She's right, so I take a deep breath and press play. As the video loads, I try to pretend that I'm watching the scene behind multiple cameras, or that I'm typing it out into a script, into . . . just a make-believe story, but I . . . I'm suddenly watching Joe hurtle through the air. I shut my eyes as he crashes into the river. There's the sound of me screaming, Courtney and Devlin shrieking, and Janet tutting as the camera pans across our empty beer cans and takeaway boxes, as opposed to Joe's battered body. And then the video ends.

Damp palms and difficulty breathing. I try to calm myself, scrolling to see the accompanying caption:

**Stupid new trend for cliff diving off the Transporter Bridge!
Bloody teenage idiots! Not in my town!**

'This is bullshit,' I say. 'She's completely misrepresented it. And she
filmed so much more than this. She was filming for ages. This doesn't
tell us anything.'

'I can . . . I'll try to find out more about her,' replies Mam, clicking
on Janet's profile.

Footsteps approach from outside, and Liev re-enters the room,
clutching Step-Nan's hand with more tenderness than I'd have thought
possible. He sits her down on the sofa, lets her sink into a crushed
velvet nightmare.

She's shrivelled and hardened since I last saw her, as if the wrinkles
in her flesh couldn't even be ironed out these days. But her gaze is
distant, focused somewhere beyond me, between fake silver roses
and glittery candles.

I open my mouth, planning on berating her for not attending
Joe's funeral, but Liev speaks before I can.

'You be nice, Elizabeth. Her mind isn't all it once was.' A look
passes between him and Mam, before he adds, 'She needs treating
gently, these days.'

I almost laugh, for 'gentle' isn't a word I've ever associated with
Step-Nan. But there is something different about her – her lips are
slightly parted, her eyes are half closed, as though she's been powered
off, as though she's slowly shutting down. I'm certain I'm not just
parroting Callum's opinions of her; I, too, recall her as an embittered
woman who'd seemed permanently fuming to have inherited two
step-grandchildren. For as long as I've known her (from the age
of four – far too many years, in my opinion), she's been almost
amusingly horrible: gifting Callum and me presents which seemed
to get worse as the years went by. Revision books for subjects we
weren't even sitting. Free toothbrushes from a coach trip she'd taken.
A roll of clingfilm. 'It's perforated clingfilm,' I remember her telling
me, rolling her r's. 'From Sainsbury's.' I'd rolled my eyes at Callum,
and she'd seen me, given me a sharp slap across the chops. A swollen
cheek for being cheeky.

But what now? Has age softened her into a near lifeless shell, or are my own memories inaccurate?

'You're not still scrolling, are you?' Liev asks Mam, and my focus shifts from Step-Nan.

'Yes,' says Mam. I watch as she clicks through Janet's profile pictures.

'There's no need, like,' Liev says. 'Callum pushed Joe. I know he did. You don't need to track down lying witnesses.'

I shake my head. 'You can't know that for sure.'

'I saw him,' Liev says. 'About a month before Joe's death.'

'What?' I say.

Liev sits up a little straighter. He clears his throat and says, 'Aye. Can't say either of us were too happy to find ourselves in the same pub, like. But I try my best to be civil, went up and said hi. Said that Joe missed him, his mam missed him. That you missed him, Elizabeth.'

'You said that?'

'Of course. All been trying to get in touch with him for years, haven't we?'

'And what did he say?' I'm nervous, as though I've just asked someone out on a date and I've no idea whether they'll accept or decline.

Liev snorts. 'What d'you think? Said, in as many words, that he didn't give a fuck. That he was glad to be rid of us all. That he hadn't kept in touch for good reason.'

I'm reminded of Callum's distance at Joe's party. The fact he spent more time with Courtney and Devlin than with me. That he didn't even bother to show up to Joe's funeral.

'He was pissed, I could tell,' continues Liev. 'Slurring his words, went from zero to a hundred real quick. Brought up the arguments we'd have when he was growing up, started blaming me for everything that went wrong in his life. Said Joe was a miniature version of me. Said he was going to teach me a lesson. Get some revenge.'

My mouth opens and closes. 'Did he? Did he really?'

'Didn't think too much of it at the time, like. The ramblings of a violent alcoholic. But . . .' Liev exhales and seems to blink back tears. 'But I'm seeing it in a fresh fucking light.'

My stomach sinks. It turns, flips, churns. I look at Mam. 'Is this . . . did this happen?'

She looks not at me but at Liev, and then she says, 'Yes. That's what Callum said to him.'

'What?' The shape of the word seems to get stuck in my throat, almost as if I can feel the sharp points of the 'w' digging into my flesh. I feel lightheaded, suddenly, as if the last of any faith I had in Callum has drained from me, tipping my body out of balance. I may not be sure whether Callum loved me and Joe. But I do know that he hated Liev.

I cough. 'Fuck. Well, you . . . you have to tell the police that.'

Liev guffaws. 'Did the police listen to you? What makes you think they'll listen to me? Not a chance. Not a fucking chance. They see it as an accident. Case closed and onto the next. My whole life, the police have never helped me.'

'You have to try,' I say, but my voice is weak, wobbly.

Liev seems to growl. The buttons on his shirt strain, incapable of containing the anger which bubbles up inside him. He starts talking. About Callum. About the things Callum said in the pub, the things Callum did when he was younger, or whenever Mam tried to reach out to him. How he'd been stupid not to take Callum's threats seriously, how it made sense that Callum had finally chosen to attend one of Joe's birthdays. Liev speaks of how angry he is. What he could do. The air in the small room grows stale and hot. I watch as fumes from Mam's vape drift about, dancing between photo frames and climbing the striped wallpaper.

Liev finishes his cranberry juice but keeps the cut-glass tumbler held under his chin, as if catching all the hate foaming from his mouth, saving it for later. His eyes narrow. He licks his lips. I need to leave. I really, really need to leave.

With an effort, I haul myself from the armchair. I take a few wobbly paces to the door.

'Toilet,' I manage to mumble.

The air outside the living room is cooler. I slide down the wall and try to steady my breathing. I should slip my trainers back on and turn right, out the front door and away from an evening which is turning more agonising by the second. But I look left, up the stairs, instead. I pick myself up and start climbing.

Mam and Liev's bedroom is at the front of the house, and Joe's is at the back. Callum and I shared the attic, into which a stairlift now leads. Seems Step-Nan has finally wormed her way into the house. That'll account for Mam's fresh Botox binge – the need to hide what I imagine is near constant irritation at her mother-in-law's proximity.

It takes several attempts before I make it into Joe's room. That smell again. The smell of him. I stand in the centre of his room and squeeze my palms shut. Not in an aggressive way. Not as though I'm about to punch someone. Rather in a desperate attempt to feel something, to feel he's here once more.

It's stuffed full of memories, this room. The attic was always too cluttered with beams and boxes to play in properly, so Callum and I would head to Joe's room, spend many a rainy afternoon creating marble runs out of rulers and duct tape and bits of pipe. Or cleaning up the treasures we had found in the industrial estate, so that Mam might not notice them, and they could remain, rather than being lobbed out the window with a cry of, 'Get that effing bit of metal out of my lovely house.'

I smile at the shiny red 'Danger: Keep Out' sign, pilfered from the fence of Scott Bros, and still sitting in the corner of Joe's room. I smile at the cactus on his windowsill, the one he called 'Callum' in the hope that doing so might stop Callum from leaving. I smile at the big flannel shirt he got caught in the barbed wire outside the local Londis, as we were making off with a giant slab of chocolate. He refused to rip it, refused to leave it, more terrified about Mam's reaction to a damaged piece of clothing that was supposed to see him through to adulthood than whatever the shopkeeper might do to him. I remember the glee of freeing him and outsprinting our pursuer keenly.

I smile at two ugly wooden boxes Callum and I made in year eight engineering class – him first, me two years later. We both hated them, but Joe loved them, displaying them side by side on his desk and stuffing each with old coins and his favourite sweets. I smile at all the signs that Joe was turning into a man: four cans of Lynx aftershave and a book on whisky and his driving test certificate. And I smile at his frayed blanket and toy giraffe and collection of *Horrible History* books, all signs that he was still my baby brother.

I'm smiling that wrong, stupid smile again. Smiling so hard that tears leak onto my lips, seemingly drawn to the black hole at the centre of my face.

I wipe my mouth and pick up Joe's guitar. Pluck one of the strings and then head back downstairs.

I stick my head back into the living room while sliding on my trainers.

'I'm leaving. And I'm taking this,' I say, brandishing the guitar.

Neither Mam nor Liev object. But Liev looks at me, and I hadn't imagined it – the glint in his eyes has returned.

'Joe needs us, Elizabeth. You'll be back,' he tells me.

I shake my head.

'I won't.'

Chapter Four

I don't go back, but I don't exactly leave, either.

Haverton Hill Hotel is an isolated little contractors' hotel with a good view over surrounding industry, and a decent pub beneath the rooms. There's a chair in my room – red, a little faded, likely once belonged in the pub – and I sit on it, watching the curtains, which are half-drawn across the window, flap about in the breeze. It gets dark. It gets light. At some point I sleep, I think. There's a crick in my neck. Pins and needles in my right leg.

I go downstairs for breakfast: good old greasy stuff, served on plain, practical plates in the pub. The landlady smiles, but I don't return it. I think I'm done smiling.

Back in my room, I sit on the bed this time, a single with a thin, striped duvet. From outside, there's the trundle of distant machinery. From inside, the hum of the small fridge in the corner. And the few other inhabitants of the hotel, their voices rumbling through thin walls.

I'm back down for dinner. Back up for . . . I'm not sure. Wall staring, I suppose. And then back down for tea, the meals serving as a helpful indicator of the passage of time. I overhear tired men grunting about lorries and the cost of fuel while I shovel beans into my mouth. The men are nicer than me; they smile at the landlady.

Up. Down. Sit. Stare. Turn the box TV on and take in nothing. Push food into my mouth. I should be leaving for Newcastle, or Manchester, but I find myself handing the landlady money for an additional week: £85, which includes my evening meals. I should be moving on. I'm getting weird looks.

But I . . . I'm up the stairs, down . . . not out, never out, always here, in this hotel, among men with weary eyes and the smell of chips and gravy.

There's no desk in my room, so I drag the chair over to the half-fridge and open my laptop on top of it. I had rough plans of what I might do once I'd finished uni. The long, penny-pinching slog of trying to work in television or film, perhaps. The safer route of teaching. I type *Production Runner jobs Manchester* into Google, but my finger gets stuck above the enter key. It starts shaking. My finger, and then my hand, and then my arm. My entire body is shaking. My eyes feel wide and dry. The words on the screen, the attempt at a future for myself, seem to merge, to become indecipherable. I can blink, I know I'm capable of blinking, and yet I can't.

My lungs, heart, everything enclosed by my ribs seems to burn, making breathing hard and then impossible. I can't . . . I can't breathe.

'Huh – huuuuh.'

I push the chair away from the fridge, needing more room, needing space to breathe.

It passes eventually. I take two white pills and stand as still as I'm able.

I google-diagnose it as a panic attack, but I suppose I could google-diagnose it as near anything – cancer, an exorcism. Regardless, ten hours later, after a fitful sleep, I can still feel the attack, as if it's stuck in the back of my throat.

Joe's death seems to infiltrate me more with every passing day. I marvel at everything I do – from brushing my teeth to sprinkling sugar onto my Weetabix – with a newfound disgust. To continue as normal, to take steps to increase my wellbeing or enjoyment of something feels unimaginably inappropriate. At one point I catch myself at the window, late afternoon sun warming my skin, and feel repulsed. It takes all my willpower to not scratch my freshly warmed flesh into shreds.

I spend a number of hours googling celebrities who lost siblings at a young age, marvelling at photos of them smiling after their loss. Or the fact that the loss in question is merely a footnote in their Wikipedia pages, rather than a gaping hole at the centre.

'They are OK. I will be OK,' I say. But I don't believe myself. I don't believe any part of it. I want the person who knew me better than anyone back. I want the person I'd send book recommendations to and discuss films with. The person who would Shazam a song at the same time as me, and then laugh upon the realisation that we were preternaturally in sync. I want the person who would let me tease him about all the embarrassing things he'd said as a child, before getting me back with a reminder of the time I made brownies with salt rather than sugar, or caught nits as a teenager. I want the person who would know exactly what I mean when I reference a particular game, or place, or television show. The person who would be hit by the same flavour of nostalgia upon hearing the opening jingle of *Deadly 60*, or the particular peal of the ice-cream van which used to trawl our streets. Joe and I would never be allowed an ice-cream, but we'd hear the manic, too-fast quality of the tune, and the fact that the ice-cream man hadn't been able to get such a simple song right would lead to a shared, secret smile.

The sun still streaming in through the window reminds me of the last time Joe and I heard the tune which indicated the approach of frozen, sugary goodness. We'd been on the old swing set in the garden, far too big for something so broken – me seventeen and wishing the next year away. Joe not yet a teenager – voice still high-pitched and face still flushed from the races he'd competed in earlier that day. I'd ducked out of the library to see him zoom round the 800m competition, pipped on the line by a boy in the year above.

'Sports day next year, it'll be yours,' I'd said to him as we kicked the dry grass beneath our feet and listened to the erratic ice-cream van drive away.

'Oh, I don't know.'

'What's not to know? You're so fast. Way faster than me and Callum.'

Joe had laughed – bashful, not quite believing.

'Callum said he'd come watch me next year,' Joe had said.

I remember being hit with a fresh bolt of hurt and confusion – that Callum would occasionally text Joe but never me was something which caused me more pain than I cared to admit during my teenage years. I swallowed down the lump in my throat and said, 'Oh yeah? Well, I'll be there too.'

Joe had looked up at me, a dark curl concealing one of his eyes, but the other on show – a warm chocolate colour that seemed to gleam as he smiled.

'I know you will,' he'd said. 'And I'll always be there for you. When you graduate. When you get your first production credit. When you need help because you've fallen asleep on the bus back from town again.'

I'd laughed, for my kid brother had cycled to meet me at the wrong side of Middlesbrough more times than I could remember. 'Hey, there's something about the crazy muttering of bus people that sends me to sleep.'

The joke no longer makes me want to laugh. It makes me want to cry. The brother who was always there, taken away by the brother who never was.

I draw my curtains, shutting the sunlight out.

The grief will never go away, but I daresay I'd learn to live with it. But it's this . . . this anger. An anger so hot it makes my heart ache and tears prick my eyes. People talk about how anger affects you initially. The burning sensation that grabs hold of your heart and squeezes it, so that you view all your surroundings in a red haze. They rarely talk about how anger affects you later on. The way it relinquishes your heart but seeps through the rest of your body, infecting every cell, poisoning them. It's always with you, smouldering in the background, tainting your vision black. My anger twists with my grief, until I don't know which is which anymore. Until it doesn't matter, until I'm changed thoroughly – on a cellular basis – by both.

I take to staring at the landlady as she counts out my money or sets rice pudding down in front of me, stumped by the fact that she can't see the darkness which now pollutes me. That to her, I'm the same girl who checked in who knows how many weeks ago.

She parts her lips as if about to say something to me, and in this moment, her features seem to shift: cropped blonde hair turning to a chestnut bob peppered with silver. Soft body becoming more angular. Smile puckering into a scowl.

Back in my room, I replace the Janet Braithwaite of my imagination with the Janet Braithwaite of the internet. And there's so much of her on the internet, that her address doesn't prove hard to find. She's a busybody parish councillor, Neighbourhood Welfare volunteer and frequent dinner party host who likes to post everything, including the kitchen sink (a marble deVOL number), on her public Facebook profile. Ahh, the naivety of the middle-aged. It's almost quaint.

I return to the video she took of Joe falling, but I don't press play. Instead, I drift into a daydream, imagining seeing the video in full and having the truth confirmed in thousands of pixels: Callum pushing Joe. I imagine showing this to the police, watching their eyes widen, hearing them declare that they need to arrest Callum. I imagine the truth acknowledged in court and in the newspapers: that Joe's death wasn't a clumsy accident. That I didn't drag his dying body from the water because of his own recklessness. No. It was Callum. It was all Callum.

My first good daydream in a long time.

I exit the hotel, blinking up at a sky which seems aggressively bright, despite an abundance of cloud. I cross from north of the Tees to the south, and then catch the 28 bus to Nunthorpe, the posh part of Middlesbrough (if any part of Middlesbrough can be classified as such).

Janet's house, when I eventually reach it, leads me to the conclusion that yes, a chunk of the town is, in fact, dead upmarket. Her house has red bricks, big bay windows, a well-groomed front garden and a double garage. The whole street is lovely, to be honest, and I reckon I stick out like a sore thumb in my hoody and ripped jeans. The back of my neck tingles, as if there are eyes trained on my flesh, so I pull my hood up and lean into a sizeable oak.

My tongue pulses back and forth against the roof of my mouth, as indecision takes hold. I've toyed with the idea of attempting to orchestrate bumping into Janet in the wild, but it seems farcical. My request is simple: I'd like to be shown the video she took of my brother being pushed to his death. My approach should therefore be simple too: a knock at her door and a level-headed explanation.

I know she's home; she's been spamming Facebook with pictures of the various vegetables she's grown for the upcoming Stokesley Show. Mini-Moo, her skeletal Italian greyhound, poses among a variety of oversized root vegetables. The dog has a bigger wardrobe than mine: dinky booties, knitted jumpers and tartan bows. A particularly large parsnip wears a matching ribbon.

Once I can procrastinate no longer, I remind myself that shy bairns get nowt, and stride towards her door. I knock three times, loudly. Even with a few inches of wood between us, I hear her raised voice as she says that she'd rather I wasn't a Jehovah's Witness because she's 'a staunch believer that Jesus is part of the trinity'. I plaster a smile that I hope looks affable but not devout onto my face and wait as the door opens.

'I don't give to the homeless directly,' she says, as soon as she sees me. She's clutching her phone to her chest, as if ready to call the police or pest control on me at a moment's notice. For now, she restrains herself from doing so and adds, 'You'd only spend any money I give you on drugs.'

'Uh, I'm not—'

'I mean, I'll give you enough for a banana and perhaps a sandwich. But I only use cash on holiday, so it'll have to be Moroccan dirham or Swiss francs. You'll have to get it exchanged.'

'I'm not homeless,' I finally manage to spit out.

'Intriguing,' says Janet, her gaze moving up and down my body. 'In which case I'd advise you to return to your home.'

'No, I . . . I'm . . .' I take a breath, hoping to recoup my composure after the assault on my appearance. 'I need to speak to you. About Joseph Karev.'

'And he is?'

I pause, as the fact that Janet doesn't even know who Joe is sinks in. I'm aware that the world stops for no one, but Janet Braithwaite witnessed – no, *filmed* – his death and she doesn't even know his name. It stings.

'He's my brother.'

'A brother. How fun,' replies Janet, as if talking to a particularly unintelligent child.

'Not really. He died. A few weeks ago. And I think you can help me.'

I watch Janet's indecision play out on her face in slow motion: the slight softening of her narrowed eyes, her two front teeth making their way onto her bottom lip and gnawing at the dusky flesh, a twitching left eyebrow which seems to indicate an insatiable yearning for gossip, no matter how morbid.

Eventually, she says, 'That's awful. Truly awful. I'm not sure what help you think I can give, but I do a lot of charity work and I must say, it is my forte.'

I nod. 'I just need to talk to you. Please.'

For a second, Janet seems torn between her neighbours witnessing her talking to someone who evidently looks like a beggar, and letting the beggar into her house. Eventually she says, 'Come in.'

I nod, and step over the threshold and into her home. It's a predictably chintzy affair, with one too many jarring floral patterns, and an array of fruit and animal ceramics which look like they were picked up at a car boot sale, but are probably sickeningly expensive.

Janet leads me into her living room and points me in the direction of a miniature sofa on which Mini-Moo currently perches.

'Probably the best place for . . . someone like you,' she says, scooping Mini-Moo up and patting the hairy cushion. 'I think you'll find it particularly comfortable.'

'Sure,' I say, as Janet and the Italian greyhound spread out opposite me on her Chesterfield.

'Tea? Coffee? Biscuit?' she asks, placing her phone onto the coffee table between us.

I shake my head, envisaging Janet watching me hawk-eyed as I chomp through a Rich Tea, revving her vacuum every time the crumbly biscuit approaches my lips.

'No, don't worry, I only meant for this to be a very quick visit,' I say.

'Yes, I imagine you don't want to dwell on Jamie's death.'

'*Joe's* death.'

'Yes.'

'OK, well . . .' I take a breath and fix my gaze on the drinks cabinet to Janet's right, wanting to dissociate as I once again relay details of the fateful night. 'Joe was pushed from the top of the Transporter Bridge. And I saw you on the river path, filming it all.'

My gaze shifts to Janet and I watch her bristle, caught off guard.

'You might be mistaken.'

'No. You posted some of the video on Facebook.'

Janet purses her lips. 'I didn't realise he'd died.'

I bite my tongue, resisting the urge to remind her that I begged for help, that my desperate wails that he was bleeding into the afterlife are likely caught in the full version of her video.

'I think the video was longer than what got posted on Facebook. The police have decided that Joe's death was an accident. This video could help me prove that it's not.'

Janet takes a thorough, nasally inhale and exhale, so deep that her nostrils flare and Mini-Moo, still curled on her lap, shivers.

'I don't think I can help you,' she says.

'It's longer, isn't it? It is? The video's longer? It can help me?' I press.

'No, I don't think it can help you.'

My bottom lip wobbles but I blink back tears; this situation is too important to allow emotion to overcome me.

'Look, I know the whole thing maybe doesn't show you in the best light,' I say, 'but maybe we could mute the part where I'm begging for help? I'll say that you did try to help, I'll make you sound like a hero.'

Janet tuts. 'The video shows me in a perfectly moral way. Filming gangs with bad reputations doing stupid, reckless things to mess our town up is very much a pursuit I'm known for.'

'That wasn't what happened. This isn't a gang thing.'

'Oh no? Devlin Mackenzie was there. I've been tailing him for a little while, trying to catch him doing something illegal. Trying to make a dent in the scum of the town.'

I don't have the energy to delve into her kitsch Batman/giga-Karen act, so I leave the vigilante shit and say, 'OK, so what's the issue? You're trying to make the town a better place. Letting me show the full video to the police is the perfect way to do that.'

'I'd really rather not get involved.'

'You involved yourself by being there and filming it,' I counter.

'And my intention was always to hinder Devlin and his gang, not help the gang out. No, I'm sorry. It just wouldn't do for me to get myself involved with the town chavs. I've got the church and my charity work and my reputation as a councillor to think about.'

It's increasingly hard to keep my expression neutral. I battle against eyebrows which want to rise, against a bottom lip which wants to drop open.

'OK, so supply it anonymously,' I say.

Janet laughs. 'I somehow doubt it would stay anonymous. You've seen the shows, haven't you? All the true crime about women trying to help and getting on the wrong side of gangs?'

'But I . . . but you wouldn't . . .' I flail, for it's hard to argue with someone so illogical. Eventually, I say, 'But this is Joe's *life*.'

'Joe doesn't have a life anymore,' replies Janet.

I glance down at her phone, still on the coffee table. She catches me looking and moves with a speed which surprises me, shoving Mini-Moo from her lap and lunging towards it. I'm slower, but I'm closer, and my hand wraps around the all-important object at the same time as hers does.

'Get out of my house,' she says, face now so close to mine that flecks of spit land on my cheek. My only response is to apply more pressure to the phone, but her bony fingers are vice-like.

'Get out of my house or I swear to God I'll call the police,' she says again, volume and hysteria rising.

'Be hard for you to do that without a phone,' I say, yanking it towards me with all my might. Janet wobbles but remains on her feet. Mini-Moo starts barking as Janet huffs in exhaustion.

I could be more brutal about this – I could gouge Janet's eyes or wrap a hand around her throat, but, selfish as she is, I'd rather not hurt her. I begin jerking the phone left and right instead, certain she'll lose her grip at some point.

'Get – out of my – house!'

'Just let me see the video!'

'Get – *out*!'

I yank the phone diagonally left with such force that Janet finally loses her balance. She stumbles, and then she falls. For a split second, a smile crosses my face, before Janet's head makes contact with her drinks cabinet. It jerks to the left with a sickening crunch. Time slows, so that her body seems to hit the ground one inch at a time. And then, with a catastrophic thud, time returns to its usual, frantic pace.

'Oh my God. Oh my fucking God.'

I drop the phone and rush over to her, crouching down. My hands pulse to and from her; I'm unsure whether to touch her or not.

'Oh my God. Janet. *Janet?* I'm so sorry. I'm so, *so* sorry.'

I'm waiting for her to jump up and screech at me, but nothing comes. A stream of blood slips from the side of her head, down her cheek and onto her jumper, where it stains the beige material. Blood and a compromised skull. For a second I'm reminded of Joe, and I dry heave in the direction of the coffee table.

Once I've controlled myself, I turn back to Janet and say, 'You'll be OK, it'll be OK. I'll get you an ambulance and they . . . they'll fix your head and I'm sorry, I'm really sorry.'

Still no movement from her. I force my fingertips to her arm, roll up her sleeve and place my index and middle fingers against her pulse. Nothing. Nothing.

'Fuck.'

I push myself away, landing with a thud on my arse. Mini-Moo approaches Janet and then starts growling at me. Hardly threatening, but enough to raise my heart rate even higher.

I haul myself up and pace about the living room, occasionally glancing back in Janet's direction, each time hoping she might jump up with a yell of 'surprise!' or 'I bloody knew you were trouble!' But her body remains lifeless, the only movement the blood that continues to trickle down her face.

This is bad. Really bad. The worst. I am fucked. I run my hands through my hair, thinking through my options. Call the police? Hand myself in? Hide her body? Chop it up? The mere thought of this makes me want to gag again. I heave, but manage to contain my revulsion; even in my shocked state, I know that vomiting all over a murder scene isn't going to do me any favours.

But is this a murder scene? Janet's own momentum is what propelled her to her death, really. I certainly had no intention of hurting her. It was an accident. People might even believe it was a solo accident. Condemning Janet to the same fate as Joe doesn't feel great, but I can't just turn myself over to the police.

So I tidy. There are anti-bac wipes in the kitchen, which I use to carefully wipe down everything I recall touching: the door handle, the dog sofa, a rogue velvet cushion. Janet's phone, of course, which I find underneath the coffee table. I'm about to wipe it, when a thought occurs to me. It's dark but . . . fuck it . . . if I don't find out, her death really will have been for nothing.

Cringing as though I'm plunging my hand into a grimy washing-up bowl, I reach for Janet's thumb and press it against her phone. Once unlocked, I release her thumb and scroll through her videos. And she did like to stick her nose in, did Janet. There are videos of matchday pain and matchday triumph, as men with hearts the size of dustbin lids celebrate or commiserate the fortune of their town football team. And the occasional dickheads who chuck glass and start fights. These are the ones Janet focuses on, of course, in her one-woman mission to see the worst in everything.

There are videos of scraps over the border, bins being set alight outside Tesco and teenagers racing shopping trolleys into Hemlington Lake. I scroll past them all, until I find the video taken on the night of the 18th of August.

Heart thumping, I click play. And I'm met with Janet's face. Just a close-up of Janet's face. She looks confused, and then irritated. She hisses the word 'drat' and then her finger approaches the screen. The screen flips just in time to capture Joe in the air for a couple of seconds, and then his body hitting the water.

She missed it.

I place the phone down, feeling numb. I've been holding back tears for the past fifteen minutes; I allow myself a brief period of crying.

There will be other chances. The video felt all-important, but I need to believe that there will be other chances for justice. Convincing Courtney and Devlin to change their statements, perhaps. Or appealing to the man with the dog, begging him to tell the police what he saw. Or Callum. If I had any idea where he lives or where he works, I might be able to trick him into confessing, record him, perhaps.

Mini-Moo barks, and I'm reminded that there's a dead body mere feet from me. Once again, I'm stupefied that Janet doesn't just get up. I should know better than most how easily broken humans are, but I'm shocked to my core.

The barking intensifies, and I realise that, if I have any chance of not being arrested, I need to get out of here as quickly and sneakily as possible.

I think about texting someone in Janet's contacts a message which might pre-empt her death, but what on earth would that be? It's not as if people commit suicide by falling on sharp corners. And some sort of 'oops, feeling extra clumsy today, hoping I don't have an accident' is too on the nose. In the end, I wipe Janet's wrist and thumb, wipe her phone and then lay it next to her.

Then I straighten the coffee table and chuck Mini-Moo a biscuit. Exiting via the front door feels too conspicuous, so I haul myself out of an open ground-floor window, pull my hood up and scarper round the side of the house.

'This is mad. This is mad. This is fucking awful,' I say, as I stride down the street, certain that eyes are following me.

I'm no closer to having Callum arrested, no closer to getting justice for Joe. And, behind me, someone is dead. And she was called Janet. *Janet.* I murdered someone whose name conjures up an image of a sweet, elderly neighbour. Granted, what appears sweet can often be sickly, and she wasn't exactly a delight, but still. Janet Braithwaite is dead. And I am in big trouble.

I've no idea what to do with myself. As if on autopilot, I start walking north, back in the direction of the river. It's a canny trek, and I do most of it in a daze, passing by shops and houses and eventually into the industrial estate. If the industrial estate wasn't so familiar to me, I might struggle to find my way through it. But it was my playground; Mam would shove Joe, Callum and me out early on weekend mornings with a stottie and a Cheestring and tell us how lucky we were, that the barren brown kingdom was ours, and she was generous enough to let us explore all day. I walk past the scrapheap we pretended was a treasure trove. Burned-out houses we believed had been scorched by dragons. Abandoned caravans that housed the ghosts of gypsies. Scraps of metal that became swords. Cooling stations that were the towers of enemy castles.

And finally, just when I feel on the verge of collapsing, I reach Mam and Liev's house. Where the real danger has always lurked.

Despite the danger, this is where I've ended up, in my hour of need. I remember Mam's eyes, so reminiscent of Joe's, as she looked over the photographs of him outside the church. The sensation of sharing the pain, of easing our mutual burden.

So I stand outside, practising delivering words I can't believe are real.

'I . . .'

Cough.

'I kill . . .'

I dry heave. My throat feels as though it's lined with razor blades. With some difficulty, I swallow.

And then I say, 'I killed Janet Braithwaite.'

Chapter Five

There are messy hiccups caught somewhere between laughter and crying coming from inside the house, which stop when I knock. It takes a few seconds, but eventually the door opens and Mam peers out at me.

'Lisbeth,' she slurs, pulling me into a hug, and we both practically fall into the hallway. I wriggle away from her and into the living room. Three of her friends are sitting on the sofa, chugging prosecco from flutes which were once expensive but have since lost their shine. I recognise them as Mam's 'girl gang' or 'dancing queens' or 'group of stuck-up pricks' depending on Mam's mood and how recently they've all argued. As far as I can tell, they originally bonded over an unironic love of *Mamma Mia!* and an unwavering belief in horoscopes.

I turn to Mam. Her cheeks are damp and red. She's swaying slightly and staring at her *Live, Laugh, Love* mural.

'I need to talk to you. Alone, preferably,' I say.

'Oh, Lizziepoo!' cries the faux-posh one, who wears Louis Vuittons from China and drives fifty miles to the nearest Waitrose every week to do her shop.

'Come have some bubbles!' says the largest of the trio, who I recognise as my childhood favourite – a woman who gave good hugs and slid Dairy Milk bars into my pocket.

Alas, I've not broken up with someone, I've murdered them. Chocolate and cuddles are not what I need. I tug at Mam's sleeve, trying to drag her from her daze.

'Please. It's important. Your friends need to leave.'

She's drunk enough to find this funny, thank God. But she's just sober enough to be somewhat helpful as we collect the various belongings of her friends and bundle them out of the door.

'Sorry . . . I know it looks bad,' Mam says. 'They've been trying to cheer me up but think I just feel . . . feel sadder and sadder.'

I nod. I've been so wired and on edge from killing Janet, that my grief for Joe has taken a back seat for the past couple of hours. It comes rushing back to me now, with such force it's thirty seconds before I feel able to speak again.

'How've you been?' I eventually ask. Stupid question.

Mam shrugs. 'Trying to forget.'

I've been doing the opposite, of course. I've been attempting to squeeze every morsel of memory from myself and from others. And now, across town, a woman is dead. And I need to tell someone.

'Where's Liev?' I ask. All the things I hate about my stepdad – that he's cold, calculated and ruthless – are exactly what I need now. He's the one person who might be able to view what I tell him with an analytical eye. I need a practical take, as opposed to the hysteria currently rattling about my own whirling brain. Plus, he feels the same way about Joe's death. For once, he might understand me.

'Liev's at work,' Mam says.

'When's he back?'

She shrugs. 'Uh, an hour or so.'

'Just enough time to sober you up, then.'

We move into the kitchen at the back of the house, and I butter her bread and pour her a glass of water. She sips and chews dutifully. I attempt to force down some bread, but it seems to turn to sawdust in my mouth, and the urge to vomit returns. I focus on Mam's selection of slogan mugs ('I'm not basic, I'm a triple shot bitch', 'Well-behaved women don't make history' and 'Classy, Sassy and a bit Bad-assy') rather than my churning stomach.

'We're cursed,' Mam mumbles through a mouthful of crust. 'I'm cursed. Your dad dying . . . everything with Callum . . . now Joe.'

I don't reply, for there's no saving the woman when she's stuck in a spiral of self-pity. Besides, I'd likely only argue that my dad's death benefited her: she got a sizeable chunk of his money, and a brand-new husband barely a year later.

I sit at the broken kitchen chair, the chair whose shattered wooden legs have been taped back together with rolls of duct tape. I remember

Callum picking it up, lobbing it the couple of metres across the room, towards Liev. But while this image is razor sharp, my recollection of whether Callum's rage had been justified or not is blurry. He'd shoplifted or played truant, I think. Had Liev punished him? How badly had Liev punished him? I think harder, attempting to recall their expressions. Callum – aggressive? Liev – worried? Scared? Protecting Joe?

No. It had been me protecting Joe, on that occasion. All five of us had been in the kitchen. I've no idea why I didn't leave. I think I froze, staring as Callum and Liev fought one another, almost overwhelming the little room with their brutality. Callum had been sixteen at this point, and almost as big as Liev. Joe had been clutched between my arms, I'd been trying to block his view with my fingers. Mam had been sitting on the kitchen counter, smoking and staring past it all, staring at her *This Kitchen is for Dancing* poster and doubtless feeling that the broken relationships before her were not her fault. She was simply cursed.

The chair wobbles, and I have the sudden urge to get away from it. I stand up, move to the sink and run a bit of kitchen roll under water before returning to Mam. She lets me dab at the mascara tear streaks under her eyes, still chewing at her bread.

I became hyper-aware of Callum in the weeks following the chair incident. I'd try to catch his eye, but Callum devoted all his attention to Liev, the muscles in his shoulders clenched, his jaw set, his dark eyes harder than they had been at the start of the year. For four long months, I truly thought one might kill the other.

It didn't happen, of course. Callum left early one March morning. We'd all sensed it was coming, but it still took me by surprise. He was too quick, and I was too sleepy to do anything other than race out of the house after him. I knew how angry he'd be if I shouted, so I kept quiet, my gaze following his retreating back and feeling rejection and regret twist around inside me. I watched his bulky backpack as it got more and more distant, and all I could think about was how painful it must have been, the heavy bag pushing into the scars on his back. Or maybe Callum had enjoyed the pain – his future impressing itself upon his past.

There's a banging from upstairs, and I'm returned to the present. I look at the ceiling, and then at Mam, who's polished off an entire loaf.

'We need to get the witch,' Mam says.

'Step-Nan? Can we not? I need to tell you and Liev something and I'd rather it not get out.'

Mam cackles. 'Christ, I bloody wish there was a risk of Step-Nan venturing out of the house. The general public are lucky these days, me and Liev are the only people she talks to.'

'Really?'

'Really. She stopped being able to look after herself, so it was either we have her, or off she'd go to a nursing home. And all her savings – all our inheritance – would be gone, in a plume of smoke. Course, not that she has much in the way of savings, but . . .' Mam sighs and looks around her clean, disintegrating kitchen. 'Every penny helps.'

The banging comes again. Mam yells that she's coming, and we both exit the kitchen.

'Seems a bit mad, keeping an eighty-one-year-old in the attic,' I say, when we're halfway through the rigmarole of helping Step-Nan down from the second floor to the ground.

'Does it?' Mam asks, raising an eyebrow.

Step-Nan gives me a sharp pinch as I'm helping her down the final stair, and starts muttering about the house stinking of eggs. I look over the little woman's head and back at Mam.

'I take it back. The attic makes perfect sense.'

The three of us sit in the living room, biding our time until Liev arrives. If I think about Janet's cold, bloody body, I'll scream, so instead I focus on the past, recalling the period of time spent waiting for Callum to come back, which had seemed to stretch on for aeons. Joe blamed himself for Callum leaving. He would mumble that it was his fault, that it was his daddy who'd pushed Callum away. The pair of us would hunt the industrial estate for him, and each Callum-free lap would result in a little of the magic slipping away from the place. I hadn't wanted to get Joe's hopes up, but privately I'd been convinced that Callum would return. He had no qualifications, no other family members and, until he turned eighteen, no access to his inheritance. But I'd underestimated his stubbornness. We heard no peep from him for over a year. This ended one Saturday morning, when Joe came racing down the stairs, his Nokia brick held above his head.

'It's Callum!' he'd shouted. Liev was out working. Had he not been, I trusted Joe would have had the good sense to be more subtle.

'Really?' I'd asked. Half my friends at the time had been in love with Callum, and it hadn't taken much convincing for them to monitor any online presence he had. Their lack of success had convinced me that Callum had gone fully analogue.

'Mm-hmm,' Joe said, beaming. 'Got his new number from Marty. He's going to come pick me up today. Take me camping.'

Had Mam been more sceptical, she might have objected. But her preference was for a child-free house in which her girl gang could better enjoy themselves, so she just shrugged.

'Are you sure it's Callum?' I'd asked, wanting to temper Joe's expectations, and feeling a little jealous that it was with Joe, rather than me, that Callum was communicating. Joe showed me the text: *Now then, little man. The prick still works Saturdays, right? Got myself a car. I'll pick you up, take you camping? Be ready for 3pm.*

I'd nodded. It did sound like Callum. Joe had started secondary school that year, and I could tell he was struggling to fit in. I'd thought the camping trip would be beneficial, that Callum (to whom popularity came easily) might be able to assist. I helped Joe pack for the trip. He was meticulous about it: making a list, checking the weather. He picked out his favourite shirt and the Adidas trainers that had once belonged to Callum. He had a shower and gelled his hair, styled it in the way Callum did his. He emptied his makeshift engineering boxes of sweets, and made Callum's favourite jam sandwiches. He laid everything out and then sat on the crushed velvet sofa, kicking his legs back and forth and staring out the window.

Callum didn't show, of course. We waited an extra hour. Two. Three. The girl gang arrived, so I took a bereft Joe out into the garden, tried to teach him how to be a successful man from the perspective of an unpopular girl.

Joe's forlorn little face looms large in my mind, even now. I'd found ways to excuse Callum at the time, had been convinced that my brothers had loved each other. Bullshit. Love had only ever flowed one way.

The door clicks open, and for a second, I think it might be Callum. It's not, of course. It's Liev. The smirk that crosses his face upon seeing me is so wide, I'm certain fresh wrinkles will press themselves into his cheeks.

'Well,' he says, kicking off his boots and moving over to the coffee table. He doesn't sit down, instead preferring to loom above me. 'Thought you said you weren't coming back?'

I nod, allowing him his small victory.

'Yes. Wasn't always my plan.'

'Didn't expect to see you so soon, did we, Kim?' he says, looking at Mam.

'Are you done?' I flinch; that was cheeky. For a second, Liev freezes, deciding how to respond. He settles on the smirk once more, too smug to think about punishing me.

'Aye. I'm done, I'm done. We don't see you for a year, and then we get you twice in a couple of weeks. To what do we owe this pleasure?'

I glance around, as if checking for bugs, or a police officer lurking outside the window. I take a final look at Step-Nan, absently staring at a biscuit, before I turn back to Liev and say, 'When I was last here, we spoke about a woman called Janet Braithwaite. She'd filmed Joe's fall and uploaded some of it onto Facebook. We thought maybe the full video might be on her phone, that it might show what really happened to Joe.'

'What really happened to Joe was that Callum pushed him to his death,' says Liev, with an authoritative boom. 'But I don't know about all this "we" malarky, like. As I recall, this was more you and your mam.'

Mam sits up straighter, leaning a little closer to me. 'Ahh, mmm, about that. I did contact her, asked her to send over the whole video. She said no and I had a few choice words for her in response.'

'Oh. Oh well, your choice words might be a bit unfortunate,' I say.

'Why? She is a kitsch bitch who couldn't get a man if her life depended on it.'

I take a deep breath, and then I whisper, 'Because she's dead. Because I accidentally killed her.'

Step-Nan bites into her biscuit. Mam's bottom lip drops open. Liev lets out a deep laugh.

'Yeah. And now the real story?' he says.

'That's what happened. It was an accident. She wouldn't show me the video either, so we were fighting over her phone. She fell and hit her head.' Even as I say these words, they don't sound real. The absurd nature of this confession seems to seep into the room around me, rendering my companions immobile, statues frozen in shock.

Liev slowly returns to life. 'When did this happen?'

'Earlier today.'

'And you came straight here?'

'Yeah . . . yes.' I can't articulate the pull of familial bond, even when that bond has been severed and abused more times than I care to keep track of. Twenty-three-year-old Elizabeth is not so different to three-year-old Elizabeth – in need of her mam when her dad died, and in need once more after the death of Joe. It feels both primal and pathetic.

'Fucking fool,' says Liev. 'So you've implicated us?'

I throw my hands up. 'I panicked. I thought you might be able to help. Besides, Mam has implicated herself if the police check Janet's chat history.'

'What the fuck, Elizabeth?' Mam finally speaks. Her eyes are wide and wet.

'I didn't mean to. I feel awful about it.'

'Like father, like daughter, eh?' says Liev. 'Mitch Mandeville lives on in you.'

'My dad was a conman. He never killed anyone,' I reply, looking to Mam for her agreement, but her eyes are fixed on her mural, as if she's convinced she can *Live, Laugh, Love* her way out of this.

'Did anyone see you?' asks Liev.

'No. I mean, not inside her house and not on the street outside,' I say, ignoring the sensation that someone's eyes *had* been on me. 'I walked here, so I obviously passed people. But it's not like I'm dripping in blood or wielding a machete.'

'Those clothes need burning,' says Liev. 'Kim, go get her something to change into. Nothing nice, like. Maybe some of my mam's stuff.'

Mam shakes herself from her daze and dashes upstairs. A few minutes later, she returns clutching an armful of Step-Nan's clothes.

'Really?' I say, turning my nose up at the floral smock and knobbly cardigan.

'Really,' says Liev.

I came here for advice from a calculated man who cares little enough about me to be rational, but hopefully just enough to keep me from jail. So I listen to what he has to say, accepting the clothes and changing into them in the downstairs toilet. Liev tells me to dump my jeans, trainers and hoody by the front door. I do so, and then sit back down, looking and smelling half a century older. I think this might finally warrant a reaction from Step-Nan, but she remains distant.

'We'll burn them. Or you can dump them in the river on your way out, or something,' says Liev. 'What did Janet look like when you left her?'

My stomach flips as I recall her fractured skull and bloodied face. 'She looked like a woman who'd just fallen into a drinks cabinet. I tidied up as best as I could, tried to make it look like I hadn't been there.'

Liev nods. 'What about CCTV?'

My armpits are hot and sticky, which seems to make the mothball stench of the flowery smock extra pungent. I cough and then say, 'Uh, I don't know. I hadn't considered that.'

Liev smacks his hand against his forehead, so I add, 'But I kept my hood up whenever I was outside her house.'

'Even more reason to burn those clothes. Does she have kids? A husband?'

'No,' Mam interjects, brimming with Janet Braithwaite knowledge she's mined herself. 'Just a sister and an Italian greyhound.'

'Right. So, she might not be found for a little while. Having three friends over all day is a decent alibi for you, Kim. But what are you thinking, Elizabeth? Going on the run?'

The *run*? I almost scoff at this suggestion for it seems wild, the type of thing done by criminals in films. But a split second changed everything. I *am* a criminal. The very worst kind. Someone who needs to be discreet, keep moving, get away from the police. But I shake my head. 'I can't leave. Joe's death is still recorded as an accident. I need the truth, and to get the truth to the police.'

Liev rolls his eyes. 'The police will not listen to the daughter of Mitch Mandeville. Whatever you bring them. Revenge on Callum might be possible, but that kid will never see the inside of a prison cell.'

Mam looks from Liev to me. 'The video . . . Janet's video. Did you see it?'

'Yeah. But Janet did that thing old people do where they accidentally take a selfie before switching the camera round. The key bit wasn't captured.'

Mam swears. Step-Nan mumbles something too, as if compelled to join in.

'But I have other options. We both know Callum pushed Joe,' I say, looking at Liev as a strange sense of camaraderie swells within me. What I saw aligns with what Callum said to him. For once, we're in agreement. 'And maybe the police will never listen to me. But I'll speak to Devlin, or maybe Courtney. Or the man with the dog – he witnessed the whole thing.'

'Oh aye, just speak to them, ay?' Liev says, mocking.

'Yes, just speak to them.' But even as I say this, I recall the feelings that flooded me after killing Janet. Paranoia and panic and a twisted sort of justice, and a complete absence of grief in respect of Joe. A bleak yet beautiful break from the desolate sadness which has ensnared me for the past month. I shake my head. 'I just need one of them to tell the police what really happened.'

Liev scoffs. 'Yeah. See how far that fairy tale gets you.'

I'm tempted to ask him what his solution is, but something about the desperate glint in his eye stops me. Instead, a silence hangs in the air. Eventually, it's filled by the mumbling of Step-Nan and then by Mam saying, 'Tell you what, I'll get my . . .' She trails off as she dashes from the living room. She returns a few seconds later clutching her phone. She dons her fluffiest pair of pink slippers and then says, 'Recent – Middlesbrough – murders,' tapping disjointedly into her keypad.

'Don't google that, howay, Kim, come on!' Liev says. He bats the phone away from her. 'Fucking dizzy cow.'

Mam doesn't even flinch. This is the treatment she's always believed she deserves. Some days I want to hug her, other days I want to shake some sense into her. Because she's not evil, Mam. No, she's just pathetic, and completely reliant on men. For her sense of self-worth, for her identity, for her survival. A uni friend of mine, someone who would make me blush from her lack of filter, once asked if I was gay because of my mam's relationship with men. I'd laughed off her comment, told her she had a basic misunderstanding of sexuality which bordered on homophobia. And then I'd thought about what she'd said for too long afterwards.

'Shame we don't have Joe's phone,' Mam says. 'Not like the police would have checked that.'

'They would have,' I say, a little too quickly. 'They'd have combed through it. Like cracking open his skull and sifting through all his secrets.'

Liev snorts. 'Bit dramatic. You've not seen his phone, like?'

'No,' I say, shaking my head.

'Well, maybe I could just type something vague about Janet into my own,' says Mam, reaching for her phone once more. I push myself away from the armchair and prise it from her grip. I get it easily; all her acrylics have now fallen off, and without them she seems to possess half the strength of the woman she was before.

'I think we should press pause on googling anything right now. Just to be on the safe side,' I say, sitting back down and placing her phone on the arm of the chair. There's a silence which feels almost accusatory. Mam's gaze keeps flickering to and from me, while Liev fixes me with a cold, hard stare. I think of the hard thunk Janet's head made as it hit the cabinet. I think of blood and cold bodies and a prison cell that should contain Callum but might end up housing me instead.

'I can't leave Middlesbrough,' I say. 'Not right now. So I'm going to change as much as I can about myself. Anything that might connect me to Janet's death. Any part of me which could be considered . . . not innocent, I guess.'

'Finally overhauling your witchy appearance?' asks Mam.

I tug at the floral smock. 'I don't seem to have a choice. But maybe . . . just in case the police find the messages you sent to Janet and think you killed her . . . maybe you should do the same. Dress like someone who would never commit a crime, I mean.'

Mam laughs. 'Oh, here we go.' She takes a drag of her vape, almost as though she's trying to hide from me behind a curtain of smoke. 'Sounds like this is just an excuse to tell me to stop wearing fun clothes? To get rid of low-cut tops and make myself invisible?'

'You could just look a bit more mumsy,' I say. 'Nothing so extreme that the girl gang will question it, but perhaps just a bit less leather. Maybe only one piece of leopard print at a time. No Juicy Couture tracksuits – especially not the bright pink one. Maybe tone down the makeup. Sadly people – especially the police – still make snap decisions. If they do end up questioning you, plain and forgettable is probably how you want to look.'

Liev guffaws. 'This the kind of shite they taught you on your drama degree?'

'Film degree.'

'Howay then. Four years at uni, let's put it to use. The police have come to question me about the death of Janet. What would you have me wear so that your mam's not accused?'

He's mocking, but even so, I can't help but scan my stepdad, wondering what I would change about him. He's always struck me as immoral, but immoral very much within the limits of the law. To outsiders, anyway. He's a smartly dressed man who would look ridiculous in anything softer; there'll be no suggestion of knitwear going his way. I almost tell him he needs to smile more, before remembering how disturbing the sight of his small teeth is. 'Maybe, I don't know . . . you could take up golf or something?'

He guffaws. 'Think I'm made of money? You and Callum are the rich pricks in this family.'

I sigh. 'Fine. OK. I don't know. Walk around with a book, or something. But a nice book. Not *The Wasp Factory* or *American Psycho* or *A Clockwork Orange*.'

'Glad to see all those thousands of pounds you spent on a degree didn't go to waste.'

I stand up, sensing that my interaction with the three of them is turning ridiculous and surreal.

'I'm going to go.'

I scoop up my jeans and hoody, instinct telling me it's best to destroy them personally. I shut the front door behind me, but not before hearing him say, 'She takes after Mitch. Mitch, Callum, Elizabeth. The Mandevilles. All killers.'

Chapter Six

I wrap my clothes around rocks and dump them in the river. A sense of catharsis floods me as I watch them sink, as if I'm relinquishing a key link to Janet, but also committing to my goal. For the first time in forever, I have a sense of purpose. Granted, things haven't exactly gotten off to an ideal start with Janet, but I won't make the same mistake again. I'm learning. I'm inching towards Joe's cause of death being corrected.

In order to do this, I need to make changes. I need to shed everything that connects me to Janet's death like a second skin. I need to turn myself into someone that no one would ever think is capable of ending a life.

My first thought is that I need to change my name. Just a little bit, nothing drastic. Continuing to go by Elizabeth is ruled out on account of Elizabeth Bathory, a Hungarian countess who was accused of killing hundreds of women at the turn of the sixteenth century. I can't go around with the same name as the most notorious female killer in history, can I? Lizzie feels too sharp, too many z's. El is what my ex called me, and is consequently quickly dismissed. I finally settle on Ella, deeming it suitably sweet sounding.

'Ella. Ella, Ella, Ella,' I mutter as I stride up Haverton Hill Road.

The dark mass of grief and anger inside me finally has an outlet, and it feels good. I picture Callum as best as I can. Gelled brown hair, intense dark eyes, a strong chin and bad teeth which he somehow got away with because . . . well, because he was Callum. I'd seen so little of him since he'd left home (a cluster of incidents I can count on one hand) that the legend of Callum had grown in my head. But had tales of his immorality been exaggerated? After he ran away, Liev would update us on how Callum's tirade against him was continuing, even from a distance. There was the time his bus was set on fire overnight – a burned-out shell, symbolic of rage and revenge by the time Liev arrived at the bus station in the morning. Another occasion, when Liev had gone to watch the football and returned with a broken nose and a deep gash above his eyebrow. Callum's mates, he had said, while Callum watched, a fully grown man now with a face hardened and stony, expression icy. It hadn't been difficult for me to picture Callum as a rock-like human being; a newfound lack of emotion at least went some way towards explaining why he had never bothered to reach out to me.

Mam would soften in these moments, wiping blood from Liev with a tenderness I recognised from a childhood of cut knees and bloody palms. Sometimes I think I fell over just to bring her closer to me.

Joe, meanwhile, would listen to Liev's stories with concern etched into features which were shifting with each passing day – from a boy to a man. A man who couldn't escape biology. A man destined to look like Liev.

'That's why he kept in touch with Joe and not me,' I whisper, shaking as everything clicks into place. This – this ultimate revenge on Liev – had been Callum's plan all along.

I'm breathless with anger by the time I reach the hotel. The urge to scowl at the landlady comes naturally. But no. I'm Ella. I'm nice now, incapable of ever hurting anyone. I flash the landlady my brightest smile, and her eyes widen in surprise. She wobbles, as though she might faint.

No collapsing occurs, so I head upstairs and open my laptop. Patently, I can't stay here any longer. Nothing screams 'I kill middle-aged women' like living in a budget hotel. It would be far too Richard Ramirez of me. Half my belongings are here, and the other half are back in Newcastle. I'm reluctant to head back up there, and – having lost Joe – material possessions don't seem nearly as important as they once did. I'll get by with what I arrived here with.

My intention is to search for flats, but I'm weak, and I browse the news before doing this. A South African restaurant is opening in Billingham. More jobs are being axed in the town centre. Food bank usage is at a record high, and people being incapable of budgeting is apparently what's to blame. Men accounted for three-quarters of suicides in the country last year. Nothing about a woman found lifeless. No 'wanted' posters featuring me in my hoody. I feel as though I'm sitting on a sordid secret. The clock is ticking as to when the rest of the world uncovers it.

I shut down the news page and begin searching for rooms which are cheap without being horrific. Liev's right in that I do have a lot of money. My dad's inheritance. But it's grim, immoral money – made from swindling vulnerable people or selling dangerous drugs to desperate addicts.

She takes after Mitch. Liev's words echo in my head. I'm not like my dad, and I'm not like Callum. Janet's death was an accident.

'I didn't want to hurt her. I don't want to hurt anyone,' I mutter, continuing to skim through flats.

I've got a little money left over from my shifts at The Bridge Tavern, which I can put towards a deposit. Afterwards, I'll need to find a job.

God bless the Northeast for its reasonable rental rates; I find half a dozen decent-looking rooms for around £400 per month and send out messages. No one replies instantly, and I'm impatient, so I move on to my next task: removing unimportant people from my life.

I'm torn on this one. Being devoid of friends certainly doesn't scream 'completely normal', but it will allow me to focus on the task in hand.

That's not the real reason, I think, sighing. The real reason is that it's increasingly hard to imagine an interaction with them which isn't agonising. Most were intertwined with my breakup, and none of them know about Joe. I'd have to tell them, I'd have to make it even more real, see their faces twist in shock and pity, listen to an awkward silence which speaks of an inability to articulate a correct response that doesn't exist.

It takes a solid five minutes of searching before I finally find my phone wedged down the side of the mattress. I haven't turned it on for . . . for . . . God, how long have I been down here? Two weeks? Three? When it flickers into life, messages await me.

Holiday this summer or nah?

Hello Elizabeth, are you going to graduation? Would be nice to have a buddy to head over with

Alreet Bonnie Lass, ya working the morra?

Hey, you OK?

Elizabeth, why didn't you go to graduation? Have I upset you?

Yalright, pet?

Hey, did you come pick up some stuff last night? Neighbour said he heard someone

Happy birthday! I've sent you a card but not sure you've received it. Please let me know just so I know whether to complain to the post office again

Happy birthday! Ganna get mortal tonight like?

Elizabeth?

Hey hey, you ignoring me? We fallen out?

Elizabeth, I'm getting a bit paranoid I've upset you. I remember I said the colour of your new dungarees didn't match your skin tone, but in retrospect, I take it all back

Howay, pet, what's the marra? Kayin says you're ignoring her and all

You've not been home in weeks. WTF? Do I need to call someone?

And on and on. I try not to read any of them. I need to delete, delete, delete.

Delete Facebook, before I see tributes to Joe and they make me start crying. Or before I don't see any tributes to Joe, and that makes me cry even harder. Delete Instagram, delete TikTok. Keep my email. Delete friends.

Kayin, first. No, shouldn't call her Kayin. Should just call her Ex Friend #1 – the first person who spoke to me in Newcastle, and probably also the nicest person I met up there. The girl who showed me Riley's Fish Shack and the art of smuggling booze into Cosmic Ballroom. The girl who introduced me to The Ex.

On the off-chance that the police question her about me, I send the sweetest message I can muster – that I've moved away for a job for the foreseeable, that I meant to tell her but have needed a break from my phone, will pay any bills I've left her out of pocket for. That I hope she's OK, etc etc. And then I block her number.

Ex Friend #2 is the girl who once sent me into a sexuality tailspin, the girl who exists without a filter. There's beauty and chaos in this trait, in near equal measure. If you look bad, she'll tell you. If you cause her the slightest inconvenience, you'll be made aware in staggering detail. If you clock someone attractive at a bar, she'll drag them over regardless of how many embarrassed protestations you make. If you tell her something, it will be passed on – to anyone and everyone. She's marmite, and I've always found myself on a knife's edge with her, entertained, but never far from being pissed off enough to cut her from my life entirely.

The time for indecision is done. I press 'block'.

Ex Friend #3 is almost the opposite. She's by far the most popular person I've ever known, and I can attribute this only to the fact that her personality is either a mirror or a blank page, depending on how generous I feel like being. She has no strong opinions. She's utterly apathetic, entirely passive. People fall over themselves trying to get something out of her. But . . . nothing. Truly nothing. A nod, a smile, a vague shrug of agreement. I've always had the impression that – at the age of twenty-two – she's bored by life. It helps that she's hot. You can get away with all kinds of character defects provided you're in possession of a symmetrical face.

I block her number.

And The Ex. She's been blocked for a while, of course.

There's a ping as an email lands in my inbox. A landlord has replied to my query. Hardly a cause for excitement, yet a thrill surges through me.

I reply, confirming my viewing. Pace from the fridge to the door and back again a couple of times. Look out the window, at the dark sky and distant fires. Take three white pills.

Sleep.

The following day I head to Central Library as soon as it opens. It's a large, regal building with a generous collection of books. Once again, I can't help myself; as soon as I'm online, I check the news. And there she is. Janet Braithwaite. A picture of her face looks out at me underneath the headline '*Local woman found dead in home*'.

I glance around the library, certain that eyes are on me, certain that the heavy pounding of my heart will be enough to summon the police. I turn back to the news article, but I can't linger; every time a picture of Janet arises, the thought of her bloody, broken face occupies my mind. I skim the article, satisfied that the word 'murder' hasn't been used, and then I whisper 'sorry' at a picture of Janet clutching Mini-Moo, before closing the page.

The urge to run is overwhelming. Her death might not be being treated as suspicious at the moment, but surely it's only a matter of time. And I'm just here in Middlesbrough, like a sitting duck.

'Joe. Joe, Joe. Doing this for Joe,' I whisper.

I return to the task in hand, printing off twenty-three copies of my CV. Between looking for rooms to rent, I rush about Hill Street Shopping Centre, handing out physical evidence of my meagre achievements, and getting weird looks, mainly.

'Where d'ya think you are? The 1970s?' asks the puzzled shopkeeper dishing out glazed goods in Muffin Break.

'It's all done online, babes,' a hairdresser in The Copper House tells me.

I'm not dissuaded. I target nurseries, beauty salons, the local art gallery, making my way up and down Linthorpe Road, and slipping into unassuming house shares whenever my appointments arrive. The rooms I view are baffling, and would be comic if I didn't potentially have to live in them.

There's the 'mezzanine studio' which is merely a bed above – yes, *above* – a kitchenette. I view another room which contains a bunkbed, and I start to wonder whether raised beds are in fashion these days, whether not having to clamber down a ladder first thing on a morning is a luxury confined to the past. The next place is bunkbed free, but so small the door opens onto the mattress, and you have to slither in and out of the room like a snake. I know that the fourth flat is going to be shit even before arriving; the landlord insists we take the 'scenic route' to reach it. She spends an inordinate amount of time highlighting how close Dorman Museum and Albert Park are, and significantly less time on what can only be described as a blatant, almost artistic fire hazard: the corner of the room in which a mini-fridge, television and microwave live, all stacked one on top of the other.

She tells me – with a sincere smile on her face – that this half-room, with a crack of natural light, a single bed, and its entertainment/kitchen menagerie can be mine for £700 per month plus bills. I look at the sharp edge of the microwave, and briefly consider shoving her into it.

A joke. I'm joking, of course. I merely smile back, tell her that the space is 'quaint, but not for me,' thank her for her time and then head north, under the train tracks and towards the river. Edging closer to my neck of the woods. It's here that industry starts to envelop you, here that the smell of chemicals replaces that of petrol and sausage rolls. It's by the river that your imagination can run wild, wondering what once occupied vast expanses of gorse, empty land. What the pile of debris had once been. Where the road – now cracked with grass and moss – once led. What the streetlamp with its coat of ivy once illuminated. Who the beggars and the drunkards were, before times had gotten so tough. So much nothing, with the potential of having been anything. It's the home of lost souls and roads leading nowhere. All of them drifting, seemingly following the river as it trickles out into the cold, grey sea.

Potential Flat #5 is among this. The cracked white walls of the building rise from the thistles and nettles. A very definite something. The landlord is quiet, and I like her all the more because of this.

She shows me a small living room, with threadbare carpets and boxy black sofas. The bathroom, with a window so low it would be inappropriate in a less desolate bit of town. The spare bedroom in question: with its high ceilings and big window, with afternoon light dancing across dust and cobwebs. Three other bedrooms, into which I sneak glances. They're all half-rooms, rooms caught between what they should be and what they once were. A man's bedroom which, judging by the chequered tile floor, used to be a bathroom or a kitchen. A woman's bedroom, in which a border of faded teddy bears still exists. An empty bedroom which seems to have been carved into the heart of the flat, warm and windowless.

We pause in the kitchen, and we're soon joined by one of the existing flatmates – a tall but boyish man, who takes a family-sized bag of Kettle Chips from one cupboard. I watch his movements, the clumsy way he shovels crisps from the bag into his mouth.

'Any issues? With this place?' I ask him as he's chomping down on a handful of crisps.

He glances at the landlord while chewing. He ponders my question, before saying, 'The washing machine's a prick.'

I mull this over. 'Washing machines are always pricks. They're never honest about how much time's left. Don't think I've ever met one I liked.'

He nods, before offering me a crisp. With the taste of sour cream and sweet onion whirling around my mouth, I tell the landlord that I'll take the room.

I begin moving my things over straight away. I don't have much; it takes me two bus trips, and arguably would only have taken one if I didn't have Joe's guitar.

I have my own space, but not nearly enough to fill it. Thank God the room is part furnished, or it really would look barren. I'm forced to give items that might ordinarily have been cast away special prominence, if only to add a little life to the room. I blue-tack a map of Middlesbrough bus routes to the wall. I spread a *Big Issue* magazine out across the chest of drawers. I line up what I can scavenge from the space outside on my windowsill: four pinecones, a broken China doll and a rusty lighter.

My blanket is thrown across the bed, and Joe's guitar is placed in one corner. I'd also packed my typewriter (in my most pretentious move to date, I purchased one after getting into uni). In retrospect, packing it was an insane decision, but I suppose I wasn't exactly thinking straight at the time. Regardless, I set it atop my desk.

Home. For now, anyway.

I meander over to the mirror and take a good, long look at my reflection. It needs altering, of course. In an ideal world, I'd have done so before meeting my flatmates, but leaving Haverton Hill Hotel was my priority. Perhaps I'll just tell them I have some sort of dress-up YouTube channel.

My gaze lingers on my clothes. My usual attire of dungarees, astrology t-shirts, flannel shirts, boots and a leather jacket – often all at once – seems too dark, too masculine. The Ex would have laughed me out the room had I ever described myself as butch (she categorised me as a Plant or Chapstick Lesbian), but I could definitely do with being girlier, a touch more innocent-looking. I need makeup and glossier hair. I need to take inspiration from Ex Friend #3, need to heed the fact that pretty privilege exists, and might just allow me to get away with murder.

I push my hair back behind my ear and allow my finger to trace the small, grey snake I had tattooed there post-breakup. That'll need covering, I suppose. A shame, to discard the parts which make me me, as opposed to an offshoot of my mam and dad. Though, to be fair, even without the tattoo and the dark clothing, I look nothing like Mam. That much has always been apparent to both of us. If she'd messed with her appearance a little less, and I'd messed with mine a little more, we might have met somewhere in the middle. Who do I look like, then? Joe? Not really, bar the dark curls. Callum? Not a chance; I'm not deluded enough to think I might ever possess the brooding look which characterises his face. Dad, then. Mitch Mandeville's grey-blue eyes. Mitch Mandeville's thick brows.

She takes after Mitch.

I turn away from the mirror and pick up my phone. For inspiration, I google the most recent batch of *Love Island* contestants – surely the cultural marker for twenty-something-year-olds who appear too vacuous to cause society any real harm. Bright, bodycon clothing. Orange skin, perfect white teeth. Full lips and impossibly long, thick hair.

I tug at my shoulder-length hair, pulling a curl taut and noting the minute differences in each dark strand.

Some might argue that Myra Hindley ruined blonde for female killers. But I disagree; I think I'd look positively angelic with a halo of golden curls. Plus, if I am captured on CCTV with my hood down, a drastically different hair colour should throw the police.

None of this is cheap though – as approximately thirty seconds of googling tells me.

I sigh and collapse onto my bed.

Flat = sorted. Job = pending. New appearance can't occur until my first paycheck. Next task = get a boyfriend. Absolutely essential. The normality of this has long been drilled into my head. An unassuming XY-chromosome-shaped accessory is the ultimate indicator of mild-mannered mediocrity.

I'll need someone traditionally unattractive. Someone who's on the cusp of incel-dom and will thus tolerate what is likely to be a lopsided and sexually inactive relationship. Someone who will still be keen to hang out, even if I haven't messaged him for five days and point-blank refuse to suck his dick.

I download Hinge; even for a fake boyfriend, I can't bring myself to use Tinder. And even for a fake boyfriend, I know there are certain things I won't be able to tolerate: bad hygiene, clinginess, anyone who captions a photo with the words 'Uncle Duties'. Anyone who calls me a 'Good Girl' under any circumstances. Anyone who thinks that telling me they really love their mam automatically makes them a stand-up guy.

I upload a handful of group pictures to my profile, and offer up some generic information: I've just turned 23, graduated from Newcastle Uni, live in Middlesbrough. I'm made to fill out prompts, so I go as bland as possible:

Don't hate me if . . . I end up loving your dog more than you!

Give me travel tips for . . . anywhere and everywhere! Lol.

My simple pleasures . . . coffee, sleep and Netflix.

A bark of laughter escapes me as I see my first suitor: Sonny, who suggests that *Together, we could . . . get blackout drunk*. Not the vibe I'm going for, so I cross away his profile and am greeted by Will, whose *Most irrational fear is . . . the pre cum of tomato ketchup*. I laugh again and have to remind myself that I have two flatmates, who will likely think I've got a screw loose if I keep up the unrestrained giggling.

It's impossible not to laugh, though. There's Kaheel, who says that *Dating me is like . . . having a migraine and an erection at the same time*. There's Aidan, who *Goes crazy for . . . Middlesbrough FC and a Stella*. Shane, whose *Typical Sunday is . . . crying and eating Chinese*. And Chris, who's *Looking for . . . someone who's STD free*. The bar is on the floor, people. The bar is on the floor.

I have to remind myself that I am actually looking for someone, and not just browsing for my own entertainment. They're all much of a muchness, though. They love *The Office* (US), their typical Sundays are a roast, a walk and Netflix, they all have strong opinions on pineapple on pizza and all love dogs. They all want to travel and want someone who doesn't take themselves too seriously. The best way to ask them out is by courier pigeon, which struck me as witty on first read, but less so on the fourth. They all go crazy for parmos and memes. The Gen-Z northern lad, summarised in four sentences.

I send messages to the meekest-looking among them, and then search for a suitable café in the vicinity. Replies trickle back to me, and I start scheduling dates at hour-and-a-half intervals between the opening and closing times of Bedford Street Coffee.

Who the hell goes on a date at 9am on a Saturday morning?!?!?

That's from Potential Fake Boyfriend #1, a guy who's fallen too far from what society deems attractive to be acting like such a diva. I remind him of this, and he agrees to the 9am appointment. Within an unsurprisingly brief amount of time, I've filled Saturday's four date slots. I perch on the edge of my bed. For now, there's nothing more I can do, and this makes my skin crawl. I scratch at my arms. Stand up and rearrange my pinecones, lighter and broken doll. Re-fold my clothes. Swat away the cobwebs. Search for tasks that keep me from the abject nothingness of grief that keeps threatening to overwhelm me.

There's the panic of paranoia, of course. I feel in the pocket of the leather jacket I've hung from the back of my door, and my fingers wrap around something cool and smooth. Joe's phone. An object I grabbed while trying to rescue him, and something I always intended to hand over to the police. At least, I intended to until experiencing first-hand how callous and robotic they are. I've been keeping it here instead, plucking up the courage to look through it and find things I might not want to. But it's also a final piece of him to keep safe.

Now, I use his phone to google Janet. There are more tweets and articles in respect of her death. And each one seems to twist the narrative, painting her untimely demise in increasingly suspicious-seeming circumstances. I'm refreshing Teesside Live when a new article appears: *Foul Play Suspected in Local Councillor Janet Braithwaite's Death.*

This shouldn't come as a shock, yet still, my stomach turns. A quick scroll of the article informs me that her death has become a murder investigation. Heart pounding, I fight the urge to head to my window and look out for watching eyes or approaching police officers. Instead, I pull my pill box from my jacket pocket and give it a shake. Empty. My mental health is a slippery beast, and I know I'm close to losing hold of it. When my emotions aren't being channelled into something, they'll spill out and I'll lose control of them.

I pick up Joe's guitar and stand with it in the middle of the room. He had received it for his twelfth birthday, and it had been an unusually expensive present; Mam's share of my dad's inheritance had run out about five years earlier – since that point, the thought of new clothes or new toys had inspired within me a strange sense of anxiety which I carry to this day. But Mam would hold the fact that she'd spent

£50 on a guitar over Joe, demand he learned the chords to songs that weren't exactly made for the instrument: Ibiza club dubstep and whatever she'd just rediscovered by N-Dubz and Abba's back catalogue. Her performing monkey would be summoned whenever the girl gang was over, and they'd howl at him attempting to play 'Blurred Lines' for them. Dance around him clutching their glasses of prosecco, shimmying close to the poor boy's body, giggling when he fucked up or shuddered at their proximity.

Mam has this glint in her eyes sometimes, this glint that lets you know she's at an emotional precipice, balanced precariously between misery and ecstasy. Joe would hone in on whatever had made her laugh – being behind the beat or bad dancing or an attempt at singing – and rinse and repeat this. Try to tip her into ecstasy or wait for the prosecco to do its job, to dull her emotions – so that her smile stretched false across her face, but her eyes glazed over.

When I left for university, I'd sometimes ask Joe to play me songs over FaceTime. They were songs I assumed he liked – 'Under the Bridge' and 'Come as You Are' and 'Glory Days' – but after a time I noticed his gaze would always be fixed on me, searching, searching to see if he was keeping me happy. Each finger could have been bleeding and he'd have played on, I'm certain. I stopped asking for songs, and he never offered anymore.

I put down the guitar, wanting to get it as far away from me as possible. I return to my pill box and open it. Empty. Definitely empty. I change into my pyjamas and turn the light off. Lie still on my bed. If I have to think of a brother, I'd rather think of Callum. I'd rather feel the heat of anger than the abyss of grief. His face comes to me. The sharp cheekbones, strong jaw, dark eyes which look through you. His lips, always slightly open – teasing, almost, teasing all the things you wanted him to say but he wouldn't.

The first time I saw him after he left home was complete happenstance. Ex Friend #1 and I were out in South Shields, and I clocked him across the bar. Wearing a black jumper and a bored expression, surrounded by half a dozen gooey-eyed girls. It took two hours and seven shots before I dared approach him. He'd nodded, stood up and hugged me. He smelled of cigarettes and sweat, and I couldn't understand why the girls behind him looked so jealous of me. His hands had moved up and down my back, searching.

It didn't take long for him to find what he'd been looking for.

'I'm sorry,' he'd said.

I hear those words again now, a deep, Smoggie timbre echoing around my room.

I shake my head.

'No, Callum,' I say to the darkness. I scrunch my fists. 'I'm sorry. Because I'm coming for you.'

Chapter Seven

I wake up sweating on Friday morning, having dreamed of handcuffs and arrest, cells and interviews. I paw at my brow and then head into the kitchen. There's a ringing in my ears that sounds uncannily like police sirens, so I turn on the television in an attempt to drown out the noise. The news – not what I wanted. I'm about to change the channel when Janet's face appears on the screen.

'An arrest has been made in the murder case of local councillor Janet Braithwaite,' says the news reporter. 'Police confirmed that they detained forty-seven-year-old Brandon Pearce late yesterday evening. Pearce allegedly confessed to the killing.'

'What the fuck?' I whisper. 'What the fuck?'

Lying. Liar. He's lying. But why? I tap the remote against the kitchen counter, staring at the screen in disbelief.

'Hey, Els, whatcha watchin'?' The Manbaby Flatmate, who I met in a whirl of sour cream and sweet onion when I viewed the place, enters the kitchen, carrying a sizeable orange sombrero.

'The news,' I say, too shocked to ask why he owns such a hideous object. The television remote slips between my sweaty fingers, clattering onto the kitchen counter. I wipe my hands against my jacket and pick it back up, fighting the urge to switch to a channel not showing something so aggressively untrue.

'News, huh. Oh shit! They caught the guy who killed that woman!'

'Looks like it.'

The Manbaby Flatmate puts down his sombrero (on top of the fruit bowl, of all places) and rests his hands on his hips. He whistles, overdramatic. 'Brandon Pearce, huh? Can't say I'm surprised – the guy looks exactly like a murderer.'

I nod, heart pounding hard in dizzying disbelief and confusion. 'Yes,' I say, 'he really does.'

Chapter Eight

Brandon Pearce's batshit confession dominates my thoughts so much, I almost miss my string of date appointments the next day. I even toy with the idea that I might not need to find a sweet little fake boyfriend to couple up with, but reason that he might well come in useful for helping me to get close to Devlin or Courtney. Besides, I don't trust Brandon's confession at all. It seems like a dream, or a trap. And if it is, having a fake boyfriend to vouch for my so-called good character might come in handy.

So, with one eye on every relevant news article I can find, I make my way to Bedford Street Coffee. I order an espresso from a barista whose long neck and sizeable nose are strangely reminiscent of a heron, and then find myself a seat at the back of the café. I'm doing approximately my fifty-eighth deep stalk of Brandon's Facebook profile (he likes clay pigeon shooting, lemon tops and The Smiths and the only photos he's uploaded are of Stonehenge and Whitby seafront; alas, I don't find any statuses declaring a penchant for self-destructive attention seeking) when my phone rings.

An unknown number.

Finger shaking, I answer.

'Hello?'

'Hello, is this Ella . . . ?'

'Ella Mandeville, yes, speaking,' I say, just as the barista arrives with my espresso. He lingers, until I give him a strained *please stop eavesdropping* smile.

'Yes, Ella Mandeville. This is Atha & Co solicitors.'

Fuck. Have I been accused of Janet's murder alongside Brandon? Have I been accused without even knowing I've been accused? Are the solicitors ringing up pre-emptively, offering me legal representation before I've been arrested? I glance outside, certain a police car is about to arrive.

'Err yes. Hi,' I say.

'I'm just calling about your receptionist application. Unfortunately, you've been unsuccessful on this occasion, but we do appreciate your interest.'

'Oh. Oh, thank God,' I say, which leads to confusion at the other end of the phone. I hang up instead of explaining that, while I'm sad to miss out on the job, I'm happy that I'm continuing to get away with murder.

I take a sip of my coffee, push thoughts of Janet and Brandon and jobs (and Joe, of course . . . always Joe's slippery, broken body) to the back of my mind, and await Potential Fake Boyfriend #1. Despite his protestations about the early hour, he's only three minutes late. And he's got the potential to fulfil my requirements, at least on first glance: near bald at the tender age of twenty-five, yet sporting large metal braces. A simultaneously young and old-looking head, which is a peculiar sight. He's confident, though, barely pausing to draw breath as he prattles on about his job as an IT teacher. The kids must have gone soft; in my day, a man with his appearance would have been eviscerated by 10am on his first morning.

He's an over-sharer, much in the way that Ex Friend #2 was: he tells me that male privilege doesn't exist, that he begrudges teaching gender identity to his students. I assume gender neutral toilets don't fall into his curriculum, but he spends so long talking about them, there's surely no room left in his head for anything else. I make desperate eyes at the heron-esque barista, and make four toilet trips during his slot.

It's a struggle to get him out the door at 10.30. He's promising to send me podcasts from some God-awful sounding alpha males as Potential Fake Boyfriend #2 rounds the corner. This guy is painfully thin, with mousey hair flustered by the early autumn breeze. He pats it back into place as he enters the café. I order my third coffee of the day, and a croissant. The barista's beady eyes, from behind his glasses, linger on me for just a little too long, as though he's attempting to figure out what I'm doing here. Let him wonder. I'd offer up the entirety of my wicked inheritance if he was able to guess that I'm auditioning men to act as normalisers and unwitting accomplices for the snooping I'm going to do while getting justice for my murdered brother.

I smile and then turn to Potential Fake Boyfriend #2. He's not bad, you know. Less self-assured and less bigoted than Potential Fake Boyfriend #1. I'm able to chat to him without wanting to pour hot coffee over his head. But, alas, he's in possession of one of the most ridiculous, high-pitched giggles I've heard in my life. I seldom say anything amusing, and yet out the giggle comes, bouncing about the café and raising the eyebrows of the barista. I imagine using him as a prop to spy on Courtney or Devlin but it's impossible; he'd draw attention to us within a minute.

Reluctantly, I let him go at 12pm.

Potential Fake Boyfriend #3 is a non-starter. He's twenty-four minutes late, and he's also far too good-looking for my requirements. He's one of those men who just doesn't understand the power of angles and lighting, and is actually perfectly reasonable-looking in real life. Even if I hadn't been planning on treating him as a glorified accessory, I suspect he'd be out of my league. His reaction when I tell him I've got to cancel our date reinforces this: complete indifference, perhaps even a little relief.

I return to the table at the back of the café, sip through another coffee, place my head in my hands and stare at the knots of wood in the tabletop. My job application rejections have been numerous and have nearly all come back electronically. I browse through them, before emailing out a few more CVs – having to lower my expectations and accept I might need to take on a job in a pub, rather than as an innocent-seeming nursery nurse or dog groomer.

Potential Fake Boyfriend #4 arrives at the same time as an application rejection from the local Chinese buffet. I groan and then have to apologise. I needn't have bothered; Potential Fake Boyfriend #4 is his own unique brand of awful. He has the voice of Paddington Bear, and a wide-eyed, innocent manner which makes the shit that comes out of his mouth sound even more ridiculous. He tells me that he'd rather make girls think than cum, and he hopes I'm OK with that. He tells me that his ex was obsessed with him, but that he had to end things because they weren't on the same level intellectually, and that he refuses to date girls with emotional baggage or daddy issues. When he says that Patrick Bateman is his idol, but 'don't worry – predominantly in respect of his morning routine,' I put my head in my hands again and groan until I hear his chair scraping back and footsteps moving away.

'Another flat white?' asks a voice from above me.

I drag my head up to see the bird-ish barista.

'If I have any more coffee, I think I might die,' I say.

He smiles in agreement and returns to the counter. I pack my things into my bag, shuddering at the prospect of another evening of trying to wheedle out men who aren't misogynistic or bonkers on Hinge. I've no idea how straight girls do it.

'See you,' says the barista as I'm leaving. His voice is soft, an unconfident mumble, despite the fact he's being perfectly lovely. I pause and turn to face him. He's tall with floppy hair – both of which sound good on paper, but he doesn't quite carry either off. He's almost too tall, and clearly uncomfortable about the amount of space he's taking up, for his long neck has tucked itself into his shoulders vulture-style, and his back is stooped. The floppy hair could do with a good wash, and keeps falling in front of his thick glasses. And his nose, oh bless him, his nose. If you were making a sculpture of him, you'd reach his face and think, 'I really should knock a centimetre or two off this, just to give the poor boy a chance'. But biology doesn't really give a shit, so here is the barista, with his comically big nose.

Baggy clothes, big nose, bashful smile. Perfection. Absolute perfection.

'Can I get you a coffee?' I ask.

His eyes widen. 'Oh God, am I going to be subjected to whatever you just made your previous candidates do?'

I laugh. *Yes, yes you are.*

'No. Not unless you want to audition to perform at my niece's birthday party.'

'That's what they were doing? There was a distinct lack of balloon sausage dogs. Or face paint. Or jokes. Apart from the second guy. But I think he just had a nervous giggle.'

'My niece is a very serious child,' I say. 'Her birthday entertainment is going to be speeches on endangered species and environmental damage.'

'Good for her.'

We stare each other out for a beat or two, him trying to figure out whether I'm lying, me trying to figure out if I can trick him.

'But seriously, can I get you a coffee?' I ask again.

His cheeks turn crimson, and I know I've got him. He knows I'm lying, but he doesn't care.

'I don't actually like coffee, believe it or not. And we're closing.'

'OK. Well, can I help you pack up?'

'That's not exactly protocol . . . I suppose you can wipe the tables, if you really want to.' He raises a sceptical eyebrow. I need to shift myself out of the tragic category I've just fallen into, so I flash him a smile and set about seductively making the tables spotless. He washes cups and plates and packs leftover goods into boxes, and he keeps sneaking glances at me, his cheeks never losing that delicious, helpless blush. I gather up biscuit wrappers and drop them into recycling bags.

'Like auntie, like niece, hey?' he says, a small smile on his lips.

'What? Oh, ah yes, my environmentally friendly niece. Totally unforgettable.' And completely made up.

I stack chairs, and as I do so I ask him easy questions – where he grew up, what he's having for tea tonight, whether he bakes the cakes on display and if so, which his favourite to make is. He gives me one-word answers and then, slowly, ever so slowly, he starts to open up. About the correct ratio of butter to flour in a Victoria sponge. About growing up on the outskirts of town and never quite feeling like he fitted in. He identifies the constellations dotted about my t-shirt and tells me the story of Orion. The muscles in his shoulders relax, he stands a little taller, he stops fiddling with his glasses. He seems to melt for me. And I'm reminded of how much I love shy people. How genuine it feels when they hold your gaze instead of looking away. How special it is to be treated to the thoughts they normally keep quiet, to be trusted by them.

We finish our jobs and I stand still, sneaking glances at him.

'Can I take your number?' I ask.

'So I can send you my speech on salamanders and Indian elephants?'

'Something like that, yeah.'

I didn't think it possible, but his cheeks turn an even deeper shade of red.

'What did you say your name was again?' he asks.

'Don't think I did.'

'Oh, maybe I just overheard you earlier. Ella Mandeville, right?'

'Err, yeah.'

I must look slightly creeped out, for he quickly adds, 'Just so I know what to save you as in my contacts.'

'OK, well, your digits first please.'

He nods, cheeks still burgundy, and reads out the eleven all important digits. I tap them into my phone, save him as The Fake Boyfriend (I certainly don't share his interest in learning names) and then kiss him on the cheek.

'I'll call you,' I say, acting every inch the sweet girl who might date a nerdy type such as himself.

He nods and I leave, one key task completed, but the all-important job still evading me. I've not received a single interview request, hair extensions don't come cheap, and there's only so long I'll be able to sneak oranges and slices of bread from my flatmates' stashes. I flip my phone over while the prospect of turning to my last resort twists in my mind.

I sigh, and call Marty Deng.

My godfather, the best mate my dad ever had, and a 'slimy, low-life weasel' by Mam's account agrees to meet me the next day. He's waiting in the betting shop he owns in Grove Hill, sipping from a can of Monster and perched on a stool. He's gone straight, or so he tells me, although profiting from other people's addictions is probably as straight as I am.

'Me and your dad used to be hell raisers, mind you,' he says, repeating what I already know, and what I'm told every time I find myself in Marty's orbit. I'm simultaneously surprised and unsurprised that this is his opening gambit. I'd thought he might mention Joe's death, but he sticks to what he knows – reminiscing about his and Mitch's glory days: ripping off pensioners and getting into fights.

'Fascinating,' is my reply. I should be trying to butter him up, but I'm two parts irritated by him and one part bored.

'Used to get called the modern-day Ronnie and Reggie Kray,' he continues.

'Oh yeah. Which one of you was gay?' I ask.

'One of the Krays was gay?'

I nod, and Marty raises his sparse eyebrows. His appearance has always been characterised by his size: small eyes in a small head and a build which seems comically slight whenever I see him in pictures with my dad. But he seems to have shrunk further into himself since the last time I saw him, leaving creases where flesh used to be.

'You look like Mitch,' he says. He's one of those people who's uncomfortable with silence. I let him wait a few seconds before I reply.

'Not sure you're meant to tell daughters they look like their dads.'

'Ahh – ahh – yeah am sorry. Silly of me. Meant no offence, like.'

There's a hesitancy to him; I think that's what's making him appear smaller than ever. His attempt to go straight is genuine, I realise. He's put thought into this conversation. I can picture him standing in the bathroom at the back of the shop prior to my arrival, rehearsing what he might say to me. How he might break the ice with a few comments about the person who links us. Looking in the mirror and checking he's still in possession of some of his youthful charm: white teeth which look good in a grin, and friendly crinkles around his eyes.

'I need a job, Marty,' I tell him.

'Ahh.' He gestures around his betting shop, pointing with his can. 'I'd love to give you a job here. Y'know I'd love to have you. But I've got nowt.'

'Doesn't have to be here,' I clarify. 'You know everyone. There must be something.'

'Not everyone likes me.'

'Well, that kind of comes with the territory when you fuck over as many people as you and Mitch did.'

He looks past me, and it's as if he's visualising himself in the safety of the bathroom, figuring out what to say next.

'Have you really stopped everything?' I ask.

He takes a drink and returns his gaze to me. 'Aye. Was never as good at it as your dad. Began to leave a bitter taste in the back of my throat. And I'm trying to get Lexi back.'

I nod at the mention of his kid daughter. I'm proud of him, in an odd way. He's got one of the strongest Middlesbrough accents I've ever heard. It's flatter than Geordie, softer than Scouse, a touch livelier than the Yorkshire burr. Vowels which always seem that bit out of step with the rest of the country: too short or too long or too deep. I'd always wished my own accent was stronger, until I watched a television interview in which a Southern news reporter attempted to teach a local man the so-called correct way to say 'butter' ('butt-er' as opposed to 'butt-ah') and a school kid said he wanted to change his accent so that people didn't think he was 'crazy'.

I look to Marty, taking nervous sips from his can. I'm as bad as that reporter, have always pigeonholed him based on his accent.

'D'you need a job? Like, really? Cos Mitch left you and Callum all that money,' says Marty.

'I'm never using that money.'

'You mad? Half a million? Just sitting there?'

'I'm going to donate it. When I figure out the best place to donate it to.'

Marty shakes his head. 'You look like him, but you ain't him, that's for sure. Good girl. Good girl.'

But I haven't been a good girl, and I need his help to avoid the consequences of my actions.

I smile as sweetly as I'm able and say, 'Yep, sticking on the straight and narrow, just like you. Honestly, though, if you could get me a job. Something nice and cute, preferably.'

'Righto. Nice and cute.'

He laughs.

* * *

I should have paid attention to his laugh. He calls me less than forty-eight hours later and asks to meet at Thorntree Cemetery. I hope to God that we'll be moving elsewhere.

We don't.

Marty stands under the shadow of a tower block, between gravestones. A large man in a long green coat stands next to him.

'Hello,' I say, struggling to keep the agitation from my voice.

'Got you a job. Had to scrimp on the cute element, mind. Not so many puppy-cuddling jobs about these days.'

'Scrimp or sacrifice completely?'

Don't say it, Marty. Don't say it.

'You'll be—'

Don't say it, Marty.

'—doing some gravedigging.'

He said it. Gravedigging. A gravedigger. A fucking gravedigger. That's exactly the kind of job a killer would have. I can't say this to him, of course. Instead, I say, 'A gravedigger? I'm a twenty-three-year-old girl.'

'I don't see gender, I don't see race, I don't see age. Completely PG.'

'PC.'

He introduces me to the man beside him, a man who can best be described as someone who would be really easy to draw. And I'm shit at drawing. Big bushy beard, sleepy eyes, plum-shaped nose . . . you know what, this guy isn't important. I turn to Marty.

'Was there really nothing else available?'

'Times are hard. Not a lot floating around. It's honest work. You get paid weekly.'

I look down at my nails: short and chipped. My outfit: decidedly dark and slightly sinister. My stomach: dissatisfied after a breakfast of a stolen banana and handful of ice cubes.

'Fine. Thank you. I'll take it. When do I start?'

'You can start now.'

And I do.

Marty leaves, and I'm left alone with Employer #1. (I insist on putting #1 because I swear to God this won't be the only job that I have. I shudder at the thought of digging my own grave as a withered octogenarian.) He's an adequately nice man, getting me a rain jacket and a flask of tea and explaining in monosyllables what I'll be doing. In fairness, it's more of a groundskeeping role – I'll be cutting grass, trimming grave markers and helping keep the grounds in good condition. He tells me, with a smile beneath his beard, that he'll let me arrange the flowers at the corner of the graves. Crikey, he really took my 'I'm a twenty-three-year-old girl' spiel to heart.

I nod. His attention to detail has kept the graveyard immaculate. Newer marble headstones are shiny and buffed, while stone headstones are in as good a condition as you could expect, given their age. And there's so much love in this cemetery, it makes my heart ache. Almost every plot is decorated with fresh flowers, coloured gemstones, balloons, angel statues, brave notes written by pained parents. I think of Joe's grave, in a different cemetery a few miles away. The fact I haven't visited it yet. Whether I'll ever feel up for doing so. My eyes land on the grave of a boy who passed away at an even younger age than Joe. His plot is decorated with pictures and balloons and toys and a signed Middlesbrough FC shirt.

'I loved you too, Joe,' I say stupidly, as if I'm in a competition. But I'm struck by the same urge that the young boy's family clearly have: the desperate desire to show a dead kid how deeply he's missed, when the odds are that what I say or do won't make a blind bit of difference.

It's an uncomfortable thought, and one that I try to push away by throwing myself into the work. The volume of physical labour makes me stiff, sore, hungry. Wet, cold and boiling, all within the space of a couple of days. Flushed with a strange sense of pride whenever I look back at the work I've just done and figure I'm helping to maintain the dignity of the deceased. Muscles I didn't even know I have grow sore. My palms swell with blisters, which are pushed off by the lawnmower handle. Blood dribbles down to my fingernails, and I hold my hands up, recalling the last time I had blood beneath my nails. A part of me regrets washing him off.

I comfort myself with the knowledge that Pete Doherty once worked in a graveyard, and that I'm inching closer to being able to splash out on a parmo and a new wardrobe.

And splash out I do. The minute that my first week's pay arrives, I gorge on cheesy chicken goodness and then I take myself round Hill Street Shopping Centre. I pause outside Primark for a minute or two, wondering if, what with Brandon Pearce illogically taking the fall for my crime, I need to bother altering my appearance. But I recall how quickly Janet judged me by my attire, how standoffish she was. If I'm going to get Courtney onside, it's probably best that I look like her. Not exactly the same – I'm not going to copy her hairstyle or buy matching jewellery – but similar enough that she might instinctively warm to me. Besides, it's surely only a matter of time before the police decide that Brandon is insane and re-start their search; I need to look as different from past Ella as possible.

I splurge on my hair (not trusting myself not to fuck up blonde hair dye) but scrimp on everything else. I purchase clip-in hair extensions, fake tan and hot pink dresses. Fluffy jackets and glittery eyeshadow and heeled boots.

I stuff my old clothes underneath my bed and watch makeup tutorials by women who tell me – with agonising vocal frys – that I'll be a bougee girlboss if only I learn how to overline my lips and contour with seven different shades of stick. Yassify yourself IRL, they say. Yassify yourself until you're totes goals. I follow their advice religiously. I cover up my snake tattoo with foundation, and I paint my nails bubble-gum pink, marvelling at the contrast between shiny nails and calloused palms.

And then I stand in front of my mirror. I am the girl who will be shown in history lessons a hundred years from now, to summarise this period of Britain. I am pretty by the mad standards of the fucked-up society we currently live in. I am glam and made-up, and somehow this makes me completely inconspicuous.

I've removed unnecessary people from my life. I've found myself a room to live in. The Fake Boyfriend is merely a text away. I have a stable, if sinister, job, and I've overhauled my appearance.

What stands before me is someone entirely dedicated to a mission. And I never thought I'd say this, but that mission is to put my remaining brother behind bars.

Chapter Nine

The next day, I head to work with a spring in my step, pausing only to buy a stottie from Greggs and chuck a few crumbs to the sky rats above. However, an influx of corpses steals the excitement from my plotting.

'Minibus crash on the M19,' grunts Employer #1 as he hands me a tape measurer. 'An' I preferred your old look.'

It's the first time he's seen me with blonde hair and a contoured nose. I'm not sure whether to take his dislike of it as a positive or negative. A mid-fifties gravedigger who wears exclusively waterproofs is hardly the barometer for what's in and what's out.

'D'you become desensitised to death?' I ask, and he shrugs.

'Fact of life. All you can hope is to go as peacefully as possible.'

On my lunchbreak, I buy a newspaper, purely because it features Janet's face. Smashing into a cabinet is most definitely not a peaceful way to go, but at least, unlike Joe, her death was instant. Her soul didn't seep from her body in slow motion.

'Stop it,' I hiss. 'Stop it, stop it.'

I skim-read the article: it's full of speculation as to whether Brandon and Janet were secret lovers, whether he broke into her house to try to reason with her, and an argument turned violent. A strand of her hair was found on his jacket and her spare key was later discovered in his car glovebox. It all sounds so convincing that for a second even I'm confused, wondering whether my encounter with Janet was in fact nothing more than a grief-fuelled fever dream.

There's a bit about his previous offences, most from twenty or thirty years ago: possession of firearms, drug trafficking, fights. I flip a page and his mugshot stares up at me: beady eyes, a sizeable nose and a hairless skull, slick like the head of a seal.

I recall Manbaby Flatmate declaring that he looks exactly like a murderer. He does, but there's something else. He also looks uncannily familiar.

After a few seconds of staring fruitlessly at the picture, I return to the text. Janet was an honourable woman, apparently. She hosted fundraisers in St Bernadette Church, she campaigned for the mayor, she organised litter picks and headed up the Neighbourhood Watch. She's described as capable, a hard taskmaster, hyper organised. Her loss is a tragedy for the whole town. There's to be a mass funeral. A minute's silence at a local Sainsbury's, her preferred place to shop. So much fuss and effort. The wrong person is being held accountable, but at least *someone's* being held accountable.

This thought is what spurs me into finding out more about Courtney as soon as I get home. I've already googled her plenty, of course – between trawling for updates on her, Devlin, Callum and Brandon, my phone has seldom seen so much use. But her social media accounts are private, so I use Joe's phone rather than mine, looking for anything that might give me leverage when I do approach her. A favourite band we could bond over, perhaps. Or a dark secret I could use to blackmail her with.

I sit on one of the stools in the kitchen and sift through her social media pages. As I do, my flatmates come in and out, making their respective dinners. The Manbaby Flatmate, tall and boyish, is over-friendly as ever. He's desperate for the flat share to be an extension of his uni experience. Impossible. You can't recreate that magic, not when each flat member has a two-hour round commute, a ten-hour working day and a metabolism that can no longer handle a diet of jello-shots and baked bean wraps.

'What was the maddest thing you did at uni, Ellie?' he asks me, while tearing into an Amazon delivery.

'It's Ell-*a*,' I say. Of course, I don't know his name either, but this is a conscious decision, as opposed to generic incompetence. Besides, my name has been carefully selected. It's important that I'm strict in respect of its proper usage.

'Sorry, Ella. But go on then, maddest thing you did at uni?'

I shrug and watch him unwrap a plastic duck mask. 'What's that?'

'Secret Santa present,' he says, pulling it over his head and quacking. I cringe into the tub of spaghetti in front of me.

'It's September.'

'Yeah, but Sarah's going to Malta, Ewan has to go home to Scotland, Jonny is turning vegan after next week—'

Too many unnecessary names. I interrupt, hoping to end the conversation. 'The maddest thing I did at uni was ten tequila shots and then cycle home.'

The plastic duck head tilts to and fro in consideration. 'That is quite mad.'

I pause before replying. He clearly started this conversation just so he could tell me about his own 'wild' escapades, and my time with him won't end until he does. I could also do with humouring him somewhat, just in case he ever becomes a character witness for me.

'Go on then, what's the maddest thing you ever did?'

'Did so much wild shit, man. So much.'

'Uh-huh.'

He removes the mask, as if signalling that things are getting serious. 'Used to try to get drunk using vodka-soaked tampons and shoving them up our . . . you know where.'

'Oh for God's sake. I'm about to start eating. And that's not mad, it's just gross.'

'It was quite mad. But not as tricky as you'd think – the plastic applicator bit sort of held in all the liquid until we got them . . . you know . . . *up* there. And then the alcohol wouldn't even pass through your stomach, it would just go straight into your bloodstream so woah-ho, the results were wild. Good times. Gooood times.'

I nod and turn my gaze towards my phone. 'Truly insane. You are a legend of the uni game.'

'Thanks, El!'

He opens a bag of Kettle Chips, and it takes me dwindling my replies down from four words to one word to no words before he finally leaves.

He's almost immediately replaced by my second and final flatmate, a pristine woman who must be pushing thirty-five, that I have cordially christened the Too-Old-For-This-Shit Flatmate. She takes a tiny, sad portion of salad from the fridge and mumbles about no one having taken the bins out in a week, while looking pointedly in my direction. I keep my head bowed, shovelling spaghetti into my mouth and keeping my eyes peeled on Courtney's god-awful TikTok dances.

Too-Old-For-This-Shit Flatmate is joined by a sickly-looking man she half-heartedly introduces as her boyfriend. He's dressed entirely in black and makes soup in a manner which is entirely new to me. Without cutting them up, he boils an entire carrot and an entire parsnip, before eating both from the pan. Christ, between a bag of Kettle Chips, a rocket salad and two root vegetables, my tea of spag bol seems practically indulgent.

Eventually, I wash my plate and then take Joe's phone back into my room. I flop onto my bed. What have I learned about Courtney? Not much, really, bar the surface shit she shares online, which is predominantly selfies and her miming along to clips which came out before she was born. I roll my eyes and scroll a little harder, past pictures of her kissing female friends and captions which are mainly along the lines of *MA MAIN BITCHEZ*. She seems to go out almost every weekend, always in a different dress with monstrously big shoulder pads. Perhaps I need to update my wardrobe again. She practically lives in Empire nightclub, and though she's left school, she doesn't seem to have headed to uni yet.

Who is Courtney? But who is anyone at that age? A mirror image of their surroundings, mainly. And who do I think I am, only a handful of years older? I'm no more clued up than she is, and yet here I am, judging hard.

I click away from Courtney's TikTok profile and do something I've scarcely dared to do since taking Joe's phone. I use it to find out more about *Joe*. I've already looked through all his interactions with Callum, of course, in the hope that I'd be able to find concrete evidence of threats from Callum. But they only ever called one another, and call logs aren't exactly going to put him behind bars. I've also prodded Callum's number into payphones in the hope that he might pick up, that maybe I'll be able to talk him into a confession, but he's never answered. So I head to Joe's dealings with other people: his WhatsApp messages, his saved Snapchats, his Instagram DMs. It feels gross, stalking through my little brother's phone like this, so I only half-look at things, eyes set in a squint. Scanning for interactions which might give me some kind of information. I'm not entirely sure what I'm looking for, but all I find are memes. I click into Joe's texts, on the verge of giving up, when a message from Courtney catches my eye.

Yeah, we can go on a date. If you get me some cigarettes. Lol that you fancy me, thought you were a massive fag.

The final word stings. I think back to the pictures of Courtney kissing her friends. Being gay is hot and quirky, provided it's specifically for the consumption of others. The caveats around homosexuality have always infuriated me. But the fact that Joe fancied Courtney stings too. Why? How? I keep scrolling through their messages, my gaze lingering on any which seem especially brutal.

I'll show you my tits if you tell Madame Dupont it was you who broke her window.

Wouldn't dare hold your hand in school, you're a fuckin weirdo. More fun if we're secret anyways.

Tell your pikey mam thnx for the brownies, hope we don't catch STDs off them tho lol.

Gives me the ick every time you cry.

You'd better not tell anyone about the stolen watches. U know I can make ur life hell. No getting away from me, lol.

My chest feels hot. My finger shakes as I reach their most recent exchange.

Courtney: Tell your carpet muncher sister not to try get with me tonight, I don't swing that way

Joe: Don't talk about my sister like that. Would rather you didn't come tonight

Courtney: Was a joke, course am still coming to your bday lol, u still getting the booze? U better be or else

Everything in my head becomes unfastened. Thoughts rush in and the air in my room feels stifling. I turn the phone off and escape. Not just my room, but the flat too. The sky outside is grey, dusk approaching, lights in the neighbouring houses flicking on as I pass them. I pass the river, pass the bridge, pass the big blue monster from which Joe plunged to his death. My vision is tinted red again and I see Courtney's face. Her thin eyebrows and the mean curve of her mouth, how wide it became whenever she laughed, its ability to swallow whole any joy in the people around her.

Red. I see red.

I walk until night falls, and then I return to my room, reaching for my pill box – replenished, but untouched for the past few days. I take out a little white pill and then put it back. Take it out and then put it back again.

Courtney's squealing laughter is out there, in the dark, echoing around the bridge. I walk over to my window and slam it shut. Pick up the rusty lighter and flick it on and off.

I can't let the awful messages change my plan. Painful though it might end up being, I still need to play nice with Courtney, I still need to get her onside, to get her to go back to the police and change her witness statement.

I force my mind to go *there*, to go to that awful night on the 18th of August. My memories are still hazy, still incomplete. From pain and shock, yes, but primarily from alcohol. To remember exactly what happened on the night of Joe's death, I need to think about the reason I was so drunk. I need to think about The Ex.

I reach for my pill box and then stop myself. I look at my outstretched hand and recall her skin on mine. How vivid this feeling used to be. The odd sensation of knowing it's fading day by day. I say her name, her real name, once.

Her feelings for me had seemed instant, her infatuation there from day one. It . . . confused me, I suppose. It struck me as near impossible to be so invested in someone you hardly knew. My feelings irritated the hell out of her because they crept up on me, slowly seeping through my body, one cell at a time. The eventual depth of them surprised even me. Because here I am, months later, decidedly alone and with no inclination to move on. Meanwhile, she's near half a year into an entirely different relationship.

I sit down. Slot a piece of paper into my typewriter. I'm getting side-tracked.

She met the girl she's with now, The Replacement, as the dust settled on what we'd been. They met on a family holiday to Blackpool, of all places – proof that good things do materialise under the illuminations and the shadow of the tower, perhaps. When I think of them meeting, I picture The Replacement as both a seaside gimmick (ice cream in hand, blonde hair pulled back with shell clips, long legs as sturdy as the tower beside them) and the antithesis of me: a better gay. Louder and prouder about it. Someone not to be cheated on, because a line would be drawn in the sand early on; there'd be no bouncing around between different levels of commitment, different degrees of mistrust. Or perhaps this is wishful thinking on my part. Despite her promises, down in the dark cracks between jokes shared and evenings curled into one another, she'd entertain snatched encounters with others. Because people seldom change, often regardless of who you mould yourself into.

I realise I've been holding my breath. Exhale. Recall the ciders I had on the train to meet Joe, the way they hindered my observations from the get-go. How much I'd craved them at the time. I tap into my typewriter:

```
                                        FADE IN:
                                               1
INT. TRAIN CARRIAGE - AFTERNOON
   WE OPEN in carriage E of the train from
Edinburgh to London, as it travels between
```

```
Newcastle and Darlington. The weather is warm
but grey. ELLA (22) opens a can of cider.
She takes a drink, wondering what it would
be like to have sex with The Ex again. She
doesn't get very far. Not beyond the way her
hair felt - soft at the roots, increasingly
twisted and knotted as it snaked down her
back - and her skin, textured with moles.
The bits of her that Ella avoided touching -
a scar on her left hip, the ticklish area
just below her ribs. And the bits of her
that Ella always wanted to be touching. The
emotions that would be present if Ella and
The Ex ever got within touching distance
again - confusion and regret and familiarity
and loneliness and
   BURN PAGE
```

I tear out the piece of paper and set it alight with the flick of my lighter. Jam a new piece of paper into the machine and try again:

```
                                    FADE IN:
                                        1
INT. TRAIN CARRIAGE - AFTERNOON
   WE OPEN in carriage E of the train from
Edinburgh to London, as it travels between
Newcastle and Darlington. The threat of rain
looms. ELLA (22) takes a shaking sip of cider
as she thinks about The Ex having sex with
The Replacement and she
   BURN PAGE
```

I push the ashes of my memories across the desk. Shake my head. I'm doing it again – lingering in the past. My emotions need direction; I need to control them carefully. So I slip another piece of paper into my typewriter. And I type:

FADE IN:

1

INT. ELLA'S BEDROOM - EVENING

WE OPEN with Ella, as she inches closer to righting the wrongs surrounding Joe's death.

~~Target #1 - JANET BRAITHWAITE~~

Target #2 - COURTNEY TEASDALE

Chapter Ten

After I've completed Wednesday's mandated eight hours of sprinkling sawdust in freshly dug graves and scraping bird shit off headstones, I meander the long way back to the flat. Courtney messaged Joe with her address around this time last year, inviting him to her birthday party, provided he came with a bumper pack of cigarettes. So I head to the Teasdale residence, planning an entirely innocent walk-past.

It's on quite a nice street, as it transpires. Each house is semi-detached, and they all have big bay windows. Oak trees have made the paths wonderfully lumpy, with roots pushing up through the concrete and the first orange leaves starting to smother the surface. Nature prevails, as it should.

It's a peaceful scene apart from the sound of squelching and high-pitched giggles.

'What the . . . ?' I round the corner and am met with the sight of two girls of nine or ten, each brandishing a stick and prodding the carcass of a mangled mouse.

'What the fuck?' I ask, and the girls halt their poking to stare at me.

'What are you looking at?' asks Brat #1.

'We didn't kill the mouse, honest,' says Brat #2, following my gaze. 'Someone ran it over and we wanted a look, for science.'

'Right, OK. I'm not the RSPCA, don't worry,' I say, not wanting to get into a fight with two baby hooligans – who, despite their age, could probably still fuck me up. I'm about to walk on when I clock the number of the house they're outside of: 26. Courtney's home.

'I like your dress,' says Brat #2.

'Thanks,' I say, identifying her as the twin whose bun isn't tied quite so tight, and thus seems less angry with the world. 'Fifteen pounds from Parisia.'

'Nobody cares where you got your millennial girl dress from,' says Brat #1.

'D'you want something, like?' asks Brat #2, as I stay glued to the spot.

'Uhh, yeah. I've got a birthday present for Courtney. Was going to give it to her.'

'Courtney's birthday's on Friday, duh,' says Brat #1. She rolls her eyes and uses her stick to flip the mouse over, giving the three of us a fresh but equally gory view. 'Give it her in Empire, like everyone else.'

Brat #2 nods, her eyes wide and earnest. 'You don't want to see Courtney now. She's due on.'

'Always a proper bitch at this time of the month,' adds Brat #1.

'I'm going to be lovely, whenever I get my period,' says Brat #2. 'It'll smell of roses and be a pretty blue colour like on those adverts.'

Good luck with that pipe dream. Brat #1 shares my thoughts, giving her sister a shove and telling her she's acting like a millennial, which seems to be her go-to insult. I leave Courtney's little sisters to their squabbles and continue, a plan forming in my mind.

The plan involves texting The Fake Boyfriend and asking whether he's free Friday evening. He is, of course. I don't tell him where we're going, but I do tell him he needs to wear shoes that are nice but not so nice that a splatter of WKD-infused sick would ruin them. At this he's less enthusiastic, but he doesn't cancel, so I accept my victory and move on.

Moving on involves staring at myself in the mirror and practising exactly what I'm going to say to Courtney. The little I do know about her suggests any sort of weakness or begging won't go down too well. Neither will appealing to a greater sense of good, for I'm not sure it's something she possesses. I'm yet to find something to blackmail her about, so my best bet might well be an angle focused entirely on Callum. I think about lying, pretending that I've managed to speak to him (ha – chance would be a fine thing) and that he's plotting to dob Courtney and Devlin in, to tell them he reckons their bullying contributed to Joe's death. *Get Callum before Callum gets you. Tell the police you saw him shove Joe off the bridge, and voila, the threat disappears.*

The bottle-blonde, perma-tan stranger in the mirror mouths this line of reasoning back at me, her glossy lips moving with the effort. I look unnatural for a whole host of reasons, but, perhaps most tellingly, because what I'm saying isn't true.

I need to get better at lying.

I need to get better at lying fast.

I make it to Friday with a few more practice goes under my belt. The more outrageous end of my new wardrobe gets an outing; I doll myself up in a shoulder-pad-heavy lime-green dress, a big silver necklace and three-inch flatforms. If things go tits up again, I don't want to be running away in heels. I may be new to the game, but I'm not an idiot.

In my bag, I pack a number of props I think might help endear me to Courtney: a raspberry vape, tampons, cigarettes, deodorant, spare razor, ibuprofen, chewing gum, sweets, lip gloss. Insulin crash, bad breath or influx of sweat – I'm ready to swoop in.

'Interesting new look,' says The Fake Boyfriend, when I greet him by the Bottle of Notes, a sculpture in Central Square.

'Not a fan?' I ask.

He squirms before saying, 'I preferred your old look.'

'You're the second person to tell me that.'

'Maybe you should listen.'

Neither he nor Employer #1 have exactly been style icons, so I'm taking both of their opinions with a pinch of salt. I don't tell him this, for I want him to give me a glowing character testimony should the time ever come, so I say, 'Maybe I should. You do dress nicely.'

The Fake Boyfriend blushes and readjusts his glasses. 'It might surprise you to hear no one has ever told me that before.'

He's wearing jeans that must be three or four sizes too big, a bright red belt that's working overtime to keep them up, and a jumper which reads 'I'm not lazy! I'm just on battery saving mode!' Tonight, of all nights, my normaliser is looking distinctly un-normal.

Again, not a thought that should travel from my brain to my lips, so I say, with as much sincerity as possible, 'That does surprise me.'

His cheeks are crimson, so, to give him space to de-blush, I take out Joe's phone and click onto Courtney's Instagram.

I have to remind myself that I can't watch anyone's stories without fear of freaking them out, so I'm left at the mercy of actual posts, which no one seems to do anymore.

I check the time: almost ten. Stroke my bag, feeling the shapes of the various knick-knacks within. My stomach churns, nerves mixing with excitement. Callum, locked up where he belongs. Tonight might be the night that that dream begins to set down roots in reality.

A wave of distant drum and bass hits us, as if Empire has just turned up the volume on its sound systems, a pied piper for the scantily clad, the overly drunk and all those in possession of a fake ID.

The Fake Boyfriend moans, and I return my attention to him.

'Please don't tell me we're going to a nightclub,' he says.

'What else did you think we'd be doing at this time on a Friday night?'

He glances upwards, at the night sky.

'Stargazing?' I ask. 'You really thought we were going on a stargazing date?'

His cheeks, which had returned to their normal shade, colour once more. 'You were wearing an astronomy t-shirt when I met you.'

I almost tell him how much I'd have enjoyed a stargazing date, how much I do like space. Not from a scientific point of view, mind you, just from . . . I don't know, an aesthetic one? It's vast and beautiful. Whenever my modules featured camera work, I'd always have to resist the urge to tilt my equipment skywards.

I shake my head. I'm Ella, not Elizabeth, and Ella needs the pair of us to dance in a sweaty abyss. So we move across the green and towards the nightclub, past a hissing group of girls with #BeKind across their chests and hate in their hearts. One of them mocks The Fake Boyfriend's jeans, and I sense him stiffen beside me.

I up my pace and get us to the nightclub queue as quickly as possible.

'Everyone looks so young,' says The Fake Boyfriend, when we come to a stop. 'When did everyone get so young?'

I scan the queue and do indeed see a handful of boys who look yet to spring a facial hair between them.

'I used to babysit that one,' I say, motioning in the direction of a boy in possession of both a baby face and a tattoo of a gun. 'He'd projectile vomit at exactly 9.03 every evening, and it was always bright blue.'

The Fake Boyfriend laughs. 'Punctual bright blue sick? Never heard of that one.'

'He ate more blueberries than I'd have thought physically possible.'

'You're a liar, Ella.'

'I'd never lie to you.'

He catches my gaze and I hold it for a second or two, until something vulnerable seems to dance across his eyes, and I feel compelled to look away.

'What about that one?' he asks, pointing out a boy with a stretcher in his ear and grills across his teeth.

'Yep, he'd sometimes visit when I babysat. Always with his dog-eared teddy bear, of course. Couldn't separate him from it.'

We invent histories for each boy in turn, reducing them to some long-forgotten innocence – childhood folly as opposed to adult apathy.

'What about me?' The Fake Boyfriend finally asks.

'You were . . . the type of kid who learned to read when he was like two and a half or something ridiculous, but also sometimes you'd eat dirt. So you know, you were really clever but no one ever felt jealous of you because you had quite a sizeable dirt-eating flaw.'

He laughs. 'That is . . . worryingly accurate.'

There's a comfortable silence, and a question I can't resist asking. 'And me?' I eventually say.

The Fake Boyfriend looks at me for ten or twenty seconds before answering. 'Loyal but holds a grudge. A sensitive soul – a kid who'd cry in the sandpit for three hours if one of her friends ignored her, probably blinking back tears to tell off the child shoving dirt in his gob. Wants everyone to stay safe, or something. Sickly sweet.'

When I don't reply, The Fake Boyfriend adds, 'How did I do? Accurate or not?'

I've accidentally murdered a middle-aged woman, nearly everything that's passed through my lips in the past six weeks has been a lie, and I think I'd do almost anything so that what I think should happen happens.

'Accurate,' I say, eventually. 'Sickly sweet. Painfully accurate.'

He nods, and the queue starts moving.

We pass by tatty rainbow flags – hung up for Pride and (unusually) not yet taken down. For a reason I've never been able to put my finger on, I don't especially identify with the flags. And this makes me feel bad, ungrateful for all the suffering and sacrifices which have allowed me to freely fuck girls (in this country, anyway). But I just . . . don't feel particularly strongly about them. Not because I don't believe in what they represent, and not because I'm not proud to be represented by them, but I've always perceived myself as such a neutral-to-dark hued person that rainbows strike me as the antithesis to this. They're loud, proud, bold – everything the LGBTQ+ community has fought for and everything we should be able to be, but I still find myself staring at the flags, not entirely sure how I fit in.

I turn back to face The Fake Boyfriend, feeling every inch the guilty gay. He readjusts his glasses, not even clocking the flags. The queue inches forward, and there are new things to look at: smudged band posters and ripped takeaway menus. My gaze slips from them. I'm impatient, and can sense that The Fake Boyfriend is too.

Finally, just when I fear he might leave, we're allowed into the building. It's a massive nightclub, and I worry that Courtney will be almost impossible to keep track of.

We head into the cavernous main space, only half full but made to feel busier by smoke and strobe lights and the sheer energy emitted by the teenage crowd: Teesside Twostepping to Maximo Park or snogging one another at a furious pace. I've never seen so many people look like they're attempting to consume someone else.

I head over to the bar to get drinks, while The Fake Boyfriend assumes his position: lofty, out-of-sync awkwardness. The option of sticking to soft drinks is toyed with, but in the end, I settle on a cider – just a little something to ready myself for the task in hand.

While our drinks are being poured, I scan the room. I'll need to locate Courtney – the sooner, the better. To do so, I hand both drinks to The Fake Boyfriend, and tell him I'm going to the toilet. He nods and then gestures to the speakers.

'They've murdered Kate Bush. They've killed a classic. How am I meant to dance to this when I'm used to the tempo being 108bpm? How am I meant to suddenly adjust to it being doubled?'

'The most pressing conundrum of modern times. I'm sure you'll figure it out. See you in a minute.'

I meander around, not expecting to spot Courtney straight away. She'll probably be fashionably late, or surrounded by so many friends it'll be hard to pick her out. Will Devlin be here? What were they to each other, anyway?

A flight of stairs leads me to a smaller, slightly busier area. EDM music floods the dance floor, and an artist paints reveller's faces for £5 a pop in one corner. I rest an elbow against the sticky bar, looking and listening as best as I can.

There are a group of Southerners next to me, gawking around as if they're on safari and furiously discussing how this compares to a night out in somewhere called Infernos. Eventually, their chat turns to dating, and my attention drifts until one of the boys – with a long, horsey face and floppy hair – knocks into me while collecting his espresso martini. He apologises and then turns to his friend and says, 'Yah, when she saw my guacamole skills – game over.'

'You pulled Saskia?'

'Pulled Saskia, bloody nearly had her angling for marriage, that's how good my guac was. Almost pulled Hettie, too.'

'Yah?'

'Yah.'

They take their drinks, still debating the ideal viscosity of guacamole, and move away. I miss their presence nearly instantly, for I'm suddenly struck by the sensation that I've switched from watcher to watchee. My neck tingles, and I scan the mass of bodies pulsating around me. It's hard to pick out anyone in particular, for the revellers around me seem to move as one impenetrable being, like seaweed swaying at the bottom of the ocean. Nauseous, I turn back to face the bar, pulling out my debit card and tapping it against the counter.

A couple of minutes of fruitlessly attempting to attract the attention of the barman pass when a girl knocks into me as she shoves her way to the front. Her long, dark ponytail almost burrows up into my nostrils.

I'm about to shove her away, when I realise who she is. Courtney. Wearing an 'IT'S MY BIRTHDAY' badge, a thin black dress and, bizarrely, a feather boa. (Are feather boas back? How did I miss this in all my hours of research?) Her long, delicate neck is encircled by a gold necklace which reads *Libra*.

Her handbag pushes against my leg – sticky fake leather against my own sweaty flesh. I attempt to swallow my nerves, deciding on the greeting that might best work to my advantage. The comparable conversation with Janet started badly and ended terribly, I'd like to think that the only way is up.

'Nine pounds for a mojito! This place thinks it's The Ritz! Thank God we necked all the pre-drinks vodka,' says Courtney to one of her friends.

'Oh, it's your birthday! I'll get you a drink,' I say, and instantly regret such a desperate statement.

Courtney shifts her gaze in my direction, and I slap a friendly expression onto my face, anticipating confusion mixed with gratitude. Perhaps even a warning that she's not gay and I'd better not be trying to chat her up. This isn't what I get.

'Elizabeth. Oh my God.'

She grabs me, wraps me in her arms and squeezes me. I freeze, not sure how to react.

'Oh God, oh Elizabeth. Oh my God. I'm so sorry.'

She withdraws but keeps hold of my hands. She looks at me as though she's assessing a stray dog.

'I'm so sorry about Joe. Really, he's all I've thought about recently. All anyone's talked about,' she says.

And now there's not just two emotions churning in my stomach anymore, but hundreds. Confusion and shock and, and . . . this deep, damp sadness. She's sorry about Joe? Is she truly sorry about Joe, when she laughed him up to the bridge he fell from? It's as if The Replacement has just come up to me and said she's sorry that me and The Ex didn't work out.

'I'm . . . I'm surprised you recognise me,' I manage.

'Well . . . it is an interesting look. Little bit last year, but I'm glad you've found an outlet for your grief. 'Course, a better outlet is getting shitfaced. Drink?' She removes her hands from mine and replaces them with an overpriced mojito. I take a sip.

Her friends are behind her; they're staring at us and wearing eyeshadow in matching shades, as though they all got ready together. Courtney tells them to go and dance, and then she turns to me.

'So, how are you holding up? They didn't uncover anything shocking about Joe, did they? Nothing that would make this any harder, like?' she asks, leaning in close so that I can hear her over the music. She's softer spoken than I remember. Where's that horrible, high-pitched giggle? I search her eyes for signs of malice but find only curiosity. Courtney the vicious bully crumbles so quickly I begin to wonder if I made her up.

She's tactile – her hands on my arms, a squeeze of my shoulders. She coos about how much of a shock Joe's death was, how hard it's all been. She buys me another drink. I shouldn't be edging my way towards drunk when I've got to bargain with and manipulate her, but . . . but will I have to? The way she's clucking over me, I'm sure the truth alone will render her more than ready to help.

Lime and sugar swirls up through the straw and into my mouth.

'Fancy a cigarette? Or a vape?' I say, after swallowing.

'Aye, wouldn't mind that, like,' she replies, shooting me a smile over her drink.

As we exit, I catch a glimpse of The Fake Boyfriend, caught in a pit of bodies.

'That's my boyfriend, by the way,' I say to Courtney. 'We came here together. I didn't come alone. He loves clubbing.'

'Oh right, uh-huh, didn't have you down as a clubber or a boyfriend girl, hun.'

'Well, that's me. Boys and clubs. Clubs and boys.'

The Fake Boyfriend is so tall, his head sticks out above everyone else's. I mouth 'five mins' at him before turning away.

Outside is a relief, at least initially – air that doesn't taste of armpits, nor surge with the blasphemous reimagining of hit eighties tracks. Courtney and I lean against a wall, and I take out my packet of cigarettes.

'Ta,' she says, accepting one. She spends a second twisting it back and forth between her long acrylic nails before lighting up.

I opt for the raspberry vape; as a non-smoker I figure there's less potential for embarrassment, though it does make me feel like Mam, which is never a sensation I actively seek.

'I did actually want to speak to you about Joe,' I say, after a tentative inhale.

'Oh God, of course babe, of course.'

'Just about what you told the police, you know?'

Courtney takes a drag and flicks back her ponytail. She looks cool enough to singlehandedly re-popularise smoking among the youth. I take another cautious inhale of my fruity vape, suddenly feeling childish in comparison.

'Told them everything I remember. Joe climbing up of his own accord. Joe tripping off the top. Dangerous up on that bridge, you know.'

'But you . . . are you sure that's what you saw?' I press.

'Well aye. Wanted to be as helpful as possible cos I knew you were a bit too drunk to be of much use, like.'

A patronising response which sends a tingle of indignation rippling through me. A *teenager* has just berated my alcohol consumption. I'm flustered, and this throws me off my smoking; I inhale too much and end up coughing.

'There, there, I know, hun,' says Courtney, stroking my arm with her free hand. 'I was low-key glad you were so pissed, like. Protected you from the worst of it, in a way.'

'I wasn't that drunk,' I say.

Courtney chooses not to answer, so I continue, 'Or maybe you think I was, and that's OK. But Joe didn't just trip off the top. I saw Callum push him.'

Courtney inhales in such a dramatic manner that the entrails from both my and her last puffs rush between her lips.

'No? Callum? Eee, he seemed dead nice when I met him. Are you sure? That's a hell of an accusation. Joe always made it out like they got on?'

Courtney rubs my arm harder, as if she's trying to start a fire.

'I mean, I always thought they got on, but—'

'You were *very* drunk, Elizabeth. Can't say I always remember things right when I'm drunk.'

I know I shouldn't, but I can't help it, I disentangle myself from her. Courtney shoots me a strained smile and then takes another puff of her cigarette.

'Callum pushed Joe. The police don't believe me, but if *two* witnesses say the same thing, they'll have to take it more seriously.'

Courtney nods, and her gaze flickers away from me.

'Fuck me, getting cold out, isn't it?' she says, rubbing her feather boa up and down her arms, as if that'll make a blind bit of difference. I silently curse myself for not packing a spare cardigan.

'I mean, a little, but—'

'Shall we go inside? Could do with topping up me makeup.'

I have so much more to say, but no time to say it, for Courtney stubs out her cigarette and turns on her heel. I have no choice but to follow her back into the nightclub and in the direction of the bathrooms.

'Fuckin' hell,' she says, upon seeing the women's bathroom. It's absolutely packed, with girls tripping over themselves to take mirror selfies, reapply blusher and generically tell one another they're boss bitches and all men are dicks. I could stick my head in and shout out each of Mam's quotes and I'd likely make more friends than I've had in my life.

'Never mind,' says Courtney. 'Staff toilets are upstairs and round the back. My mate Decca used to work here.'

We wind our way up through the various sections of the nightclub, sampling different music and revellers as we go. Occasionally, we get stuck in a crowd or on a staircase, and I seize my opportunities to say things to Courtney.

'It would mean everything to Joe, his death being properly investigated, you know.'

No answer.

'Would help it all seem less . . . futile and hopeless.'

Still nothing.

'And to me . . . it would mean . . . everything to me. If you could help.'

The crowd shifts as a new song starts, and a gap onto a staircase appears. Courtney manoeuvres into it, and I follow.

'I know you're maybe . . . maybe you're scared of the police? But it would just be like doing what you did last time, except adding the bit in about Callum. I could come to the station with you, I don't mind coming to the station with you.'

We've finally reached the top of the nightclub. It's darker and quieter, and the crowd is thinner – just a couple of stragglers and the odd passing person who strides with such an air of authority and urgency, they can only be staff. One of them hurries past me leaving the smell of nicotine and hair gel so pungently in his wake that I dry heave.

Courtney ducks past the cleaning cupboard – bulging open from an overload of mops, bleach and brooms – and into the empty staff bathroom.

'Elizabeth.' She stops abruptly, and turns to me. 'I know you're upset about Joe, but I'm not going to lie to the police for you.'

The light in the bathroom is ugly, the grimy grey of a half-dead lightbulb which hasn't been dusted for some time. It gives Courtney a ghostly glow.

'You wouldn't be lying,' I say. 'You were just behind me. You saw what I saw. You saw Callum push Joe. You couldn't have missed it.'

She shakes her head before turning towards the mirror.

'If I went in and poked Callum, d'you not think he'd poke back twice as hard? D'you not think he'd accuse me of shit?'

I can't help myself. I say, 'What? Cruel messages you sent to Joe? The way you picked on him all night? The fact you told him to climb up the bridge?'

I see Courtney's reflection roll its eyes. 'Oh my God, Elizabeth.

96

Joe had a mind of his own. It's *pathetic* he did everything I told him to.'

For a second, I don't realise that I, too, am reflected in the mirror. I look ashy, stoic, like a statue. With some difficulty, I crack open lips that feel like concrete.

'Please. Please. I know you saw what I saw.'

I feel as though I'm a toddler trying to smash a star-shaped block into a square hole. No one is behaving the way I want them to, and it makes me want to throw a tantrum. I am behaving like a child. And yet nothing has ever mattered so much to me. Right and wrong seem so blindingly obvious, I can't believe others can't see it.

They can see it. Of course they can see it. They'd just rather save their own skin.

'What I saw was Joe – who was, by the way, renowned for being fucking weak and weird and pathetic – being weak and weird and pathetic by doing a stupid dare I'd given him, and then being so utterly useless, he just fucking fell to his death,' says Courtney.

She smacks her lips together and then laughs – high-pitched and horrible. The laugh that chased Joe up to the top of the bridge.

She turns and heads into one of the cubicles, locking the door behind her.

My eyes dart to and fro, taking in my grey surroundings. The hard edge of the sink. The sharp corner of a smashed bit of mirror. The solid base of an abandoned glass. I think of all that I packed in my bag: the painkillers and the razor. I think of Courtney, in the cubicle, think of the sharp point of her heel, the promising length of her feather boa, the pin of her birthday badge. I think of her long, delicate neck and the *Libra* necklace draped around it.

'Oh fuck, I'm on,' says Courtney, from inside the cubicle. 'D'you have a spare tampon?'

I'm snapped from my daze.

'Err yeah. Yeah, I do,' I say.

I open my bag and extract the tampon, removing it from its packet. And then I nip outside, to the cleaner's cupboard. Initially, I reach for the bottle of bleach, before clocking a bottle of antifreeze. I unscrew the lid and dip the tampon inside. The cotton swells as it absorbs the liquid, but the plastic applicator holds it in shape. I imagine it'll feel weird, though, so it's a good job Courtney had all the pre-drinks vodka.

I slip the tampon back into its packet and return to the bathroom, squatting to pass it to Courtney underneath the cubicle door.

'I opened the packet for you,' I say, 'Thought you might find that kind of difficult, what with your two-inch nails.'

Courtney's fingers close around the tampon.

'And you probably want to insert it too, don't you? Fag.'

I let go. It's as easy as that. I let go and then I leave, turning on my heel, exiting the bathroom, striding down the corridor and pushing back down into the bowels of the nightclub. The Fake Boyfriend has left, a decision I respect but one which doubtless means he's crawled back into himself.

A problem. But not a problem for now.

I exit the club and stride forward. With each step, everything seems to slow: the taxis and the drunken men falling into them. Sly foxes shifting through bins. My own heart. Neon lights from late-night chicken shops become one delicious blur.

I stretch my arms out, gliding through the still air. Noises that might ordinarily be separate – giggles and screeches and the low mumbling of car engines, the tinny music of house parties – merge together for me, becoming a single, deep symphony which shakes my very soul.

I stretch my arms wider. Keep walking. Middlesbrough wakes up. The sun rises, setting the factories and towers on fire. I blink it all in, savour the town's golden resurgence before it's smothered by a blanket of smog.

I'm smiling. My face twists into something harder, something colder, as if I'm solidifying, as if I'm turning to stone.

Chapter Eleven

Courtney's death is confirmed via social media, of course. To my surprise and relief, it doesn't sound like she made it out of the bathroom. I monitor her accounts via Joe's phone, and observe the flurry of heartbroken messages and comments. They appear thick and fast. Lamentations about how shocked everyone is, how much she'll be missed. There are rumblings about her death having been caused by toxic shock syndrome, or alcohol poisoning, or ecstasy, but nothing concrete.

How bad should I feel? This is the question that occupies my mind. While Janet's death was accidental, there was most certainly intent in Courtney's. Still though, in an abstract way, it doesn't feel like I've murdered her. It's not as if I've bashed her repeatedly over the head (I don't think I've got something like that in me), I merely gave Courtney what she asked for, albeit with a deadly twist.

Still, deep down, I feel something which has a distinctly guilty pang. If I wasn't here, if I was in Manchester editing scripts or fetching coffee for actors, Courtney would still be alive. But then again, might Joe still be alive if Courtney never had been?

'Stop it,' I mumble. Going around in circles like this is counterproductive. Besides, other feelings are stronger: the rage that surged through me when she insulted Joe. The frustration upon realising that she wouldn't help me reveal the truth of Joe's death, because she was a part of it. The crushing sense of sorrow I feel whenever I look at messages sent from Courtney to Joe. And I look at them frequently, I look whenever I clock a heartbroken post telling the world what a good person Courtney was.

But stronger than any other thought, is the memory of how I felt in the wee hours after exiting Empire. The way time and space slowed and twisted for me. The sense of freedom. The sense of release.

When news of her death makes it into *The Northern Echo* obituaries page, I cut out the little paragraph and head to Mam and Liev's. I clutch the scrap of paper tight between my thumb and forefinger and feel like a child, rushing home from school to show my parents my latest shite piece of artwork.

Mam nigh on faints when she opens the door.

'Eee. That's a look and a half,' she says, eyeing my mauve faux-fur jacket and cut-out dress (admittedly a bold choice given the autumnal chill in the air).

'Quite a look for you, too,' I reply, shocked to see that she's followed the suggestion I made on my previous visit. She's wearing sensible, beige trousers and a knitted jumper decorated with cartoon cats. She might even have overdone it somewhat – anyone would know within a couple of minutes of talking to her that she's not the least bit religious, despite her cross earrings, crucifix necklace and Star of David brooch suggesting a confused alternative. The biggest change, however, is her hair. I've gone blonde, while Mam's gone brunette. This probably says something profound about society's perception of women as they age, but I'm not smart enough to articulate what.

I follow her into the living room and my eyes land on Liev – much the same, bar a pair of wire-framed glasses.

'Now then, Elizabeth,' he says.

'I'm actually calling myself Ella, these days.'

'Hallelujah!' says Mam as she collapses onto the sofa. 'Been trying to call you Ella since you were a toddler! You wouldn't have it, mind. Such a serious kid.'

'Glasses?' I ask, eyes still on Liev.

'Aye. Glasses are for nerds. And nerds are never in trouble. Plus, I look damn good in them.'

Christ. I look at his large hands and wide shoulders and suppress the laugh knocking at the roof of my mouth.

'Pile of shite though, this,' he continues, waving a thick book at me.

I squint at the book.

'Yeah. Well, you might have been a bit ambitious, starting off with *War and Peace*,' I reply, sitting down on the armchair. The sensation of the crushed velvet against my limbs is familiar. Almost comfortingly familiar.

Step-Nan joins us, a cup of tea clutched between her hands. I squeeze the clipping between my fingers, attempting to determine how to tell them what I've done. I turn to Liev, who's muttering to Step-Nan. I should stop calling him Liev, really. I'm not naming unimportant people these days, so it no longer seems appropriate. No name has ever felt quite right for my stepdad, though. I remember Mam bringing him home, barely a year after Dad died. Despite the inheritance, we'd had it rough since Mitch had passed, with all those who hated him viewing Mam, Callum and me as easy targets. Scary men would harass us, and Mam had seemed the only safe haven in an increasingly dangerous world. So I was pleased, upon meeting Liev. Pleased until I clocked his eyes, the way they'd harden with annoyance whenever they roamed over me or Callum. Pleased until I saw how tightly he'd hold Mam, the bruises he would leave on her.

I don't think I truly remember this, of course. I was four at the time; I barely remember anything from that period of my life. Most likely, this is just a tale passed down to me by Callum, embellished for dramatic effect. It hasn't proven to be inaccurate, though.

I mouth the word 'stepdad', noting the way in which it shapes my tongue. Perhaps mine and Callum's refusal to call him 'Dad', as requested, was the point at which relations began to sour. We settled on 'Liev' and he hated it, which only endeared the name to us more. 'Stepdad.' I mouth the word again. I'd like to call him Stepdad #1 in the hope that I might get a new one but – near two decades on – this seems increasingly unlikely.

'Not that any of us need to look more innocent now though, right?' he says. 'What with that Brandon Pearce confessing to your murder.'

'Yeah. That was . . . He must be crazy. Or a massive attention seeker.' I say the only thing that makes sense. 'But I . . . well I . . . you know I was going to talk to Courtney?'

'Oh yeah, did she agree to go back to the police?' asks Mam. She picks her vape up from the coffee table and I'm immediately reminded of my night at Empire. A sweet, fruity smell fills the room and my stomach flips.

'No. She was never going to help,' I say. I hand over the scrap of newspaper. The ink has smudged against my fingertips, as if the consequences of my actions are starting to pollute my body.

'Oh Christ. Oh wow,' Mam says, her eyes widening as she reads. 'You did this?'

'It just . . . I didn't plan to,' I say. 'But you should have heard the things she was saying about Joe.'

Mam is torn, I can see it in her eyes as they dart back and forth, and in her knuckles, as they tense and relax around her vape. A normal mother might scream that this isn't how she raised me. But Mam knows she didn't raise us especially well. And she can be savage, like, she'll understand why I did what I did.

Stepdad speaks before she can, 'Wow. You get away with it?'

I shrug. Step-Nan has the mug which reads 'Classy, Sassy and a bit Bad-assy'. My eyes linger on the word 'Bad' and I say, 'I think so. They don't seem to be treating her death as suspicious.'

I'm beginning to think that my idea of avenging Joe needs to shift. Getting Callum locked up is increasingly looking like an impossible dream. I've tried to deny this, but it's felt good to see those that contributed to Joe's death suffer. Janet, for not helping me rescue Joe. Courtney, for bullying him to the top of the bridge. Devlin and the man with the dog are guilty of similar sins. And Callum, of course. The worst of them all.

This is a thought I try to articulate to Mam and Stepdad.

'I don't think anyone's going to change their witness statement,' I say. 'This isn't something that's going to be solved in a court. So I've been thinking . . . I've been thinking . . .'

I can't say it. I've been thinking that I've already killed two people. What's three more? There's certainty in death, but it's more than that, it's the feeling of control, of justice, of power. It's this brief, brilliant absence of grief.

Stepdad understands. Of course he does. He starts mumbling about tracking down Callum. About hurting him with his bare hands. I look to Step-Nan as he speaks, wondering how much of this conversation she's taking in. How much mental capacity she has left, whether, despite Mam's reassurances she might accidentally let slip what's being discussed. I keep waiting for the uncomfortable sensation of her beady eyes on my body, but she remains blank, staring somewhere beyond me.

Stepdad becomes increasingly animated, reminding Mam of Callum's violent tendencies and reckless nature. He doesn't speak of Devlin or the man with the dog. I zone out. I might have just alluded to killing three more people, but I'm not sure I have the stomach to go through with it. Instead, I look up to the ceiling, pretending that I can see not only into Mam and Stepdad's bedroom, but all the way through it and into the attic above. I picture the sandwich years between Callum leaving and me heading to uni, when I used to skulk around the beams by myself, sweating in the summer and shivering come winter. I wasn't allowed my phone for vast stretches in this period of my life, so my isolation seemed ten-fold.

I had Joe, though. Whenever he came in, we'd call it 'visiting hour' – his face and mine lighting up whenever his head popped up and into the loft. Visiting hour could last anywhere between five and five hundred minutes, and would normally start with me rolling my eyes and saying, 'Oh, it's you. Smelly little boys aren't allowed up here,' while failing to conceal the grin twitching at my lips. We'd lounge about on my bed, taking it in turns to play whatever our favourite songs were at the time. Initially this was done on my phone (if I had it). Later, Joe would haul his guitar up and happily pluck away. My brow crumples as I try to recall whether he'd enjoyed playing for me. He had, I'm certain. Visiting hours were sacred and safe.

I'm not tactile, and I don't think Joe ever was, either (he certainly never clung to Mam), but he was the one person I felt completely comfortable touching. I remember the coarse sensation of his curls between my fingers, the weight of his body slumped against mine whenever he'd had a tough day at school and needed a few forlorn minutes of comfort.

I drag myself back downstairs and into the present to tell the three of them that I'm leaving. I receive a cautious peck on the cheek from Mam, and a squeeze from Stepdad. Both actions that I'm too surprised and nervous about to enjoy.

As I walk back to my flat, I examine my chipped nails and my scuffed, impractical boots. My hair extensions are ratty, and my false eyelashes are falling out in clumps, giving me a blinkered, dozy appearance. I pick away at my acrylics, thinking about the problems with my new look.

I have turned myself into society's norm, but this also seems to have turned me into society's possession. In the past couple of weeks, I've noted that men seem to assume they both know me and own me. I clock them taking sly pictures on the bus. One man screamed that I was a slag when I accidentally walked in front of his car, as if my taste in dresses and inability to look both ways before crossing the road has any correlation to how promiscuous I am. I tried to think up a male equivalent insult that's as instantaneously degrading, but I drew a blank.

More pertinently, Courtney no longer exists, so dressing in a way which might endear me to her is pointless. I've also realised that my idea of an inconspicuous outfit is, in fact, rather conspicuous. Big hair, high heels and bright Lycra practically begs for attention. Naturally – isn't that what everyone in their early twenties craves? I shouldn't. I don't. In retrospect, leaving a murder scene in a lime-green dress probably hasn't been my brightest idea.

I let myself into the flat and head straight to my bedroom. One of my flatmates is baking shortbread; the smell of it pads across the landing and slides under my door, filling the room with a warm, strawberry smell. A welcome accompaniment to the reassessment of my appearance. I unclip my hair extensions and stand still, looking in the mirror. I need to be attractive enough that people assume nice things about me, but not attractive enough to be memorable, not worthy of fantasising about the next day.

Ha, as if that would ever be possible.

I decide to keep my blonde hair, pink eyeshadow and the prettiest of my tops, but reintroduce trainers and jeans to my wardrobe. Back before Joe's death and the realignment of my priorities, I enjoyed lining my eyes in a thick black kohl. More recently, I've been trying and failing to adopt a neat, winged eye. Heavy eyeliner feels gothic and inappropriate, while the subtler version is taking me too much time to perfect. So I stuff the unforgiving black stick beneath my bed and commit my time more wholeheartedly to completing what I've started.

'Woah, did you hear about that girl?' asks Manbaby Flatmate with such enthusiasm in his voice that it travels into my room, souring the strawberry.

'Huh?' asks Too-Old-For-This-Shit Flatmate.

'That girl? Got killed last weekend?'

'I really don't care, I'm trying to concentrate.'

I care, though. My body has frozen at the use of the word 'killed' as opposed to 'died'; my right arm is floating in the air, a lock of tatty hair extension pincered between my fingers. I put it down and move towards my door – Too-Old-For-This-Shit Flatmate is patently too busy zesting fruit to ask follow-up questions, so I'm going to have to take investigating into my own hands.

'What was that?' I ask as casually as possible, sweeping into the kitchen and pouring myself a glass of water.

'What was what?' asks Manbaby Flatmate. He's opening an Amazon delivery and getting under the feet of Too-Old-For-This-Shit Flatmate, who's furiously rolling dough and pushing blonde tendrils of hair back from her sweaty forehead.

'What you were just talking about.'

'Ewan's mega sesh at graduation?' he replies. Good God, he just won't let uni die, will he?

'No, the . . . you said someone had been killed? Kind of freaked me out.'

'Oh my God, yeah!' He takes a pair of fish flops from the cardboard box and waves them around. 'Yeah, this girl – Coco or Candice or something. Worked at Macy Brown's with Jonny. Died last weekend. But apparently didn't like die, die. Big rumours that she was murdered.'

'Wow. How?'

He shrugs, slipping the fish flops onto his enormous feet. 'Jonny's gone vegan so, like, everything he tells me is mega confused. Don't think he's discovered lentils yet, so I reckon he's just living off vegan Percy Pigs. Everything he tells me comes out in a backwards order.'

So. Much. Unnecessary. Information.

'Oh, I have heard of this,' says Too-Old-For-This-Shit Flatmate, pausing her rolling to give the pair of us her full attention. Our eyes meet, and I realise it's the first time I've properly looked at her. There's something tired yet sharp about her expression. 'Courtney Teasdale. My cousin dated her last year. I heard she died of toxic shock syndrome?'

'Yeah no, no, no. This is the thing. Apparently not. Jonny said the pathologist said her death hadn't been accidental.'

My heart is beating so loudly, I'm certain they'll be able to hear it. I open my mouth, feeling the urge to speak in order to conceal the heavy, guilty pounding from my chest, but my lips are dry. Too dry to form words.

Too-Old-For-This-Shit Flatmate speaks before I can, 'So, what?'

'So, there's a killer on the loose.'

Second time round, you'd think I'd be prepared. But I seem to have a more visceral reaction to Courtney's death being treated as a murder. The hairs on my skin seem constantly raised, as if someone is always watching me. Sleeping, already hard, becomes near impossible. Anti-freeze and bodily fluids have likely eradicated my DNA from the tampon itself, but what about the tampon wrapper? Did Courtney throw it away? Have the police rifled through bins? And what about CCTV? Will they have trawled back through her entire night at Empire? I think about breaking into the nightclub and trying to steal the bathroom footage. An idea so untenable, my brain of a few months ago wouldn't have entertained it for more than a couple of seconds. But my brain now? It lingers on this possibility for multiple fruitless hours.

I return to my pill box. Five white pills do nothing, so I take a sixth. Pace up and down my room, feeling my mind curl in on itself. A spring I'll only be able to keep pushed down for so long.

So I leave. I find Devlin's address in Joe's phone, and head there. But rather than stop in Grangetown, I head further north, towards the quiet industrial estate, where groups of lads linger, chugging White Lightning and watching – anger and resignation etched onto faces which look old but aren't – the place where they should be working. The steady, useful career which, in an alternate universe, would have been available to them. These are the lads who stood clutching 'Save

Our Steel' signs one September morning nearly a decade ago, as their dads were laid off. These are the boys who watched the government bail out bankers but not steelworkers. The boys who watched their family's finances crumble, who watched their own future options shrink by magnitudes of ten.

I squint, wondering if Devlin is among them. Wondering if Callum is. If Joe would have been.

They hurl metal poles and bits of rubble over barbed-wire fences. They cut open the fence and run, hooting and hollering around the once thriving site. Security guards with barking Alsatians come for them eventually, and I watch as the hard masks of their faces melt. They smile. For they finally feel seen. Finally, they're making a mark on the town, living out a twisted version of the future that had been promised.

It's an area I visit a few times over the coming days. The lads shout. They fight. They set fire to the scrapheaps and the dry grass which lines the barbed-wire fences. They cause enough of a commotion that police get involved, that tutting mothers share videos on Facebook, moaning about the wretchedness of youth. I daresay, at their peak, the fires would have been visible to the planes flying overhead, that happy holidaymakers might have looked down and assumed Bonfire Night celebrations were starting early. But still – despite the noise and the desperation and the disruption – most of Teesside's industry remains closed.

I move on from them, eventually. I perch on a bench close to Devlin's mam's ground-floor flat, chipping red paint from the wooden slats and vowing to make amends with The Fake Boyfriend. His presence would make mine seem far less shady. Still, everyone who passes by me is friendly enough. The girl who apologises for the delightful burbling of her bairns. A bald man with a big belly who lets me pet his Irish wolfhound. He slips me a biscuit, and the great beast becomes my friend for life. Decent people dealt hard hands.

Devlin returns to the flat in the evening. Even from metres away, I smell the ash buried deep in his hoody and his short, dark hair. I pull my own hood up and watch as life ripples through the ground-floor flat. A bird swoops through the living room. An anaemic light is switched on, casting a hospital-like glow about the room. His mam stirs and rises. She's a short lady with a stoop.

For a while, little happens, and I look around at the neighbouring houses – some done up nicely, with freshly painted window frames and fake flowers on the sills, while others are rougher: trollies in the garden and windows cracked so that the glass looks like tree roots, or a river trickling off into different directions. There's a park behind me, full of boys pedalling bikes idly, and beyond this are two things: Eston hills, turning rust-coloured as the year draws to a close, and the ghostly industrial estate. Always the ghostly industrial estate. An omnipresent reminder of what we've all lost.

I look down and scroll through Joe's phone, a habit I seem incapable of breaking. I've just started looking through his notes, when yelling from Devlin's house immobilises my finger.

'MOVE. FUCKING MOVE. I CAN'T TAKE THIS ANYMORE. I CAN'T TAKE IT.'

Voyeuristic of me, to be hearing things that are supposed to stay within the four walls of Devlin and his mam's flat. But his mam is screeching so loudly, it would be impossible not to hear.

'FUCKING MOVE!'

I can't tell if this instruction is intended for Devlin, or for one of the half a dozen birds which flap about inside her living room. Her voice softens, the shouting stops, I think I see her reach out a tentative hand.

'Sorry, I'm . . . It won't . . . WORK! WHY WON'T IT WORK? Come on, come and have a, come and . . . MOVE!'

She switches between calm and cataclysmic at a rate of knots. If there's one compliment I can give to Stepdad, it's that he's consistent. Eerily so. I'm not sure I'd have been able to survive unpredictable changes in rage. Even from out here, my heart is pounding. I feel sick and uncomfortable. I squint, trying to catch a glimpse of Devlin, see his reaction to his mam's fury.

'FUCKING WORK,' she yells again. The flock of sky rats gathered on the front garden scarper, screeching as they flap away.

Here I am, witnessing the heart-breaking cycle of bully creating bully. Where does it end? How did it begin? Who's to blame? Should

I be murdering Devlin's mam, as opposed to Devlin? Should I be murdering whoever fucked up his mam? How far down this morality hole do I really want to travel? How closely do I want to examine my motive for all of this? How well would it all hold up in my own court of ethics? Do I want to inspect this? Or do I just need to keep going, need some sense of purpose, a distraction, something to do?

Another light turns on, in the room adjacent to the living room. This light is green. It flickers. Devlin appears in the window. He places his hands over his ears, and he screams.

This is too personal, as if Devlin has just severed open his soul in front of me. I look down, at Joe's notes. Among homework reminders and favourite songs, one sentence stands out:

Devlin hates me cos my dad stuck round. He doesn't know that that's a bad thing. Doesn't realise it meant I lost Callum and Elizabeth, instead.

I leave, a sour taste in my mouth, and paranoia creeping back in. Distant sirens are coming for me, I'm certain of it. A police car passes, and I almost stumble into the road. My skin is prickly, as though ants are crawling over my body. The lime-green dress I wore to Empire needs burning. But is this enough? Can I get my hands on the bathroom CCTV? I hear the shrill, mocking peal of Courtney's laugh. See the pained twist of Devlin's face as he screamed under the eerie green light. Joe's body, plunging into the water.

When I arrive back at the flat, it's to find that both of my flatmates are in the kitchen. Too-Old-For-This-Shit Flatmate is making soup, while Manbaby Flatmate is unboxing a six-pack of party sunglasses. 'Partaaaay!' he shouts, when he sees me, brandishing a flamingo-themed pair of specs. He forces pineapple glasses onto me, while Too-Old-For-This-Shit Flatmate is given a Hawaiian pair. Our gaze, behind our ridiculous glasses, meets. Her eyes are watery, and there are dark bags beneath them. I'm reminded of my own, in the first weeks after Joe's death.

I lick my lips, trying to summon enough energy to ask if she's OK. Manbaby Flatmate places three different comedy glasses onto his head at once. Too-Old-For-This-Shit Flatmate turns towards the fridge before I get a chance to force my tongue into action.

My left eye twitches.

'Oh shit, guys!' says Manbaby Flatmate. I pull myself together and turn towards him.

'What?'

'That girl who was killed at the nightclub.'

'Yeah?' The hairs on the back of my neck raise.

'They've arrested someone,' he continues, scrolling through his phone furiously. He removes his pelican glasses but allows the parrot glasses to remain lopsided on his head.

'Who?' I ask.

'Yeah, I'm trying to . . . Jamie Sleight. Yeah, some guy called Jamie Sleight.'

'Are they . . . are they certain?' I ask.

'Yeah, looks like they are,' says Manbaby Flatmate. He stops scrolling and looks at me and Too-Old-For-This-Shit Flatmate, wearing a serious expression which is a near-perfect contrast to his immature glasses. He continues speaking. 'The guy confessed. Was overcome with guilt, apparently. He confessed to killing Courtney.'

A long, shuddering breath escapes my lips.

One confession is coincidence. Two means that someone's fucking with me.

Chapter Twelve

Someone out there is smarter than me. I mean, millions of people out there are smarter than me – I'm not completely devoid of self-awareness – but to be confronted with that fact so glaringly catches me off guard. Someone knows I'm killing people. And for reasons that I can't even begin to fathom, other people are confessing to my crimes.

I remove my stupid pineapple sunglasses and head into my room, needing to think. Think about what, exactly? A false, wayward confession is – as it was last time – simultaneously a massive fucking issue and an enormous relief. I may not be facing the consequences of my actions now, but they're coming for me, I'm certain. My punishment has effectively been delayed, but it is approaching.

It's obvious I need to speak to Brandon or Jamie – preferably both. I turn on my laptop and search *visit someone in prison*. You need to be added to their visitor list, so I adjust my goal, and search *send a prisoner a letter*. I'm met with another stumbling block: I need to know their prison numbers. I fire off an email to findaprisoner@justice.gov.uk, and then I wait.

I meet Mam and Stepdad much sooner than I'd hoped. The next day, we convene at the beach. South Gare, with bottle-green fisherman huts to our right, and the steelworks behind us. Mam and Stepdad are bundled up in thick coats, looking out over Paddy's Hole at the crashing grey waves beyond. The smell of salt is so strong, it's as if I've just polished off a fish supper and stuck my head in the greasy newspaper that it came in.

'You saw the news?' I ask, searching their faces for the worry I know must be present in my own expression. I don't find it.

'Aye,' says Stepdad. 'And what great news it is for you. A touch, from Jamie Sleight. Whoever the fuck he is.'

'Well, that's the issue. We don't know who he is. We don't know why he'd confess. Does he have something on me? Does he know something?' Questions tumble out of me. I glance around, feeling, as I so often seem to these days, as though I'm being watched. 'Why on earth would someone confess to a murder they hadn't committed?'

'Count your lucky stars and move on,' says Mam. She's holding a paper coffee cup, with pink lipstick stains on the edges. She trails them with a gloved finger, as if savouring what remains of her former glam self.

'I can't believe a *man* took credit for a tampon murder,' I say.

Stepdad laughs. 'Ahh, I'll tell ya what it is, like – Ella's jealous. Aren't you?'

'Of course not.'

'Should be buzzing, and here you are, with your knickers in a twist.'

'You two are simplifying things,' I say.

'And you're complicating things,' Stepdad replies.

I look down into Paddy's Hole, at wooden fishing boats battered by rough journeys, and the gulls flapping about around them. There's a long stretch of deserted sand across the bay, which seems to go on forever. Smoke from distant industrial chimneys drifts skywards, disappearing into the grey, omnipresent blanket of cloud.

It's going to rain.

A speck hits me and I sigh, wiping my cheek. Perhaps I am a little jealous. *Jealous*? That can't be the right word. A touch indignant that someone has claimed what is mine, maybe. But Mam and Stepdad are right; I don't want anyone to know that I killed Courtney Teasdale. I desperately don't want anyone to know. Mere days ago, I was near hysterical at the thought. So what? Why am I not relieved? Why am I not looking out across the waves with a calm expression shaping my features like the two people standing next to me?

'There's a reason Jamie Sleight confessed,' I say. 'I don't know the reason, and that makes me vulnerable.'

'Jamie Sleight is forty-nine. He's been married three times. His Facebook profile picture is a selfie of him wearing a cap. His cover photo is The Riverside Stadium, like every other man in this town. And most importantly, he's behind bars,' says Mam.

She's done the same googling that I have. Sleight also has 51 convictions for 113 offences, including driving while disqualified, drug possession and theft. The police think that they have their man, and I can certainly see why.

'I just . . . I've never really known of anyone just confessing to a murder. Especially one they haven't committed . . .' I trail off, gaze following a sanderling as it bobs about on the waves. For thirty seconds or so, neither Mam not Stepdad say anything. And then Stepdad zips his jacket up higher. He turns to me.

'It's Baltic. You coming back for a brew?' The corners of his mouth shift apart slowly, until half a dozen of his small teeth are visible. A smile. An attempt at a smile.

I hesitate. Not so long ago, a cup of tea round Mam and Stepdad's would have been punishment akin to water torture. These days, spending time in their basic-bitch living room is almost palatable.

'Howay. What are you going to do if not? Take a draughty bus back to town and cyberstalk Jamie Sleight?'

Stepdad has a point. A light but cold drizzle fills the air and I relent, following them back to their car. I watch the back of Stepdad's head on the drive back. The thick skull which houses a delicate brain I never could figure out. Beneath the bravado and the bullying, he's a sensitive man. A ceramic human, cracked with insecurities which threaten to destroy the whole structure if only tapped hard enough. I know the insecurities intimately. Mitch Mandeville. Money, or lack thereof. His own masculinity – the desire to always be the strongest, loudest, proudest. My gaze drops. He's removed his coat, and I can see the muscles tensing and relaxing at the back of his neck as he turns the steering wheel. He's fifty, half a decade older than Mam. The thought of him losing muscle with each passing year, the thought of him shrinking into a wrinkly, weathered shell of the man he once was, is a delicious one. I smile at his salt-and-pepper skull.

Once inside, I sip at tea, this time from a mug which reads 'Let the Good Times Be-Gin'. We're in the kitchen, rather than the living room. I've Step-Nan to the left of me, Mam to the right and Stepdad straight ahead. The only reason I wanted to see them was to discuss Jamie Sleight, but they're adamant that it'll be brushed off as some rare good luck. Proof that Mam isn't cursed, perhaps. Instead, chatter about rising food prices, stagnant bus wages and mould in the downstairs toilet fills the little room. My gaze is drawn to a stack of angry-looking letters on the coffee table. The words LATE PAYMENT jump out at me before Stepdad seizes the pile and crumples the letters between his fists.

I'm on the broken, duct-taped chair, and it's as if the cracks of contention worm their way up through the wood and into my body. I find myself thinking about the arguments which took place in this room. The one time I yelled at Callum and Stepdad. Perhaps I shouldn't have yelled, as they were doing the only thing that united them: sending Joe on fool's errands. But it was a bitterly cold day in the months before Callum left, and Joe had been flushed with a slowly diminishing pride having won his school cross country race – an achievement that had neither interested nor impressed Stepdad. Instead, he'd pressed a list and a fiver into Joe's hand and told him they needed the objects on it, or there'd be no tea that night. Hours passed before I saw Joe – soaked through and dejected – skulking outside, too scared to come in empty-handed. I had let him in and read the list: left-handed tablespoon, pot dividers, a grape grater and sparks for the fire. Stepdad had walked past, looked Joe up and down and told him he wouldn't be eating that night. It was at this point that I had shouted. Stepdad had laughed, and I think Callum laughed too. Even Joe had – a nervous giggle shaping his blue lips and tired eyes pleading with me not to make a fuss.

I'm holding the handle of the mug so hard I fear I might break it. Colour floods back to my knuckles as I loosen my grip. I look up, and Step-Nan's eyes are on me. There's an intensity in them I haven't seen for a while which quickly disappears as they glaze over and she looks beyond me. My own gaze drifts to Stepdad, and I find myself wondering how much he misses Joe. Whether he even has the capacity to ever truly love or miss anything.

It's at this point that I do what I always seem to: excuse myself and leave the room. I pad into the little downstairs toilet and sit on the toilet seat, allowing a finger to trail up and down the door. The hole Callum once punched in it remains, covered up with duct tape and off-white paint. The tiles – once new and expensive – are now chipped and missing in places, a pertinent reminder of the fact we used to have money, and all too quickly ceased to. Troubles which can't be scrubbed away, no matter how much bleach and elbow grease Mam uses.

Once breathing becomes a little easier, I stand up. I'm drawn to Joe's room and find myself trailing a toe over his stripy blue rug – picked bare from damp, bored afternoons when we'd have nothing better to do than loll on it and fidget. It's scuffed, too, from afternoons which were the opposite: dry and warm, when we'd roam barefoot and return to Joe's room with dirt between our toes and Mam shouting that we were ruining her house.

I rifle through Joe's drawers, pulling out a shirt which still smells of him. Not nice, per se, but warm, lived in. I clutch it tight and pick up his school yearbook, which I slip into my bag. And then I thumb through a stack of photos which lives on his desk. There's a print of me aged seven or eight perhaps, with long, dark curls flipped over my head. Exploring my very own 'hair jungle' as I used to put it. I brush back my short, blonde hair, smiling at the old memory. Beneath this photo is one of Joe on his first day at primary school: body swaddled by Callum's old jumper, mouth set in a gap-toothed grin. He was a cute kid. The cutest. Callum and I had loathed the thought of Mam and Stepdad having a baby, of course. 'Satan's Spawn,' Callum had mumbled, repeating lyrics from an Eminem song which had been his favourite at the time. I don't recall feeling so strongly, but I did have a sense that money was fast disappearing. To have another baby in such circumstances was unexpected. 'It's to keep Liev around,' Callum had told me. I couldn't decide if this was a good or bad thing. Stepdad's presence kept people away; there'd been no more fireworks through the letterbox, no more stones through our windows, since he'd moved in. But he was . . . he was his own creeping brand of undesirable. At that age, I'd found it hard to articulate what exactly was 'off' about Stepdad, I just knew in my gut that I didn't want two of him around.

But Joe was nothing like Stepdad. He wasn't even anything like Mam.

The next photo is of the three of us squished into a cardboard box, a mess of limbs, giggling and clutching long screws: our latest industrial estate find. Happy hours spent playing in our own metal kingdom, before Callum and I had grown up, and Joe had been killed before getting the chance to. Happy hours before we'd found out who each other really was. I glance outside, at the darkening steelworks, wondering if the place we'd played had ever really existed. If I return, rather than skirting around the edges as I have been, I'll probably find out it never had.

I look at eleven-year-old Callum, with a pale, protective limb wrapped around four-year-old Joe.

'How?' I whisper. 'How could you kill him?'

The image of Callum and Stepdad in the kitchen on the night we went hungry fills my mind. Their faces twist, mouths contorting into sinister, clownish grins. But who had started the laughing? How wide had Callum's smile actually been? What was going on behind his dark eyes? Had I ever known?

Am I remembering everything wrong?

Marty visits Thorntree Cemetery as I'm planting bulbs near the little chapel. With him is his squat, stubborn old tyme bulldog, whose name I once knew but promptly forgot. Marty and the dog meander over to me, and I haul myself to my feet.

'How do?' he asks.

'I'm alright,' I reply, offering up a quick smile. I'd give the dog a stroke, but it's a bastard of a beast, and would probably have my hand off.

'How's the cemetery treating you?'

'Got some gloves, so my hands aren't as wrecked.'

Marty nods. I let silence hang in the air and watch as he grows more and more uncomfortable.

'I'm sorry about Joe, by the way,' he says, finally breaking it.

'Are you?' I ask, surprised that he's finally acknowledged my loss.

His eyes widen. 'Yer jokin', aren't ya? Course I am! Savage business, losing someone you love.'

I nod. 'Yes. It was a brutal night.'

He holds my eye contact for a second or two before shuffling away to speak to Employer #1 when the silence becomes too much for him. I turn a couple of bulbs over in my hands, watching the pair of them grunting between the headstones. The dog doesn't take its eyes off me. Marty's grip on the dog's lead is so tight that his knuckles have gone white, but I know he'll take satisfaction in this, in the grisly power which accompanies him. A role my dad used to play, I suppose. My dad, with his heady supply of weapons, his quick temper and wide shoulders and bravado. And Marty, to the side or behind, cold and calculated and plotting. Always plotting. A thought occurs to me.

'Do you know Brandon Pearce or Jamie Sleight?' I ask, when he and the bulldog stroll back past me. Marty pauses, looking down and then up before replying.

'Jamie Sleight and Brandon Pearce? Eh? Uh, names ring a bell an' all but . . .'

'They're from the area. Same age as you and Mitch. You guys probably committed crimes around the same time,' I press. Marty won't – or can't – meet my eyes.

'That was a long time ago, like. My memory ain't all it once was.'

I push my tongue into my right cheek, gaze roaming round Marty's face, trying to read him. He looks uncomfortable, hates the silence, I already know this. But there's something else, too. Something calculated in the way his eyes are darting from side to side.

'Let me know if you do remember anything about them,' I say.

Marty laughs. 'Aye. I'll give the old memory a jog. Just for you.'

He leaves, dragging the stubborn dog with him. We get no more visitors until the afternoon. But this group more than makes up for the previously empty graveyard; they arrive en masse, clutching flowers and balloons, which they take to a fresh plot at the back of the graveyard. I pause my digging and squint over at them, all holding hands and wrapped up in expensive-looking coats. Two of the figures are considerably shorter than the rest, and my heart aches for the little girls who've suffered a loss. One girl pulls the other's ponytail, and gets a nip in return. My breath catches. Brat #1 and Brat #2.

This is Courtney's grave. How the hell have I missed it? I watch with renewed interest as her family add tokens of love to it. I'd be lying if I said I didn't feel guilty. Until very recently, causing people pain was never something I actively set out to do. This isn't exactly how I'd pictured post-uni life. At the rate I'm going, I'm more likely to use my degree certificate to smother someone than to get a job.

'It was for Joe. It was for Joe. It was for Joe,' I whisper, hands curling tighter around the handle of my trowel.

Regardless of how much I try to convince myself that the mourning of the group in front of me is deserved, I still feel uncomfortable. I'm about to turn away, when I spot another figure lurking on the other side of the low metal fence which encircles Thorntree Cemetery. I recognise his buzz cut and the miserable, downwards trajectory of his face, even from a distance. Devlin is present, but seemingly reluctant to intrude.

He stays on the outskirts of the graveyard after Courtney's family leave, a dejected figure against a darkening sky. I linger once my shift ends, only leaving when he does. The urge to follow him is overwhelming, and once again I curse myself for messing things up with The Fake Boyfriend; a couple meandering along seems less suspicious than me darting about on my own. Or perhaps my perception of what is and isn't shady is a figment of my imagination because I manage to follow Devlin all the way into South Bank without him clocking me. I anticipate him pressing on into Grangetown, but he doesn't. Instead, he stops and hauls himself up onto the wall opposite a row of small terraced houses. I pick my own spot on the wall – half hidden by a bush and a dozen metres away – take my phone out and bow my head.

Every so often I look to my left, keeping an eye on Devlin. I needn't have worried about him clocking me; his gaze is fixed on number twelve and the car which pulls up outside it. We watch – him from twenty metres away, me from thirty – as a man with the same Roman nose and slender figure as Devlin escorts two babbling children, both with swimming goggles on their heads and damp towels under their arms, into the warmth of the little house. It seems remarkable that Devlin's dad doesn't see him. I'm reminded of the boys by the steelworks, of how invisible they all were, despite their rage, despite the commotion they caused.

There's no rage from Devlin. His face softens as his dad and half-siblings join their mam in the front room, settling in for a sausage supper and playfights with the television remote.

Devlin and I watch – separate but united – until my arse grows numb and my fingers stiffen in the wind. I imagine we're both kept warm by a sickening sort of nostalgia which we allow to trundle through our bodies, despite the fact it's fake, despite the fact it's fleeting. The life in the window will never be Devlin's. And I will never get Joe back. Once again, I'm amazed that grief isn't visible; amazed other people can't see it trickling into the bricks below me, can't see it catching the wind and curling its way up into the sky.

Eventually, all lights within number twelve turn off, and Devlin leaves. Head bowed, hood up. I spend a few more minutes on the wall, only one thought going through my head.

I can't kill this boy.

It's a thought I try to shake on the walk back to my flat. After all, I saw Devlin bully Joe, didn't I? I saw Devlin and Courtney order Joe to the top of the Transporter Bridge, to his death. It doesn't seem right, to kill one without killing the other. I have to keep things moral, keep holding myself accountable. I laugh. Who do I think I am? Serial killer, but make it ethical? #Notliketheotherserialkillers?

I don't know who I am. I don't know what I'm doing. I'm lost, I was lost even before Joe died.

I sling my bag into a corner of my room, run a hand through my hair and turn to my typewriter. As if on autopilot, I start typing out what happened on the day of Joe's death.

```
                                        FADE IN:
                                               1
INT. TRAIN CARRIAGE - AFTERNOON
   WE OPEN in carriage E of the train from
Edinburgh to London, as it travels between
Newcastle and Darlington. It's summer in
```

```
England, so the weather could be fucking
anything. ELLA (22) is low-key pissed by the
time she meets JOE (18) at a quiet spot on
the banks of the river Tees. She watches as
DEVLIN (18) and COURTNEY (18) mock Joe and,
rather than do anything, Ella drinks more and
more, letting her mind drift to thoughts of
her lying ex
   BURN PAGE
```

I tear out the paper and set it alight. The page with my list of 'targets' is folded into the top drawer of my desk. I take it out and shove it back into my typewriter, adding to it as follows:

```
                              FADE IN:
                                     1
INT. ELLA'S BEDROOM - EVENING
   WE OPEN with Ella, as she inches closer to
righting the wrongs surrounding Joe's death.
   Target #1 - JANET BRAITHWAITE
   Target #2 - COURTNEY TEASDALE
   Target #3 - DEVL
```

I can't do it. My mind floods with the image of his body as he watched his dad through the window. He'd been simultaneously slumped in defeat and tilted forward, as if trying to insert himself into a scene that had been stolen from him. I'm reminded of his face contorting into a scream through the window of his mam's house. I push myself away from the typewriter and pace round my room, picking objects up and putting them down at random, finally settling on Joe's yearbook.

I flick to the front page, and my heart sinks, for only two people have written Joe a message. The first says:

Dear Joe, thank you for having been such a unique and inquisitive individual. Thank you for teaching me a couple of chords on the guitar! Keep your head up. I've a feeling you'll flourish outside away from your classmates. I probably shouldn't say this given I'm your teacher, but it's OK to hate school. Kids can be horrible. It gets better. Good luck for the future, Mr Downing.

The second message says:

Hope you make more friends, mate! Good job I was there for ya, eh? Brothers for life. Devlin.

I can't kill him. I cannot kill Devlin. I must have remembered the night of Joe's death incorrectly. I must have imagined the relentless bullying from Devlin. My alcohol-infused brain must have gotten things wrong. My grip on the yearbook tightens as I realise I'm going to have to stop the only thing that's kept me going since Joe's death. But what? What instead? Pills? Pill after pill? Move away, get a job? Get over it? I can't even get over what The Ex did. I am never, ever going to get over this.

I turn to Joe's phone, desperate to watch a video of him or listen to his voice message or just . . . something . . . something to feel close to him. TikTok is where I eventually end up, scrolling through the accounts of his classmates, trying to catch glimpses of him. I scroll for what feels like hours, my eyes focusing and un-focusing, before I clock his dark curls. I press play, and find myself watching a clip of teenage boys braving the freezing grey ocean. They splash about – Joe, Devlin, a couple of others. They're playfighting, pale skinny limbs flailing. I almost smile. And then Devlin grabs Joe. He submerges Joe. For a few seconds, the others find it funny. And then they start shouting. It's an age before Devlin releases my brother, who gags. He's wearing an expression I recognise from our FaceTimes, when he'd think I wasn't looking, and his happy mask would slip. I spent half a decade pretending I'd imagined the sorrow in his eyes.

Over the next few seconds or hours or minutes, I see it all. I missed so much of Joe's life, and I catch up through social media mainly, I think, and through my imagination, too. Videos end, but my mind carries them on. Confused boys becoming even more confused men. Skinny chests puffed, searching for their places in the world via Smirnoff and cigarettes and shoving one another around. I witness Devlin with his arm around Joe, and I witness Devlin pushing scrap metal into the side of Joe's head, his lips moving with something unintelligible. Beach fires with the burning industry as their backdrop, Courtney curled up to Devlin, Joe watching from a couple of metres away. Glass-smashing competitions against the walls of the abandoned youth centre on North Street, Devlin's eyes wild, lobbing beer bottles at Joe's feet, grinning and shouting that it was a laugh, it was all just a laugh. Joe was his best mate, Joe knew he meant no harm, if Joe hadn't wanted bleeding ankles, he should have moved quicker, or worn trousers. Joe's dad was still around, Joe could afford decent trousers, could he not? The hugs between Joe and Devlin that would turn into chokes. The fear in Joe's eyes. The madness in Devlin's.

Love and hate so often run close to one another. I think Devlin loved Joe. But I think he truly hated him too.

I set down the phone. Return to my typewriter. And finish typing:

```
                              FADE IN:
                                     1
INT. ELLA'S BEDROOM - EVENING
   WE OPEN with Ella, as she inches closer to
righting the wrongs surrounding Joe's death.
   Target #1 - JANET BRAITHWAITE
   Target #2 - COURTNEY TEASDALE
   Target #3 - DEVLIN MACKENZIE
```

Chapter Thirteen

Devlin comes to the cemetery most days, without ever actually stepping inside. On day four of watching him do this, I text The Fake Boyfriend, apologising for dragging him to a nightclub, telling him that I miss him and that I have something special prepared to make things up to him. He ignores me for a few days, and then he replies, as I knew he would. It's why I chose him, after all.

He hops over the low gate to meet me in Thorntree Cemetery on Tuesday evening, wearing the same expression I imagine I did when I first stepped foot in here.

'I hope we're moving on,' he says, pulling his scarf tight around his throat.

'We're moving about a hundred metres further in, so that's moving on in many respects,' I reply.

He rolls his eyes, not bothering to argue.

We head for the back corner of the graveyard, the spot which is currently empty, just waiting for death. In many ways, I'd argue this is the most sinister area in the entire cemetery. I try to make it less so: unzipping my backpack, laying out a picnic blanket, binoculars, chocolate and a flask of tea.

The Fake Boyfriend rolls his eyes again, but I can tell he's suppressing a smile. We both sit down, and I pour tea into the lid of the flask.

'Remembered you don't like coffee,' I say, handing him the steaming drink.

'Romantic of you.'

'Thanks.'

He takes a sip and then breaks off a chunk of chocolate.

'I thought I was weird,' he tells me. 'But you blow me out the water.'

I feign surprise, pretending my intention isn't to subject him to a load of highly weird shit.

'Go on then, what weird things do you do?' I ask.

He shrugs. 'Quirky enough things to be described as weird, without dragging dates to cemeteries.'

'We're stargazing!' I protest, waving the binoculars.

'We're still in a graveyard.'

'The back of a graveyard.'

'Still within the perimeters of the graveyard.'

'There's less light pollution.'

'Albert Park would have done just fine.'

'You're avoiding my question,' I say, accepting that – quite rightly – I won't win this argument. 'What weird things do you do?'

He breaks off another chunk of chocolate, dunks it in his tea and chews it while thinking. 'I mean, I don't think anything I do is particularly weird. I pickle food, for example.'

'Like . . . eggs? Pickled eggs? Or pickled pickles?'

'Use your imagination! You can pickle all sorts. Blueberries, ginger, mushrooms. Lovely.'

'Yeah, I've never heard of anyone doing that to be fair, so I guess that makes it weird, or at least unusual, by definition. What else?'

'I put ticks instead of crosses when I send text messages or write cards,' he says.

'Why?'

'Self-explanatory, isn't it? Ticks are way more positive than crosses. No idea why people think sending crosses is nice.'

'You've never sent any ticks to me.'

'I'm not sure you've ever deserved them,' he says, smiling slightly. Fair point.

He picks up the binoculars and leans back, staring up at the stars above. My gaze shifts to him, rather than the solar system. He's one of those people you could maybe fancy from some angles, in a certain light. Personally, I don't actually think he's terrible-looking. But, having said that, tall, dark and handsome was never exactly going to do it for me. He's also sweet and funny in an awkward way, which makes him more attractive. The nightclub evening was a one-off;

from now on my intention is to make our interactions as pleasant for him as possible. What? I'm a murderer, I'm not an arsehole. I'm only going to subject him to one truly rubbish date. It just happens to have been the very first.

'What's up with you, anyway?' he asks, placing the binoculars down and turning away from all of space and time to focus on my plain old face.

'What do you mean?' I ask, heart rate quickening. My changing appearance? The shifty behaviour I displayed in the nightclub? The fact that my idea of a romantic date is supposedly a graveyard?

'You're just a bit avoidant. Did something happen with an ex?'

I wouldn't have thought it possible, but my heart rate gets even faster.

'Oh.' I take a large gulp of tea and then chomp down a piece of chocolate. Both seem to sour in my mouth. 'Uh. Ish. Standard stuff, I guess.'

'We've just established that you and I are both weird. So, I need to hear about this "standard stuff" to determine whether it really is,' he says. 'If you don't mind, of course.'

I take a deep breath. Force myself to scan the graves in the distance, willing Devlin to appear and save me from something I really don't want to talk about.

'I was with someone, and I thought we were really great together. And that ended earlier this year.'

'Fair play, that does sound pretty standard. Why did you think you guys were so great together?'

Not the question I was anticipating.

'We had a lot of shared interests,' I say. 'Liked a lot of the same music and books and things.'

In the weeks that followed the breakup with The Ex, I tried to lure her back in. I'd take to reading her favourite book (*Ulysses*) whenever she was in the vicinity. It took me an age to slog through, so the book seemed almost always lodged somewhere between my eyes and hers. But no comment. I bought a new phone case – the album art for *Electric Warrior*, the lyrics of which we'd spend lazy Sundays analysing. I flipped my phone whenever she came near, but she never seemed to clock it. I posted songs she'd sent me on Instagram, until she stopped watching my stories and I consigned myself to the fact that she was no longer interested. Still, the desire to prove that we were better suited than her and The Replacement lingered. Lingers.

'I think I just put a lot of weight on cultural things,' I say to The Fake Boyfriend. 'Like, I love books. I love films. I can never understand people who can just listen to music and enjoy it and that's that. I become obsessed with music. I pick apart the lyrics, devour albums, make playlists for every mood and month and weather. So, I guess when I found someone who matched this love for culture, I got a bit blinkered. Thought we were perfect when – in reality – we were just passionate about the same random shit.'

'You need character over culture.'

'I thought she had both.' Shit. '*He*. I thought he had both.'

'Why d'you like books and films and stuff so much anyway?'

I crumple my brow. 'Isn't it obvious?'

'I wouldn't have said so.'

I mull it over. 'I think it just helps you feel connected to people.'

The Fake Boyfriend takes another sip of tea. The wind picks up, and he zips his coat all the way up to his chin.

'I feel detached from people, a lot of the time,' he says. 'Not everyone. Get along with my mam. Not so much with my dad. And then, I don't know, in groups it's as if I can't allow myself to properly relax, and people can sense this, and being near me makes them uncomfortable. It's . . . I don't know . . . not even that I feel I can't be myself, just that myself is so self-conscious, so devoid of anything interesting to say . . . I mean, what do people talk about? All the time, what does everyone have to say that's so interesting? How can they chat and chat? Are other people interested too? Or are we all just lying to one another constantly, in the name of social cohesion, in a desperate desire to fit in?'

I nod, a little taken aback. The Fake Boyfriend stiffens and looks away. I reach for his cold hand, overcome by the urge to reassure him.

'I think more people feel like that than you realise,' I say. 'Sometimes

I feel like I'm watching people interact from behind a camera. As if there's a degree of separation between me and whatever's going on. That can be a safe feeling, too. Guess that's one of the reasons I ended up studying film.'

'Avoidant.' He smiles, mocking gently. 'I'm joking. I get that. But yeah, I don't feel the same way about culture as you do. I like it for other reasons, though. I like the technical side of it all – how things are made. The pitch, volume, synthesis. Aliasing and bitrates and chord progression.'

I tilt my head from side to side. I've always been interested in the psychological element of culture – what tortured or joyful or dull event might have inspired the writing of lyrics or scripts. But I struggled through the overly technical elements of my degree. And – in respect of music – chord progression and the creation of tunes were always Joe's areas of speciality.

Eventually I say, 'I don't think that interests me much at all.'

'You don't like knowing how music's made?'

'I guess not. I just want to appreciate how good it sounds.'

The Fake Boyfriend lies back against the blanket and tugs me down with him. He points a long arm skyward. 'You don't care how stars are made? You don't want to know how many light years away from us they are? What about black holes? The speed of comets? How close they might be to wiping out humanity? The diameter of the moon? What it's made of?'

He sounds like I did, when I was trying to get Mam and Stepdad to take the fake confessions seriously. Needing to know everything, not happy to let good things simply *be*.

I laugh, squeezing his hand. 'No, I don't care about any of that. I just like looking at it.'

And so I do. The deep blue abyss that serves as an omnipresent yet unfathomably incomprehensible reminder of how tiny and insignificant we are. Distant silver pinpricks, the number of light years from which The Fake Boyfriend is probably gagging to reveal.

There's the rustle of dead leaves as they're disturbed a few dozen metres from us. I hoist myself onto my elbows and look around the cemetery. Sure enough, a thin figure wearing a hoody is traipsing towards Courtney's grave. As far as I can tell, he hasn't spotted us yet. I'm not naïve, not of the belief that The Fake Boyfriend is an invisibility cloak, but I doubt Devlin will figure out who I am in the dark, from a distance, accompanied by someone he's never seen before. He comes to a standstill opposite Courtney's grave. A glance down at my watch tells me it's 21:06.

'You alright?' asks The Fake Boyfriend, shuffling up to match me.

'Yep. Just watching.'

'Watching what?'

For someone who just told me he often feels he has nothing to say, he sure is talkative. But I'm fake dating in an ethical way, so I don't tell him this. Instead, I shrug and say, 'Just the graveyard in general.'

Devlin stands still, just staring at Courtney's grave. I prop myself up on my palms, trying to get a better view of the lone boy in the cemetery with us. I glance around, too, checking things: how many windows this spot in the graveyard is visible from; how many lights are on in those windows; how much I can hear; how distant the road and kids and dog walkers sound.

It's quiet. A quiet, near-perfect spot.

DUH-DUH-DUH-DUUUUH-DUUUUH-DUH-DUH-DUUUU H-DUUUUH

'Is that fucking *Star Wars*?' I hiss, turning to glare at The Fake Boyfriend's bag.

'Obviously,' he says, taking out his phone and making to answer it. I glance back at Devlin who, fifty metres from us, has just turned around.

Shit.

I grab The Fake Boyfriend and lunge towards his lips. I lock him in a hard, slightly toothy kiss, while whoever is on the other end of his phone grows increasingly confused. We're just a nice, totally normal couple, having an aggressive snog in a graveyard. Eventually, I release him, and shift my gaze towards Devlin, who has already turned away from us.

'That was . . . enthusiastic,' says The Fake Boyfriend.

'What can I say, I was overcome by a fit of passion,' I reply, eyes fixed on Devlin.

'I'll have to play the *Star Wars* theme tune more often.'

The kiss may have been unconventional, but it's an event I linger on long after Devlin leaves the cemetery. Long after we leave the cemetery. Long after The Fake Boyfriend leaves me.

My first since The Ex.

When I get back into my room, I find myself doing something I haven't for a long time. I scroll to the Facebook page of a country music festival held in the outskirts of Newcastle. The page on which a picture of The Ex lives, snapped by an unassuming photographer as she was leaning in to kiss another girl. The first time she cheated. Our relationship was in the early stages at this point, and we continued to let it grow after. But the roots had been poisoned, and we became an odd, delicate organism, rotting from within. I scroll through pictures, heart in my mouth. Seeing it again will hurt. It's always hurt.

The sinking feeling in my chest. The curl of my lip. The instinct to look away. The other instinct, the one which creeps up on me slowly, telling me to look. Letting the betrayal – caught on film, my favourite medium – eke back into my consciousness. The Ex with her back to the photographer, her long, dark hair slicked back with gel and sweat, half-braided with a polka dot bandanna. The girl in her arms, lips pursed, eyes closed, novelty cowboy hat askew, curly red hair brushing her shoulders. Buttery golden rays of sunlight dancing down from the top right corner. Artistic. Fucking artistic.

There was a time, not so long ago, when I was obsessed with this picture, and the pain it would produce within me. I'd spend my grey, in-between hours – the ones just before dawn, when I was drifting between a bad dream and a bad day, or the ones spent hungover on buses, drizzle dripping down the windows – with my phone in my hand, and the picture on the screen. I'd flip my phone back and forth, possessed by the belief that I might find The Ex's face on the other side.

The poisoned roots of our relationship would shiver within me, and I'd think of The Ex – drifting through grey hours of her own, perhaps, or with her arms wrapped around another girl – and I'd wonder if she was ever overcome by the urge to see this particular photograph from another angle.

I hadn't thought so. She'd felt the corners of her mouth press themselves into her cheeks in anticipation of the coming kiss. She knew exactly what the picture would look like if flipped around.

She knew, or would at least come to know, other things, too. Things that I didn't. The name of the girl she'd slept with last Christmas. Whether tinsel had been present in whichever room they did it in, whether cheesy Christmas songs had drowned out any guilt she'd felt in relation to me. Whether I'd been in her thoughts at all. Names, dates, times, locations. All different. All yielding the same result.

I turn off my phone. I am, in my own way, grateful for the time spent with The Ex. For she taught me something.

People don't change.

Feigning enthusiasm for work at the cemetery is not something which comes naturally to me, but the next day I tell Employer #1 that I'd like to take my career to the next level and have a go at actually digging a grave. His bushy eyebrows rise, but he seems genuinely chuffed by such an animated show of life among so much death, so he talks me through the basics. There's a small cluster of freshly dug graves at the back of the cemetery, one of which is only half-finished. He hands me a shovel and says I can have a go at neatening it up.

For the first hour or so, I do so under his watchful gaze, but eventually he has other things to do, and I'm left alone to add my own finishing touches. Ordinarily, graves are dug between four and six feet deep. I make mine just over seven feet. I time its completion for the end of the day – too late to clear away the pile of dirt beside it. I leave my shovel out, alongside four slabs of concrete which might normally form part of cheaper headstones.

Employer #1 and I grunt our goodbyes at each other, before he locks the gates, and I head to Aldi. This is where I buy two litre bottles of vodka, and a litre bottle of water. Once back in the flat, I pour half of the water down the sink, before topping it up with vodka. I pour the remainder of the vodka from this bottle down the sink, and then refill it with water from the tap. I set the three bottles atop the kitchen table: one being honest vodka, one being water disguised as vodka, and one being a deceptive water-vodka combination which should quicken the speed at which the unsuspecting drinker gets pissed. And then I meander over to Manbaby Flatmate's room.

The sound of tinny music drifts between the tiles of his floor and the wood of his door, and I add my own noise: three knocks against the oak.

A chair groans, and the sweaty slap of bare feet against ceramic follows.

'Yo, Els!' Manbaby Flatmate opens the door to me, headphones around his neck, a family-sized bag of Sensations clutched in one hand.

'Hi. Are you free?'

He shifts his head from side to side. 'Depends what for. I'm stuck on a work call.'

Faint squealing and the sound of gunfire comes from his headphones. Behind him, the screen of his television displays the unmistakable scenes of *Grand Theft Auto*.

'Uh-huh. To be honest, I've had a tough day at work, too,' I say. 'Just feel like I'm missing uni extra hard, d'you get me?'

'God, yes. I've never got something more in my life.'

'I knew you'd understand. Anyway, I remembered our conversation about the maddest things we ever did, and just really wanted to re-enact them.'

Manbaby Flatmate pauses, before saying, 'Oh, Elsa, I think my days of tampons up the arse are behind me.'

Growth. He's grown. He has limits. He's developed as a character. Good boy. I'm proud.

'Oh, don't worry, I wasn't suggesting that! I couldn't keep up with you, not even in my heyday. Just fancied an evening of getting pissed by more conventional methods.'

He shrugs off his headphones, sets his crisps down, and points at me. 'Now that – *that* – I'm always game for.'

This is how I find myself sitting at the kitchen table while Manbaby Flatmate prattles on about freshers' flu and the time someone called 'Big Psycho Dave' glued all his dorm furniture to the ceiling, him taking swigs from the vodka bottle, me swigs of water disguised as vodka.

'I like my own bottle, just to keep track of how much I've drunk,' I say, when he asks why we each have our own vodka bottle.

'Pfft, lightweight!' is his response, the competitive, dickhead energy of uni halls still alive and well within him.

I'm deemed less of a lightweight when I tell him that I don't need water to keep going, while he guzzles at the innocent-looking vodka-water combination, pulling confused expressions, but already too pissed to question the liquid he's necking.

We're thirteen or fourteen swigs deep, and Manbaby Flatmate is passionately insisting that contracting quinsy made him a legend, and that unsticking each of his items of cutlery from his dorm ceiling 'wasn't even that inconvenient' when Too-Old-For-This-Shit Flatmate enters. I mirror Manbaby Flatmate – slouched forward, jaw hanging, eyes out of focus.

'Please don't break or spill anything,' Too-Old-For-This-Shit Flatmate says, taking a fruit salad from the fridge. 'And please don't be too loud. My boyfriend's staying, and he really needs rest.'

'Yada yada yeah yeah,' replies Manbaby Flatmate, flapping his hands about before taking another gulp from the water/vodka bottle.

'And those bottles can go in the recycling, not the bin. It's being collected tomorrow,' she adds, before stalking from the kitchen.

'Boring!' Manbaby Flatmate says at a volume I like to think he'd be embarrassed about if sober.

'What a lightweight,' I add.

'Oh my God! You said it, Elalalalala, what a lightweight.'

I don't have to put up with much more before his head hangs backwards and he starts snoring. Unnecessary death isn't really part of my plan, so I gently shift him into an upright position in the hope that, should he throw up, he at least won't choke on his own vomit.

I smile at him. I've successfully used The Fake Boyfriend as a prop, and now my buffoon flatmate is going to provide a handy alibi, should I need one. I imagine the police asking him what I was doing on the evening of Devlin Mackenzie's disappearance, and him innocently insisting I was with him all night, getting pissed and reminiscing about the good old days of illness and getting bullied.

For the sake of my alibi, I leave quietly, pausing only to set a glass of water (just water, this time) next to his hand. Then I dart out, into the night.

Anticipation bubbles up inside me, murderous magma beneath the crust of my sanity. I'm just waiting to erupt. This nervous energy propels me forward, and I reach Thorntree Cemetery in record-breaking time. I hop over the fence and make my way towards the freshly dug, extra-deep grave at the back of the cemetery. Once there, I turn the volume on Joe's phone up to its maximum, and place this within the grave. I then retreat to the outskirts of the graveyard, and wait.

Granted, Devlin might not turn up tonight. I don't really have enough data on him to guarantee it and – even if I did – it's not like I could ever account for the many random events which might throw him off track. But I don't think I'll have much trouble in getting Manbaby Flatmate pissed again, in recreating my alibi.

My stomach churns, terror and excitement writhing together, freshly hatched monsters battling for sovereignty. I stoke the embers of my anger, reminding myself of Devlin's immense cruelty.

My guts have barely had time to settle, when I spot a skinny figure making his way over to Courtney's grave. Devlin tugs down his hood, and places a teddy bear at the foot of her grave. He stays crouched, running his fingers through the gemstones and gravel which make up her pretty, over-the-top final resting place.

I leave him to his contemplation for approximately a minute, before I take out my phone, and dial Joe's number. The ringing of Joe's phone seems amplified by the hole it's in, aggressively loud against the stillness of the cemetery. It catches Devlin's attention immediately, better than I'd dared hope, actually, because it turns out that Joe's ringtone is 'Seventeen Going Under' – hardly original, but distinctive enough to pique Devlin's curiosity, to send a shiver of recognition rippling through him.

I move slowly from the shadows, in step with Devlin, as he leaves Courtney's grave and heads towards the freshly dug one. He stands at the edge of it, staring down.

Jump in. Jump in.

He teeters on the edge of the hole, swaying. I can't see his expression. How desperately I want to flip him round. I'm gripped by the sensation which strikes me whenever I see the picture of The Ex and the first girl she cheated on me with. Twisted curiosity. The need to know exactly what the person facing away from me was thinking. Is thinking.

Just as I'm growing worried that I might have to push him, Devlin hops down into the grave. And this is when I speed up. I jog the remainder of the distance to the grave, and pick up one of the concrete slabs by the side of it. In the grave, Devlin is crouched down, holding Joe's phone and twisting it back and forth in his palms.

I pause only for a second. I think about asking him to return to the police and tell the truth about what he saw. But I know he won't. They never do.

I bring the concrete slab down on his head. It's more effective than I'd dared dream, but still, I chuck a second one into the hole for good measure.

The crunch of bones. The gurgle of blood. Not even a whimper from Devlin's lips. This is unnecessary; the rest of his body is telling me everything I need to know.

I'm not cruel, not a monster, I don't want Devlin to suffer a slow, drawn-out death, so I release a third slab of skull-crushing concrete into the grave. As I do, I recall a time, not so long ago, when I thought I didn't have this kind of murder in me.

Growth. I've grown. I have no limits. I've developed as a character. Bad girl. I'm disgusted.

I steel myself to jump down and join Devlin in his bloody pit in order to collect his and Joe's phones. This has been easy. This has been easier than I ever could have hoped.

The metallic smell of blood drifts up to greet my nostrils as I take a step forward.

'Ella?'

Shit.

'Ella?' says the voice, again. A woman's voice.

I turn around to find my flatmate staring at me.

Chapter Fourteen

Half a million pounds to anyone who knows how to react to this situation. I try to run through as many different options as possible in three seconds.

'What are you doing here?' is what I settle on asking, trying to insert some righteous indignation into my voice. 'Employees only after the gates close.'

It works, somewhat, for Too-Old-For-This-Shit Flatmate crumples her brow in surprise.

'You were smashed. I followed you to check you were OK.'

Shit. I'm supposed to be drunk. Very drunk. I sway a little and, as I sway, I try to figure out whether Too-Old-For-This-Shit Flatmate saw me kill Devlin. She's still a fair way from me – two dozen metres or so – and she's a little out of breath, suggesting she ran to catch me up, that she was further behind. It's also dark and Devlin, bless him, kicked the bucket in mercifully quiet fashion, so . . . might I get away with this?

'Yeah, uh, sorry about that. Needed some fresh air to sober up. And I'm behind with my gravedigging. Thought I'd kill two birds with one stone.'

The words of a mad woman. I know it, and Too-Old-For-This-Shit Flatmate knows it, too. Still, I grab my shovel and begin frantically piling dirt over Devlin's body, wanting to completely cover it, in case she moves close enough to see into the hole.

But she stays still, watching me. Once again, I'm overcome by the metallic smell of Devlin's blood, and I shovel quicker, desperate to disguise it with the petrichor smell of dirt.

'Were you . . . was someone else with you?' she asks.

I pause, and plaster a strained smile across my face. 'Nope. Graveyards are pretty creepy though, definitely the kind of place your imagination can run away in!'

I think I see her nod. She zips her jacket all the way up to her chin, and opens and closes her mouth a couple of times.

'Sorry to be a bitch, but I really am going to have to use my gravedigger credentials to insist you leave. We open at eight-thirty tomorrow morning. You're welcome to come back then.' Said no drunk person ever.

Too-Old-For-This-Shit Flatmate nods again. Her eyes scan the cemetery for a few more seconds, before she says, 'Sure. Get home safe.'

'You too,' I say, piling another shovel load of dirt onto the dead body below me.

Avoiding her is the only thing I can think to do. What's my other option? Killing her? Nope, better to keep my head down and hope Too-Old-For-This-Shit Flatmate is secretly as dense as Manbaby Flatmate, and is none the wiser to my homicidal hobbies. I leave the flat as soon as the sun rises, and head straight to the cemetery, hoping to clean up what I started last night.

I'm too late.

'I hadn't finished this plot. Didn't think you'd be burying anyone here until this afternoon,' I say once I reach Employer #1, who's lowering a casket into Devlin's grave.

'You what?'

'This plot wasn't ready.'

Employer #1 shrugs. 'I know. Finished it off this morn. Was alright. Yer a talented grave digger.'

Ahh, a talented gravedigger. Just the accolade I've always wanted. I scan the plot, looking for signs that Devlin has been discovered. I scan Employer #1's paint by numbers face too, trying to ascertain whether he clocked anything about the hole. A hand sticking up through the mud, for example.

'Coming into flu season,' Employer #1 says. 'The oldens come flying in around this time. Coffin dodgers that can't coffin dodge no more. Got to get a head start on them. On death.'

Righto. A noble, if sinister ambition. One which I don't think I'll be helping with. For being in the graveyard, which had been somewhat tolerable, suddenly becomes unbearable. I didn't like being in such close proximity to Courtney's dead body, but being so close to Devlin's is even worse. It's as if the ground below me is polluted, as if he's trying to wrap his ghostly tendrils around me, one blade of grass at a time. Plus, despite not spotting Too-Old-For-This-Shit Flatmate, the back of my neck tingles, as though someone's watching me.

So, despite my gravedigging talents, I head to Marty's betting shop as soon as my lunchbreak arrives. He's on his hands and knees, fiddling with one of the machines.

'Marty,' I say, placing my bag down and then sitting on it, so that our faces are level. He looks up.

'Afternoon. How do?'

'I don't think I can work at the graveyard anymore.'

'Oh, right. How come?'

How long has he got? How much does he want to change the wholesome opinion he currently has of me?

I shrug, and say, 'I'm super grateful I had the opportunity. But I just need to do something different. Please.'

'Oh . . . can't say I understand that, like.'

I sigh and then say, 'Yeah, bit of an atmosphere. Slightly too much death for me. All the negative energy was causing havoc with my menstrual cycle.'

'Oh.'

That shuts him up. He breaks eye contact, and I swear a droplet of sweat appears just below his hairline.

'Mmm, well. Tell ya the truth, my cleaner quit last week. So you could do that?'

'Here?' I ask. 'That would be great.'

'Mint. Hope you're good with a mop cos the old fellas like to piss anywhere but the urinal.'

A strained smile seems to be my default expression these days. I unclench my teeth and say, 'Can't wait to put my mop skills to the ultimate test.'

Old-man piss aside, this is quite the improvement. I'm physically further from the scene of my most recent crime, plus I can keep a closer eye on Marty. He knows something about Brandon Pearce and Jamie Sleight. I'm certain of it.

We agree that I'll start tomorrow, so I head to Mam and Stepdad's, to update them on Devlin. I'm a touch giddy at the thought they might be proud of me. They're the only other people marred so deeply by Joe's death; my progress on those who contributed to it will please them. It has to.

It's Baltic, in their house. Stepdad is at work, but Mam and Step-Nan are shivering in jumpers and scarves, mugs of tea clutched in their hands. I lean against the radiator after I've greeted them. It's off, of course. This winter's going to be a savage one.

The familiar crushed velvet armchair is where I come to rest. I scan the pair of them. Mam's expression is worried but resigned. Defeated, almost. Step-Nan's is blank but for a twitch of discomfort. Much as I dislike the old hag, the cold won't be good for her. Employer #1's prediction that the elderly will soon come flooding through the gates of the cemetery looks set to be more accurate than ever this year. I toy with the idea of giving them some of my inheritance. But I haven't even used the money to keep myself warm – I recall chilly evenings in draughty ten-person house shares, daydreaming about the modern flat my money could get me. But no. My dad's money will be used to right his wrongs. And unfortunately, that extensive list doesn't include the cost-of-living crisis. Besides, Mam spent as little as possible of her own chunk of inheritance on me.

'I killed Devlin,' I say, if only to warm the room with a spark of sinister conversation.

It does the trick, for Mam stops shivering and says, 'Fuck me, Elizabeth. I didn't think you were being serious when you came over before. You're motoring through them.'

I nod. 'Ella. And to be honest, I think you guys should pick up the slack. These people fucked over Joe. You should want to end them just as much as I do.'

Mam shifts from side to side. She takes a sip of her tea before saying, 'Seems you're pretty good at doing them yourself.'

'Not really. Devlin's murder was a mess. I nearly got caught.'

'Well. You didn't. You're a talented killer.'

A talented gravedigger. A talented killer. This has been quite the day for compliments. Shame I'm looking to unshackle myself from both so-called skills. My gaze drifts from Mam to the glittery silver-framed mirror behind her, to my own reflection. I'm a mess, quite frankly. My roots have grown out. There are purple bags beneath my eyes. The clothes I'm wearing are a halfway house, neither reflective of who I am, nor who I'm trying to be. I'm reminiscent of a drunk aunt, asked last minute to model for the local bargain store.

'Want me to sort your hair out?' asks Mam, following my gaze.

'It'll cost you, won't it?'

Mam shrugs. 'Not really. I've got products left over. Besides, Liev seems to think we might come into some money soon.'

The woman has been trying to make me over since I came out of her womb. Today is the first day I allow her to. And she's good, you know. She takes me to the bathroom and strips my hair of the bleach, dies it a dark chestnut not dissimilar from my natural colour. She slaps a face mask on me, and she rifles through her wardrobe, pulling out her cast-offs – denim skirts and leopard print jumpers and knee-length red boots. Not what I'd typically choose to dress myself in, but she ties them together well enough that I'm almost drawn to the idea of strutting around town in black sequin leggings, an aviator jacket and grey Ugg boots.

I watch her work, passing a lipstick of hers between my fingers, and recall the days when the creamy, dusky rose shade used to cover almost everything I came into contact with. There'd be lipstick on poorly washed glasses, lipstick on vapes left lying on countertops, lipstick on Joe's cheek, lipstick on mine. I sniff at it, am reminded of how I'd cling to the crumbs of comfort she'd give me. She'd watch, dusky rose lips pressed tight together, as Stepdad adjusted his rules, raised his standards to heights which I could no longer reach. A kiss on the cheek, before I left for school. A kiss would be enough. A kiss would make it all better. I press the plastic tighter between my fingers and glance over to her wardrobe. Hidden deep within, inside a shoebox wrapped in scarves, are her diaries. I'd sneak in and read them on the rare occasions I had the house to myself. It had been an attempt to feel emotionally close to her, I suppose. To make up for a perceived physical disconnect. A love which only ever felt surface level, and I desperately wanted to be deeper.

It was around this time that I'd taken, on occasion, to reaching an arm around Joe – if he ever looked especially cold or despondent. He'd reach a small arm around me in return, and through my jumper, his fingers would trace the white ridges on my back without knowing what he was touching. In turn, I'd run my fingers over Joe's unblemished back, grateful that Stepdad had at least left his own flesh and blood alone.

But then I'd spot a smudge of lipstick on Joe's cheek, smell Step-Nan's syrniki on his breath and see Stepdad in his alabaster skin, and I'd have to fight the urge to push him away from me. He sensed this, I think. In the days of my study leave, I'd wake to find him watching me, swaddled by Callum's school jumper, toothpaste on the corners of his mouth and his curls half brushed, an earnest attempt at neatness. I would force my chapped lips into a smile and accept whatever token he'd decided was appropriate that day: his favourite marble, an especially interesting curl of metal, a treasured guitar pluck. A promise that he'd come back. A promise that I would stay.

I place the lipstick down, and it's almost immediately picked up by Mam. She's selected me enough clothes, now it's time to make a start on my face.

'I was just going to keep it minimal,' I say, holding a hand out to stop her from getting any closer.

'Well, I was just going to pluck your eyebrows. Put a little silver shadow on your lids,' is her reply.

I shrug; I've already allowed her to do most of what she wishes. While she powders my nose and curls my eyelashes I say, 'I guess you don't know where Callum lives, do you?'

She takes a second or two to answer. 'No. I never knew where he went.'

There's something in her voice. Something syrupy – sadness or regret, perhaps. There's so much I want to ask her – does she resent the influence Liev's had on her life? Does she regret always putting him first? Does she miss Callum? Did she miss me? – but these questions feel to me like a piece of string with no start and no end, just the capacity to fray off in different directions, each more painful than the last.

'Stepdad said he saw Callum in a pub. Do you know which one?' I ask.

'Liev said . . . ? Oh, yes. I'm not sure actually. He goes to a few different ones.'

'We need to find out,' I say. 'I don't exactly have many leads on Callum at the moment. Although if he saw Stepdad there, it's pretty much the one place he's guaranteed not to return.'

I take my phone out. Searching for Callum on the internet is pointless (has always been pointless) but still, I can't help myself. I click around various social media sites. Whenever the screen goes dark, my own strange, quizzical reflection stares back at me. My ordinarily heavy brow has been plucked to near nothingness, and I have to fight the urge to scold Mam. So much pain to produce such a comical expression.

My heart thunks as I scroll through Facebook and catch sight of posts about Devlin. It's been less than twenty-four hours, but already there are questions wondering whether he's been seen, or whether anyone's heard from him. The drama of the murder overshadowed most of the guilt I felt about it, but it hits me now. From my sole experience of watching her through a window, I'd written Devlin's mam off as unhinged. I'd viewed her as a caricature, but she'll be in pain. I know exactly how much pain.

I scroll faster, as if I'm just going to miraculously find something that leads me to Callum.

'You said a man with a dog watched you try to rescue Joe and didn't help,' Mam says, and I nod, putting down my phone.

'Yes. He did. He saw it all.'

'You're going to try to get him to go to the police?' Mam asks. 'Do you even know who he is?'

'It's complicated.'

'Do you . . . me and Liev were thinking . . . well, Callum's the priority, isn't he? Maybe the focus should be on him?'

Never have I met a woman so eager for the murder of her own son. If I didn't feel a similar sordid hatred for Callum, I might judge her for this.

Still, I'm overcome by a sudden urge to get away from her. I gather my things, thank her for my makeover and unlock the front door.

I think of seven white pills, waiting for me when I get back to my bedroom. Just need to put one foot forward. And then another. And then a—

'Elizabeth?'

I freeze. A woman has just gotten out of a car parked across the street.

'Elizabeth?' she says again, with a comforting Geordie accent.

It's . . . it's . . . I see tightly wound curls, dark, kind eyes, a red coat that I've borrowed more times than I can count on one hand.

'Fuck.'

It's Kayi—

'Fuck.'

It's Ex Friend #1.

Chapter Fifteen

I blink, trying to ensure that my mind isn't playing tricks on me.

'What are you doing here?' I ask her.

Ex Friend #1 chews on her lip. She opens and closes her mouth before saying, 'I've been so worried about you, Elizabeth. I miss you.'

Something seems to thaw within me.

'Do you?'

'Oh my God. Yes. So much.'

Her voice is so soft. But it's more than that; her voice summons within me the memory of existing beyond the house behind me for the first time. My first taste of freedom. Her voice reminds me of tipsy all-nighters and whispered exam prep and . . . and a life in which I didn't feel as though I'm fading to black, a little more every day.

'I . . . like . . . I heard about,' Ex Friend #1 says. She pauses. 'I heard about Joe.'

'Oh. Uh-huh.'

'I'm really fucking sorry.'

No. I want to shake my head. *Don't be sorry. I'm taking care of it. It's OK, it's in hand. I'm three-fifths of the way through avenging him.*

'And I was going to say you should have told me,' she continues. 'But then I realised that people deal with grief in different ways, and that I can't be mad at you for ignoring me for months, or not trusting me enough to let me know.'

A simultaneously selfish and selfless statement to which I have no answer. I look past her, towards the big blue bridge from which Joe fell. My cheeks are damp, but it doesn't feel like I'm crying.

'It was good to see you,' I say, visions of white pills and typing out the name of victim #4 swimming in my brain.

I turn to leave, but Ex Friend #1 grabs my arm.

'Please, just . . . I'm here for you, OK?' she says.

I can't look at her. My neck is damp. I'm crying. I'm definitely crying.

'I'm having, uh, it's my birthday. In a few weeks. Was just going to do a small thing for it. I'd love you to come. You could grab your stuff too, if you still want it. It's all in the loft.'

This suggestion feels so alien I'm not sure how to react to it. A birthday party. With friends. Alcohol, maybe. And . . . and . . .

'Will she be there?' I ask.

Ex Friend #1 shrugs. 'It's possible. She hasn't confirmed yet. It might be good for you, though. Closure.'

'Mmm. I don't think I need any of my things, actually.'

Ex Friend #1 laughs. It's forced, but she's so warm the laugh just about passes for genuine. She squeezes my wrist a little tighter.

'Howay, you don't want your signed *Twilight* poster? You don't want your butterfly onesie?'

I almost laugh. Ex Friend #1 doesn't let me answer, instead she pulls me into a tight hug and says, 'Just think about it, OK? Please.'

When I arrive back at the flat, there's a letter waiting for me. Having given out my new address to few places and people, I'm nervous. The envelope is a plain off-white, the colour of cheap paint and office ceilings. I don't recognise the spidery handwriting, but I do imagine a receptionist chewing a pen lid between their lips, eyes flickering between the envelope and the ceiling, feeling trapped but unable to articulate why.

I tear the letter open, suddenly claustrophobic.

My request to visit Jamie Sleight has been approved. I'm invited to visit him at Holme House Prison on Saturday, between the hours of 2pm and 3.30pm.

'Wow,' I say, hardly believing that I'm just over a day away from visiting a man I can only describe as an unfathomable mystery.

I'm more nervous than I anticipated, so, when Saturday rolls round, I fill the hours before the visit with The Fake Boyfriend: we grab lunch from a café on Stockton High Street, and end up chucking most of it to the sky rats by the river when it winds up being shite.

'Why do they always have to add stuff to tuna?' says The Fake

Boyfriend, as he lobs a corner of crust into the air. 'I always get a tuna sandwich and feel safe, and then I open it up and it's full of sweetcorn or tomato or cucumber or some rubbish.'

'Interesting. I had you pegged as a veg guy,' I tell him.

'Oh I *am* a veg guy, don't you worry about that,' he says, giving me a silly half wink. 'Just not veg that's smothered in mayonnaise and butter and fish.'

'Noted.'

'Like, why do they make sandwiches so complicated?'

'Oh no, you're not one of *those* Subway people, are you?' I ask.

'What do you mean?'

'Someone who goes into Subway and orders, like, *just* a cheese sandwich.'

The Fake Boyfriend blushes, and I'm reminded of how lush it is when he does so: cheeks splotched in a shade that matches his lips, mouth set in a crooked smile, eyes not meeting mine.

'I'd probably get ham, too. And sometimes I'd have it toasted.'

I grin. I sit down on a particularly appealing section of wall, and he sits beside me. It's probably still too early in the year to use the word apricity, but it's what I think as the sun warms my face. The Fake Boyfriend's fingers inch their way onto mine, and I let them rest.

'Is your dad called Mitch?' asks The Fake Boyfriend, after a beat or two have passed.

I laugh. 'Random. Super random. I mean he was called Mitch. My mam's called Kim, if you're thinking of doing a family tree.'

'Sorry. No, obviously not.'

'How do you know his name, anyway?' I ask.

'I think I heard it. Or the Mandeville part, anyway. It's not a very common surname.'

A cloud covers the sun, and I miss it instantaneously. I turn to The Fake Boyfriend and say, 'Well I don't think he gave you it for his coffee order. He's been dead for two decades.'

'Oh. Oh right, sorry. How did he die?'

I shrug. 'He was involved in a lot of drug and gang stuff. Think it was some sort of deal gone wrong. My mam has never really spoken about it much. Her new partner doesn't really like talk of my dad, you know? If you heard the name Mandeville recently, it's probably in relation to my brother, Callum.'

'Yeah, it was recent. Yeah, maybe you're right,' he mumbles.

I've half a mind to dig into any leads The Fake Boyfriend might accidentally have absorbed on Callum, but I store the question away for later. I'm building myself up to my brother. I'm slowly progressing to the main event. I wrap my fingers around a clump of grass poking up between the bricks and squeeze, imaging I'm holding onto Callum's hair. I slowly rip the blades out.

'And the drug and gang stuff, I guess he had people to help him with all that?' The Fake Boyfriend asks.

'I guess. Isn't that normally how it works?'

'I don't know.'

'I don't know either. Why so interested, anyway? Looking to switch the caffeine business for cocaine?'

The Fake Boyfriend bites into his sandwich – sweetcorn and all – before saying, 'No. Don't be daft. Guess I'm just always curious about things I'm clueless in. Don't think I'd last a day in a gang.'

'Respectfully, no, I don't think you would either.'

We both laugh, but mine is hollow, as my mind drifts towards this afternoon's activity, and the fact that I'm about to sit down with someone who – judging by his track record – spent many years in gangs. Thrived in them, even, depending on your definition of thriving. Jamie Sleight dealt and intimidated and stole and managed to keep himself out of jail, yet he's just waltzed in for a murder he didn't commit. The sheer *wrongness* of it all makes my head ache.

The sun comes back out, and I bask for a few more minutes, before standing up and telling The Fake Boyfriend I need to get on with my day. He offers to walk me back to my flat, but I tell him I've got errands to run in the far end of Stockton, and I need to do them alone.

'Sounds dodgy to me, Ella,' he says, smiling.

My eyes widen and my blood seems to chill. 'Not at all. What do you mean?'

'It was a joke, sorry. An offensive one, really, given what you just told me about your dad. Sorry, I'm sure you're off to help old people, or something. But none of my business.'

Ordinarily, I find his word diarrhoea endearing, but today it sets me on edge. I force out a laugh and then turn and speed walk the long way to the prison, feeling more nervous than ever. And I can't say that anything about the process of entering the prison makes me feel more relaxed: not the pat down from staff or the showing of my ID or the curls of barbed wire which line the walls. I've killed people and gotten away with it. To willingly enter a prison feels insane.

No more insane than what Jamie Sleight has done, I realise when I see him. He's in the centre of the vast visiting room, sitting on a green plastic chair and twiddling his thumbs. I scan the room before heading over to him. It's pleasant enough and well lit, with long windows dominating the far wall. There are a few dozen clusters of plastic tables and chairs, all bolted to the floor. Inmates and visitors occupy them, and guards are meandering round.

I take a deep breath and then join Jamie.

'Hey,' I say. I sit opposite him straight away, having decided that there is no correct etiquette in this scenario (handshake? Hug? Air kiss?) so I'm better off removing all options completely.

He raises an eyebrow, but doesn't say anything. I resist the urge to word vomit, instead taking a silent second to drink in his appearance. It's that of an ageing bass player, perhaps. He has long chestnut hair, a prominent Adam's apple and a strong brow bone. His dark eyes are deep set, and he's lucky to still have both, for a smooth scar runs from his left temple to left cheekbone. He crosses his legs and wraps his fingers around his bony knee.

'I'm Ella, by the way.'

Jamie nods. 'I know.'

'Thanks for agreeing to see me.'

'Thought I'd better, when I saw your name. Thought you might have . . .' He pauses to glance around the room. 'Instructions for me.'

My forehead crumples in confusion.

'No. Did . . . someone else give you instructions?' I ask.

Jamie takes his time reading my face. I feel those dark chocolate eyes search every inch of me, before he licks his lips and says, 'No.'

I nod. I have no idea how to dance around what I need to ask him, how to build up to it. I glance about to check there are no guards nearby, and then I decide to just come out with it.

'You didn't kill Courtney Teasdale.'

Jamie's eyebrows rise. He cracks a smile and pushes his hair back behind his shoulder.

'Wish I hadn't killed her. Wouldn't be in here if I hadn't,' he says.

My turn to stare. I observe every inch of him, every freckle and wrinkle and scar. Every twitch and blink and lick. Is he insane, or is this something different?

'I know you didn't kill her,' I say.

Jamie laughs. 'I'll have to introduce you to my lawyer. He'd love to have you as a witness.'

'I don't understand why you're doing this,' I say.

Jamie shrugs. He switches his left knee on top of his right and repositions his knuckles. I cast a furtive glance around the room, scanning for police officers, and then I lean as far forward as possible.

'I know you didn't kill Courtney Teasdale,' I whisper. 'Because *I* did.'

I lean back and watch as shock explodes across his face like a firework: present only for a second, but all-changing despite its brevity. Jamie runs a hand through his hair and readjusts his legs.

'That makes sense,' he says. 'Yeah, that makes sense.'

I hold my breath, half expecting he might stand up and scream at the guards to arrest me. Instead, he says, 'Is this a test? Have you been set up to this?'

I shake my head. 'No. I've not told anyone about my visit. I just need to know why you've confessed to a murder I committed.'

He laughs again. 'Fuck, this whole thing has been such a trip.'

'What happened?'

Jamie glances around, but his eyes linger on the other visitors, as opposed to the guards.

'If you speak to you know who, this conversation never happened,' he says.

'I don't know who "you know who" is supposed to be.'

His gaze returns to my face. 'You really don't, do you?'

'No. And, funnily enough, this conversation isn't helping.'

'I can't tell you who set me up to this. Can't risk fucking up the deal.'

'OK,' I say.

Jamie gestures for me to lean closer. We bridge the gap between us, so that my forehead is only a few inches from his.

'Had been sleeping rough for a while. Was begging near Saltburn pier, you know. It's busy down there, people'll quite often buy you a chip butty even if they don't give you change.'

'Go on.'

'Was approached and told to get in a car, was told doing so would be worth my while. And I knew... I knew straight away there'd be no point in resisting. I'd be getting in the car whether I liked it or not.'

A guard passes a few metres from us. Jamie pauses his story, watches until there's a solid wedge of space between his lips and the guard's ears, and then recommences.

'So I was driven for a little bit. Not in a horrible way, not with a bag over my head, or anything. Was driven to their house.'

'Where did they live?'

'You're trying to cheat,' Jamie says, flashing a wry smile. 'I was sat down and made a brew and given a biscuit, and then the bombshell gets dropped, doesn't it?'

'You were told Courtney had been killed.'

'Yeah. Was told some lass called Courtney Teasdale had been killed a couple of days before. And I'm sitting with my brew, thinking, "oh yeah, what's this got to do with me?"'

'What did it have to do with you?'

'Was made an offer, wasn't I? Was made an offer, and there I am, eating a hobnob, can hear the arcade going off, all feels very fucking surreal.'

'But it was a good offer?' I ask.

'Took it, didn't I? Though I don't think I had much choice.'

'And then what?'

'I was told what had happened to this girl. All the details, what I should say to the police. Cos they don't just believe you if you waltz in and start saying you've murdered someone. They think you're crazy, bit like you did, when you first came in here. So I was prepped with the sort of information only people who'd been very involved in the situation would know. And I was given things, too. Couple of strands of her hair, to put onto one of my jackets. Her necklace, to say I took, a sort of token, I suppose.'

'What did the necklace look like?' I ask.

'Silver. Just one word. *Libra*.'

I shiver. Shake my head. 'How would the person who set you up have gotten her necklace? Her *hair*? How would they know all the details of her death?'

'The person who set me up to this knows everyone and everything worth knowing in this area. And then some.'

I lean back, suddenly needing space from Jamie. He mirrors me, leaning back in the green plastic chair and placing his hands behind his head.

'You've got to tell me who it was,' I say.

'You know I can't do that.'

'Please.'

Jamie shakes his head. He licks his lips. 'A ghost from my past, that's all I'll say. It was a ghost from my past.'

Chapter Sixteen

I cling on to what I can from my talk with Jamie: namely that he could hear an arcade from the house in which he was taken to. There's an arcade in Saltburn, but no houses nearby. Besides, this is the spot from which he was picked up, and it sounds like he was driven a little while after. So I take a punt on Redcar, home to the most, and arguably the loudest arcades in the area.

I get Sundays off, and I use my free time to bake an incredibly basic batch of brownies. I then take a long, hard look at myself in my bedroom mirror. People are more interested in themselves than in anyone else, I've known this from the get-go. My aim should be to move unnoticed through the crowd, to invite strangers' eyes to slip through me as though I'm a billow of smoke on a foggy day. I need to channel the style of someone who's having an off day: hair gone wrong or suffering a breakout or feeling the repercussions of a big weekend. The kind of person whose raison d'être is to be uninteresting.

Mam's castoffs work relatively well for these purposes. They're fairly stereotypical of a Northern woman out and about running errands. I run my fingers over a pair of her leggings, recalling a time when the women of Middlesbrough were voted least fashionable in the UK. I'd been furious; the year was 2009, and I was still a malleable pre-teen, hoping to emulate the fashion I saw around me as soon as I scraped enough pocket money together. I still think the vote was bollocks (aren't they all?), but I spend a second or two lingering on my lost innocence, a point when my personality and opinions could be swayed by something as inconsequential as a pop magazine. I recall reading that Christina Aguilera changed her hair colour more often than boys changed their pants and taking this literally, insisting as much to Callum, even as he answered me in derisive guffaws. To laugh at this memory is my natural instinct, but I catch myself. Callum is the enemy. No good comes from him. No good ever did.

With the brownies packed in my bag, I meander over to Hill Street Shopping Centre, where I purchase two small, pretty pink coats and four pink ribbons. And then I head back to the tree-lined street where Courtney used to live.

Sure enough, Brat #1 and Brat #2 are braving the chilly weather to torture a frog with all the emotional trepidation of a teaspoon. That is to say, none at all. They pause their prodding when they see me.

'Girls,' I say, squatting to join them and what's left of the frog. 'How are you?'

'You look older than last time we saw you,' replies Brat #1.

'Tell me something I don't know,' I say.

'You look uglier, too.'

'How come?' I ask.

Brat #1 sticks out her tongue. 'Ugly nose. Big ugly hair.'

She's given a shove by her sister. 'Don't be mean. Just uglier clothes, that's all. We liked your other stuff.'

'I still have my other things,' I say.

'The pink fluffy skirt? And the leopard print scarf?'

'Yep. I've actually . . . well, I was going to sell them all for money. A lot of money.'

'How much money?' asks Brat #2, flipping the frog over with her stick so that its mangled stomach is on display. A pointy, vinegary stench drifts up towards my nostrils.

'I think I could get a few hundred. But I want to make sure they go to the right people. You know, girls who are stylish enough to look good wearing those things.'

'We're very stylish,' Brat #1 assures me.

I stick my tongue out, pretending to think for a couple of seconds. I've the attention of each girl, can feel both beady pairs of green eyes fixed on my face.

'You are,' I say. 'But do you have hundreds of pounds?'

They shake their heads. I tilt mine from side to side and click my tongue.

'OK. I suppose you could do something for me, in exchange for the clothes? But it's top secret. You can't tell your parents.'

Brat #1 laughs. 'Yeah, right. As if we tell those millennial losers anything.'

This is how I end up on a bus with the pair of them, twenty minutes later. After a bit of cajoling, they're both wearing the pretty pink coats over their tracksuits, and I've plaited their hair with pink ribbons. Alas, it seems I'm not over my incessant urge to give everyone around me makeovers just yet.

It's only once we reach Eston that it occurs to me that I've technically kidnapped Brat #1 and Brat #2. But is it kidnap if you're chomping at the bit to return your kidnappees? I can think of few things worse than having to hunker down with two obnoxious ten-year-olds for the remainder of my existence.

In the interest of getting rid of them as quickly as possible, once alighting at the seafront, I take out my box of brownies immediately.

'What *are* we doing?' asks Brat #1, tugging at her plait.

We're knocking on the door of every household within a hundred-metre radius, to see if I recognise an inhabitant as someone who might manipulate randomers into confessing to my murders. I refuse to believe that someone I don't know is behind this. I'm convinced an 'aha' moment is waiting behind a nearby door. I'm not sure how many other serial killers have to track down the person who's tracking them. I must be doing something wrong.

I can't say any of this, of course.

Instead, I say, 'We're raising money for your Brownie pack. Brownies for Brownies, or something. I'm sure you can come up with some adorable catchphrase.'

'We're not *in* the Brownies.'

'I know. That's what's so clever about this. We're only pretending to raise money for Girl Guiding. If you're really good, I'll let you keep any money we make. And all my stylish clothes.'

Brat #2, ordinarily the kid I prefer, makes an annoyingly observant point. 'And what are you getting out of this?'

I tap at the Tupperware box. 'I'm getting feedback on my new recipe.'

She doesn't really buy this answer, so I follow my statement up with, 'Anyway. Who's better – YouTubers or TikTokers?'

The brats start an impassioned debate while I peer down a row of terraced houses off the high street. My tongue pulses back and forth against the roof of my mouth. The street is quiet, bar the distant buzzing and dinging of the arcade. Despite our proximity to the sea, my nose is filled not with salt but with the damp, amber scent of fallen leaves. The sharp smell of lit matches and distant bonfires. The warmth of summer is gone, has been gone for a while. It's replaced by the rot of autumn. I had worried that the change in season would make me feel more distant from Joe, but he comes to me in dark moments – his body rotting in parallel with nature.

I shake away this image.

With forced joviality, I manoeuvre the twins down the street, and knock at our first front door.

'Act really cute, girls,' I mutter. 'I'm not just giving away my sparkly scrunchie collection.'

They're good, to be fair to them: affecting saccharine accents and babbling on about wanting to make a difference to their community. They tug at their plaits and bat their eyelashes and eventually the man who opened the door hands over a couple of pounds in exchange for baked goods. I don't recognise him. And, though I try my best to peer round him while the brats babble on, I don't see anyone else behind him.

This is a theme that continues as we make our way down the street. People either don't answer (and with these houses, I always press my face up to the window, wondering if they're genuinely out, which prompts a telling off from the literal children accompanying me) or I don't recognise the owners.

To my complete indifference, the brownies are a roaring success, with one older man buying six of them.

'It's OK honey, let me,' I say, when Brat #2 attempts to pick up all of them at once.

'Thanks,' the man says as I hand him two clusters of three. 'These adorable girls must be your daughters?'

Good God, has a life of crime and vengeance really aged me that much? I grit my teeth and say, 'Cousins. The adorable girls are my cousins.'

I pat my face as he closes the door, as if searching for wrinkles.

'Said you were looking older,' mumbles Brat #1, and I roll my eyes.

But two and a bit months of constant stress, grief and paranoia bubbling within me might finally be taking a toll externally. Sleep is irregular, and often impossible without the white pills. Memories of Joe and Callum haunt me, and I sometimes struggle to distinguish the good memories from the bad. Happy memories correlate with Joe. Sad ones with Callum. And yet that's not always how it feels. Add to this the pressure of acting a part around people I largely didn't know a few months ago, and my head seems always to be swimming, attempting to determine the correct expression, opinion, tone of voice.

And that's before adding in the murder, of course. That minor detail. The thing my life now revolves around. There's a strange sort of distance between me and the idea of murder, now. My feelings are still, at times, slippery and inconsistent. It's not dissimilar from the early weeks of my breakup – some days I'd be burning with fury for The Ex, and others I'd find myself feeling more rational. This is that, but on steroids.

I don't enjoy killing. Not by a long shot. There's still a significant part of me that regrets having done so three times. But there is, I suppose, a certain amount of power that comes with taking a life. And a neat, accomplished feeling, as though I'm checking off a task which has been looming over me. But I'm not staring down a slippery, murderous slope, not fighting the urge to knock off people hither and thither – a stabbing here, a smothering there. Murder has been, and I believe always will be, just a means to an end. My list of victims is inflexible. Five and done.

But murder is less daunting than it initially appeared. Before, the idea of killing was like staring at a collection of twentieth-century French films. The language, setting, period was unfamiliar. The pressure of interpreting them correctly seemed huge. An insurmountable task, one I didn't even know how to begin. And yet, when I did start watching, I remembered that there were subtitles to help me. That people across the Channel and a few decades ago aren't so different to those today. That certain topics – love, loss, struggle – are universal. One film would lead to another and watching each new film would be that bit easier than the last.

A better example might be cold water. Initially, getting in is one of the worst thoughts in the world. But, after a few minutes of being submerged (perhaps you edged your way in, an inch of flesh at a time, or perhaps you flung yourself in wholeheartedly), you realise you're quite capable of staying afloat in the cool and the dark. That it might not be pleasant, but it is possible.

There's a dog barking from within the next house we pass, and I let my mind drift to my penultimate victim. I'm inching closer to a goal which now seems tattooed on my brain. A goal that, despite having taken over my personality, I resist examining lest the whole thing crumble. More murder won't get Joe back. I doubt Joe would even have wanted me to murder. And yet murder I must.

'We're running out of brownies,' says Brat #2, tugging at my elbow.

I nod. We are running out, and I'm no closer to uncovering the person who has been covering for me. I change tack for the next house.

'I wanted to talk to you about Jamie Sleight,' I say, keeping my voice low and mentioning his name when the brats are busy selecting brownies. I'm not sure how many details they've been told in respect of their sisters' death, but I'd rather they didn't connect me with it. The man who opened the door responds to my question with confusion and disinterest, a reaction mirrored by the residents of the next four houses. I like to think I'm becoming reasonably good at reading people, and I'm inclined to trust their dismay.

Only one reaction veers from this norm. A pretty girl of about twenty-five opens the door of number 58. She clucks over Brat #1 and Brat #2 when they tell her they like her hair (it's long, a striking ginger shade and undeniably luscious, to be fair) and purchases two brownies.

But when I ask about Jamie Sleight, her whole demeanour changes.

Her smile vanishes. Her eyes widen. She glances back, as if someone else is there, just out of view.

'I think you've got the wrong address,' she says, before closing the door.

My analysis of this reaction is cut short when I see Brat #1. She's silent, but tears are streaming down her face. There's a faraway look in her eye, as if she hasn't even clocked the emotion that's pouring from her. I feel a pang of empathy.

'Why do you keep asking about the man who killed our sister?' says Brat #2.

I've not been as subtle as I'd hoped. I have no way of answering her question truthfully, and for the first time in months, I'm desperately reluctant to lie.

'I'm so sorry,' I say.

I've been reductive of the people around me again. I've viewed the pair of them as funny little caricatures, objects to help me achieve what I want. I don't even know their names. This has been necessary, this detachment, since I found myself slipping into murder and then committing to it. But it's polluting me, and it's polluting the people around me.

'Honestly, I'm so sorry,' I say again. I've justified Courtney's murder to myself hundreds of times. But whether I consider it justifiable or not is almost irrelevant; I've still placed the pair of them in my position – with a gaping hole in their lives.

I wipe away their tears and give them the remaining two brownies. I take them home in a taxi, with the promise I'll drop all my clothes in their front garden the next day.

And then, feeling weighed down by my recent actions, I begin the walk back to the flat. There seems to be a swelling within me – as if my organs are growing thick and heavy with emotions I have no control over. There's an unpleasant nostalgia to this feeling, for it's one that I became acquainted with when Mam's money ran out, when Stepdad had to get a job, when Stepdad turned his attention to Callum, and then to me. It's a feeling that all but disappeared when I left for uni.

I shake my head, reluctant to dwell on the past more than

necessary, but I find myself getting dragged back into . . . more of a sensation than a memory. I remember feeling hot from pain and embarrassment, but it's difficult to remember which part of my body was throbbing. Cheek? Back? Shoulder? Heart? I was . . . ? How old was I? Sixteen? Seventeen? I was so angry with Callum, but why? Why had I repeatedly blamed my raw back and bruised arms on his absence, rather than Stepdad's presence?

I recall stumbling up the stairs, vision blurry, planning on heading to the loft and packing a bag, planning an escape. My phone was locked away somewhere, but I'd convinced myself I didn't need it, when the door to Joe's room opened, and he pulled me inside.

He'd been growing his hair at this point. It was shoulder-length, fluffy – bouffant, almost. Ridiculous on a twelve-year-old who'd barely looked ten, and oddly reminiscent of Karen, our next-door neighbour. I'd taken to calling him Karen, asking if he'd wandered into the wrong house, which would make me chuckle specifically because it annoyed him.

'Alright, Karen? You're in the wrong house again,' I said, voice wobbly, organs still feeling thick, as though saturated.

Joe had rolled his eyes, bored of the joke, and said, 'Have you learned how to say "Diplodocus" yet?'

I pronounced this dinosaur as 'Dip-lod-icus' rather than 'Dip-lod-o-cus' and had therefore spent a whole childhood having Callum and Joe mock me, but this particular occasion had left me breathless. It was the sensation of feeling so deeply known by someone, I think. It was such a vintage insult that only someone who had known me before I turned ten would be able to use it, for the word no longer featured in my increasingly adult vocabulary.

I remember looking at Joe – hair fluffy and cheeks flushed and eyes bright – and thinking that he was creating a mosaic of me, and I was creating one of him, in return. My favourite month was December, specifically because of how much Joe loved Christmas lights and mince pies. I sang the lyrics to Ed Sheeran songs wrong because, for reasons unbeknownst to me, he was the one artist Joe would always muddle up. Joe had three and a half spoons of sugar in his tea and one and a half spoons on his Weetabix, because that's what I had. If meals ever involved mash and carrots, we'd both chop the carrots up and create mash castles with orange turrets, an old competition which had grown increasingly silly.

There were pieces missing from both of us, of course – I couldn't ride a bike without thinking of Callum's lessons, I couldn't eat candyfloss without thinking of the time Callum had made me a huge, hideous wig out of the stuff – but in that moment I felt lucky beyond words to have Joe piecing together my preferences and personality. I felt lucky to be formed by someone I loved.

There's a shout from the kitchen almost as soon as I enter the flat, just as I'm locking up and kicking my trainers off.

'Oh man! It's like we're living in a DC film!' is the over-enthusiastic cry of Manbaby Flatmate. With trepidation tapping at my skull, I join him in the kitchen. He's making a crisp and vinegar sandwich, while Too-Old-For-This-Shit Flatmate is nibbling on a carrot. Both of their gazes are fixed on the television.

'What?' I ask.

But I already know. The screen shows a familiar scene: Thorntree Cemetery, and a pile of earth. Less familiar is the reams of police tape and the heavy police presence. The scene switches to include a raven-haired presenter, clutching a microphone in one hand and attempting to keep her hair in place against the wind with the other.

'Engineering apprentice Devlin Mackenzie was reported missing last week. Detectives were able to trace his phone back to a grave here, in Thorntree Cemetery. This is where they found his body. His death is being treated as suspicious, and his family ask for privacy at this difficult time.'

Fuck. Fuck, fuck. His phone. Joe's phone. With the shock of Too-Old-For-This-Shit Flatmate appearing, I forgot to grab them. I'd had plans of smashing Devlin's phone to smithereens, of lobbing it into the North Sea.

My flatmate.

Slowly, slowly, I turn to look at her. She's already looking at me, of course. Her eyes are wide, and the carrot is gripped so tightly in her hand that her knuckles have turned white.

Fuck.

I'm going to have to veer off track. Despite an afternoon spent regretting the lives I've already destroyed, I'm going to have to kill this woman too.

Chapter Seventeen

I know I might end up in jail. To say I've accepted this as a potential outcome would be a bit too far; I imagine the reality of being confined to a cell would be more devastating than I could ever conceive. But I'm committing criminal acts. The repercussions of these – if caught – are not unknown to me. And I think I'd be just about OK with languishing in prison provided I'd avenged Joe by the time I arrived. This is why I look at Too-Old-For-This-Shit Flatmate with renewed trepidation. Because she might just stand in the way of my goal.

I don't want to kill her. I've said it before, and I'll say it again: unnecessary murder isn't part of my plan. Hell – murder wasn't part of my plan at all, originally.

We look at each other, and she doesn't say anything. Does she need to, though? Might she just take what she's seen directly to the police? Is it worth begging her not to? Blackmailing her? But how? With what? Having spoken to Jamie, I've an inkling that someone out there might already be scrambling to find another fake confessor to take the fall for Devlin's death. But what if whoever it is doesn't realise it was me who killed Devlin? What if they don't fancy covering for me again? What if their intentions have always been malicious?

There are so many variables, it makes my head spin.

Too-Old-For-This-Shit Flatmate finishes her carrot and leaves the kitchen. My thighs shake, as if they're preparing to sprint forward and restrain her. I look back to the screen instead, where a confused, upset-looking Employer #1 is being interviewed. I'm too linked to all of this: Devlin's body has just been discovered at the place I used to work. Might my fingerprints be on the slabs which crushed Devlin, or will the mud have wiped them away? Would the presence of my fingerprints on the slabs or on Joe's phone be considered suspicious? I might have moved the slabs while working. I might have taken Joe's phone for my own comfort.

And, of course, there's the fact that both Courtney and Devlin – present at Joe's death – have now died. But, as far as the police are concerned, neither had anything to do with his fatal plunge. Why would a member of Joe's family want to kill them?

The links are tenuous, but they do exist.

I look back in the direction of Too-Old-For-This-Shit Flatmate's door. She's the biggest link of all, of course. I'm either going to have to murder the man with the dog, and Callum, pronto, or I'm going to have to kill her.

Not a decision I have the capacity to make now, so I'm relieved when I receive a text from The Fake Boyfriend saying:

My mam is out tonight. Want to come over?

I try my best to shake thoughts of Devlin's death from my brain, and reply with:

A not-so-subtle way of asking me to come over and have sex?

His response is simple: a tick. I laugh, and send a tick in return, confident that he's just trying his luck, that he would never actually force me to do something I wasn't comfortable with. I wouldn't have chosen him as my fake boyfriend, if so.

Not that I'd necessarily rule out having sex with him. I might be towards the gayer end of the spectrum, but it's not as though having sex with a man would traumatise me. I'd likely just be incredibly bored. Potentially a small price to pay to keep him sweet.

I tap my phone against the kitchen table and think back to the last time I slept with a man, during my second year of uni. I recall lying half naked next to him, looking down past his soft stomach and clocking his antenna of a dick poking at his boxers, desperate to come out and enter an orifice of mine. My stomach had turned, and I'd decided that a life of being prodded with phalli probably wasn't for me.

Not that that stopped certain men from trying. The egotistical, in particular. Occasionally, it would be brought up in conversation that I wasn't all that fussed about sex with the male population, and their response would always be some variation of 'that's cos you haven't had sex with me yet'. These men genuinely – I repeat, genuinely – thought that, at the grand old age of twenty-one or twenty-two, they were enough of a sex God to re-write my entire history of heterosexual encounters. I'd imagine them grunting and gyrating and groaning and me lying flat, looking up at them and trying not to laugh.

God, I hope The Fake Boyfriend isn't showy. And I hope he's not the kind of guy who lasts for an hour, or something ridiculous. I hope he doesn't speak too much – I fundamentally resent being told I'm a good girl when I let a man do something degrading to me; if he spanks me, I'm out.

A recent dip in temperature has made Mam's aviator jacket and Ugg boots a welcome addition to my wardrobe. I put both on and head outside, where dusk is just starting to settle.

The Fake Boyfriend lives in Billingham so I walk along the flyover, stopping to pause halfway across the bridge. The view from here makes me feel miniscule. The town stretches out ahead of me, lights beginning to flicker on to combat the fast-approaching darkness.

People allow beauty to be prescribed to them. This needs subverting, when it comes to Middlesbrough. Because beauty is here, if you allow it in. It's in the cerulean of the sky, criss-crossed by telephone cables, a crescent moon trapped between wires. It's on the beaks of the sky rats which swoop above, lucky enough to have a bird's eye view. It's in the old industry, slowly being infiltrated by goosegrass and fireweed. The way that steel and nature intertwine with one another. It's in the hidden tunnels of Marton West Beck, and the rusted goalposts in the parks, spectators to thousands of good games. Middlesbrough's beauty is warm and sad. Like the last hug from someone you really love.

I watch for a few more minutes, and then I continue walking, eventually reaching where The Fake Boyfriend lives: a flat above a Chinese takeaway. It's a cute little home, decorated with picture after picture of The Fake Boyfriend and his mam.

'Nice pictures,' I say, picking up one of the pair of them eating lemon tops on the beach.

'Thanks.'

'No pictures of your dad?'

'He's been gone a while. I took the opportunity to bin all his pictures.'

'Oh. How long's he been gone for?'

'Couple of months.'

'Why did he go?' I ask, seemingly incapable of reining in my curiosity.

The Fake Boyfriend readjusts his glasses and then says, 'He'd done quite a lot of . . . not good stuff. Guess it caught up with him.'

Trapped as I am in the midst of my own spell of decidedly 'not good stuff', I shudder and look around for a lighter topic of conversation. I land on a jar of pickled peaches on the kitchen counter.

'Cute,' I say, picking it up.

'Delicious.'

He's gone all shy again, which is probably for the best, although not what I expected given that we're in his natural environment, as opposed to a nightclub, or a cemetery. He keeps straightening cushions and wiping tiny bits of food from the stove.

'Sorry about the smell, by the way,' he says.

'Are you kidding? I love Chinese.'

'Yeah, everyone thinks they love Chinese until they inhale the stench of it for two decades.'

'Fair. But right now, inexperienced as I am, it smells of celebrating handing in an essay. Or finding twenty quid down the back of the sofa. It smells of treats, of celebration. You should enjoy that.'

'It doesn't smell like a group of lads puking up Peking duck after a night out?'

I laugh. 'There's an element of joy in that, too.'

'You should be an estate agent.'

'Thanks, I think. But seriously, this is a nice home.' I pick up a picture of The Fake Boyfriend and his mam taken at Stonehenge. 'You really get on with her, don't you?'

He shrugs and starts twisting a line of mugs so that all their handles point in the same direction. 'Yeah, I'd say I do. She calls me her comrade. I think she's just really into Orwell. She's the person I pickle things with. And we pick blackberries in autumn. And strawberries in summer, come to think of it.'

I nod. 'That is wholesome. Shall we . . . go to your bedroom?' I ask, if only because I'm optimistic that there'll be marginally less for him to fiddle with and clean in there.

'Is this your not-so-subtle way of asking me to have sex?' he replies, some of his nervousness receding.

I shrug. Truly, I don't know whether it is or it isn't. Regardless, his bedroom is where we end up. And it's perhaps not as quirky as I'd hoped or anticipated. It's the bedroom of a boy who has grown into a man who's still figuring himself out. I'm reminded of Joe's room. I even spot an acoustic guitar in one corner, and that sense of happy sadness fills me again.

'What are you doing? Where are you going with your life?' I ask a ridiculous question in an attempt to distract myself from thoughts of Joe.

The Fake Boyfriend quite likes these questions. And that's one of the things that I quite like about The Fake Boyfriend. He says, 'I'm not working at the café anymore. I'm a shop assistant in TK Maxx.'

'Oh yeah?'

'Yeah. I quite like it. Get to spend my days telling women they look nice in X top or Y pair of trousers.'

'You're happy because you now have a permanent job perving?' I ask, sitting at the foot of The Fake Boyfriend's bed.

'I wouldn't call it perving.' The Fake Boyfriend tilts his glasses in the sassiest way possible. 'I'd call it telling eighty-year-old Marie that the blue scarf makes her eyes sparkle.'

Where was the job of buttering old women up when I was looking for something innocent?

'But do I want to do that forever?' he continues, coming to sit next to me. 'Probably not. You know I like figuring out how things work. So might look into a job of that variety.'

'Seems like that would be a good fit for you.'

Silence falls, and I look down at our feet, both enclosed by black socks and thirty centimetres away from one another. I wriggle my toes, and The Fake Boyfriend wriggles his in return. We both laugh and then, slowly, his hand comes to a rest on my thigh. We turn to face one another and kiss. It's not the hard, frenetic kiss of the graveyard. I sense his soul soften, a part of it drift from the back of his throat to the back of mine. The sharp taste of a fizzy drink greets me, followed by the morose flavour of the spam dinner it had been used to wash down. And beyond this, the metallic taste of ulcers I imagine The Fake Boyfriend running his tongue over during lost minutes spent sorting clothes or contemplating what kind of shopper might cross his path next.

'Is this OK?' he asks, once we stop kissing.

'Yeah.'

'Tell me if it stops being OK.'

'I will.'

It's all OK, truly. His hand creeping up my thigh. Him removing my jumper. Removing his jeans. His fingers against my knickers. Under my knickers.

I know what's coming, know that I'm going to be OK with what's coming. Thoughts of The Ex aren't healthy, and they're not welcome here. That's what I tell myself as he opens a condom packet and I find myself wondering how many of the dull, repetitive things men usually say during sex will pass through his lips. Whether it will be 'God, I'm so deep. Can you feel how deep I am?' and I'll have to nod, pretending to be impressed that his average-sized dick has made the journey into a relatively minimal part of my body. A gold star for the man with the erection.

In the end, there's no need for a bingo card of cringey comments, for he's mercifully quiet. This has drawbacks; I find myself zoning out at one point, before realising that I'm picking a pimple halfway down his back and that my face is completely blank. I endeavour to twist it into something that might convey enjoyment, and I throw in a moan that I hope sounds erotic for good measure.

I don't feel like lingering, when it's over. The Fake Boyfriend leads me out, and his face twists into this odd, slightly hopeless expression as he shuts the door. As if he anticipated an increased sensation of intimacy from sex, but I've left him feeling lonelier than ever. It's a feeling I know well.

I push his face from my thoughts as the flat comes into view. For a variety of reasons, I've been delaying the murder of the man who watched me trying to save Joe without helping. But the discovery of Devlin has hammered the urgency of this into the front of my mind.

I head up to my bedroom and take out my list, which hasn't been updated for a while. I do so now, using a pencil to cross through Devlin's name, and then re-inserting the list into my typewriter and adding the name of my fourth victim. The list is stupid, but it feels important somehow – tangible proof that I'm completing what I set out to achieve.

I then slot a fresh piece of paper into my typewriter and begin tapping out the names of everyone I've been in close contact with recently:

```
                                   FADE IN:
                                          1
INT. ELLA'S BEDROOM - EVENING
   WE OPEN with ELLA, trying to figure out
who's responsible for Brandon and Jamie's
confessions. She wracks her brain for something
she's missed, someone she's overlooked.
   - THE FAKE BOYFRIEND. She's been too close
to him recently, that much could certainly
be argued. He's sharp, but is he sharper than
she gives him credit for? Has she told him too
much? He was sort of present when Courtney
```

died, but absent when Janet and Devlin died. Has he guessed at what Ella is doing? He surely doesn't have the disposition to make deals with the likes of Brandon and Jamie, and even if he did, why would he? Ella and The Fake Boyfriend get on, but it's not like either is in love with the other.

- MAM, STEPDAD, STEP-NAN. They're in on it and seemed as baffled as Ella at news of the first confession. They know what's happening of course, but they're collectively too passive to frame people post murder. Aren't they?

- MANBABY FLATMATE. Can't have anything to do with anything. Surely. Ella will eat his fish flops and all of his comedy sunglasses if he has clocked on to her crimes.

- TOO-OLD-FOR-THIS-SHIT FLATMATE. Saw Ella murder Devlin and - for reasons unknown - is yet to confront Ella. Perhaps she's nervous, perhaps she's biding her time. She seems too straight-laced and too preoccupied with looking after her sickly boyfriend and moaning about the state of the flat to force Brandon and Jamie into false confessions, though.

- JAMIE SLEIGHT & BRANDON PEARCE. Ella didn't know them. Was certain they didn't witness the murders of either Courtney or Janet. And yet they've confessed to killings they didn't commit. Jamie said that he'd agreed to take the fall in exchange for something from someone. But in exchange for what? And from who? Besides, might Jamie have lied when Ella spoke to him in the prison?

- MARTY DENG. Knows everyone in this town.

```
Knows Ella just lost her brother. Knows Ella
worked at the graveyard in which Devlin's body
was discovered. Has power, has a reputation.
Has lied to Ella. Would do so again.
```

I'm breathing hard by the time I finish typing. I stare fruitlessly at the piece of paper, agonisingly aware that I've made no further progress. Admitting defeat, I fold this list over my list of victims. I toy with the idea of slipping them into my bra or Ugg boot, before abandoning this line of thought. Visions of being patted down by the police and them instantly finding such incriminating pieces of evidence are too vivid. Instead, I pick up Joe's yearbook, and slot them between the pages. And something catches my eye. No, not something, *somethings*.

I open up the yearbook to find what I'd longed for but missed at first read: tens of messages from his classmates. I exhale, and, as I do, it's as if I feel Joe's relief glisten from the crisp pages, unspooling with each glorious, jagged letter.

You're a pretty canny lad, the girls will be all over you at uni, like x

Joe, mate! Swear down you're the best French buddy I could have asked for! Will miss ripping into Madame Dupont with you.

Proper devvoed we didn't spend more time together, you cracked me up whenever we had the same class, though. Top bloke.

Joe, you're sound as a pound. You're gonna smash uni, you big brainbox. Keep in touch and that, though.

Now then, mush, don't be a stranger. You may eat chicken dinners like a psychopath (no gravy! You mad?!) but you're hilarious, and tip top at the guitar. Love you, bro.

Fuck. He was popular. Happy. Funny. I imagine his face as each message was added, the shy grin which would have stretched across his lips, the way his curls would have flopped over his eyes. The warmth of his body. I hug the yearbook close, wanting to squeeze his classmates, wanting to thank them for looking after him when I couldn't. His funeral, his small, sad birthday party, the TikTok videos: all inaccurate. He was OK. He was OK.

He was OK.

Chapter Eighteen

Brandon Pearce's plea hearing is announced in the *Evening Gazette*. It's to take place at Teesside Crown Court in a few days' time. A quick google tells me that none of the really juicy information will be discussed in a plea hearing (that comes later – months or even years later) but the public can attend. It strikes me as highly likely that whoever convinced Brandon to confess to the murder of Janet will go. I certainly would if I was in their shoes; it's the perfect opportunity to surreptitiously ensure that Brandon goes through with his guilty plea. For this reason, my own attendance is vital.

I ask Marty for the day off when he first emerges from his office on Tuesday morning.

'Uh, yeah, sure thing,' is his response. I may only be a handful of days into working for him, but he has all the makings of an excellent boss – especially if it's early and his coffee hasn't kicked in. His new existence seems to rotate around avoiding confrontation; unless I told him I wanted to kidnap his dog or daughter, I'd wager he'll agree to anything I ask.

'Will you be working on Friday?' I ask, trying to ascertain whether he's planning on attending Brandon's plea hearing.

'Yeah, most likely. Practically chained to this place, you know me.'

Could be a double bluff. I keep a close eye on him for the remainder of the day. A yellow cloth in one hand, a bottle of lemon-scented spray in the other, and my gaze always on his small, quick body as he darts between machines and between customers. My gaze occasionally flickers to his office, a tempting trove which seems stuffed with secrets. But Marty keeps it locked, and the key firmly within an inside jacket pocket.

I watch him, and he watches me. There's a knowing look in his eye, I'm certain of it.

'You knew Brandon Pearce, right?' asks one of Marty's punters. He's leaning against a roulette machine and flicking through the *Evening Gazette.*

I'm cleaning the inside of the windows; the question isn't directed at me, but my ears prick in interest.

'Eh, name rings a bell, like,' says Marty from across the room.

'Bit of a booze problem, not very nice to his wife and kid. Head so shiny you could fry an egg on it.'

'Ahh, me memory isn't all it once was, like. Struggle to remember owt that happened last week, never mind anyone from decades ago.'

'Went to your wedding, didn't he? Your first wedding, the one in Malaga.'

I set down the window spray. My heart rate quickens and sweat forms on my brow, despite the chill of the day. I'm desperate to see Marty's reaction, desperate to monitor each minute change of muscle, but I have a feeling he'll be watching me just as closely. With an effort, I pick the spray back up and apply a fresh splattering to the window.

'Oh, aye, guess I . . . guess he did go to me wedding.' Marty is sheepish, and too fucking right – he evidently knows Brandon Pearce beyond just a vague familiarity with his name, as he implied to me.

'Can't believe he's going down for murder. I mean, always knew he had his issues, but howay, *murder*?'

'Not nice. Not nice at all.'

'And to kill that Janet Braithwaite lass, of all people. Why? What did she ever do to him?'

Marty coughs once. 'Nothing. If I didn't know better, I'd say Brandon hadn't been the one to kill her at all.'

Finally, I can resist no longer. I twist round to face Marty. He's already looking at me, his small eyes seemingly scorching a hole in my soul. Does he know? Does he know what I'm doing? How could he possibly know? How could he know it was me who murdered Janet?

And then, the second line of thought: if he knows, is he the person who lined up Jamie and Brandon to take the fall in my place?

It's a question I'm convinced I'll get an answer to when Friday rolls round. Before making my way to court, I'm once again forced to psychoanalyse my appearance. I need to blend in completely. I select black trousers, a navy jumper and Mam's parka jacket, which has a hood so fluffy it conceals half my side profile. I chop a thick fringe in and pick up a pair of fake glasses from Poundland on my way over, longing for the day when I might dress how I want, rather than how I need.

The court, while being intimidating, is less so than Holme House Prison. Once through security, I sit myself by the vending machine outside the courtroom, and bury my nose in a book, so that only my fringe and bespectacled eyes are visible. I take note of each passer-by and everyone else who lingers in my vicinity, though I don't recognise any of them.

Eventually, an usher emerges from the courtroom and tells us we can come in. He leads us into a big room, containing perhaps the most wood I've ever seen in one go: wooden panels on the wall, wooden desks, a wooden witness box, and of course the judge's bench. We're led over to the public gallery, at the side of the courtroom. I up my pace, ensuring I get a spot in the back corner, with a good view of everyone.

Once in place, I make myself as small and unassuming as possible, and then I scan. Brandon has yet to arrive. A cluster of lawyers are writing and talking in low voices at the centre of the courtroom. To the other side of the room, official-looking people who I assume are the police or CPS representatives straighten their ties and tap their pens. There are no jurors, of course.

But my real section of interest is the area in which I'm sitting: the public gallery. Twenty or so other people share this space with me, and I quickly split them into one of two camps: press, or a loved one of Janet. I see no one I recognise, no one who looks like they might have forced Brandon into the position he finds himself.

I press my fingertips hard against my temples. I'd been certain that the stealer of my crimes would be in attendance today. To be staring down the barrel of yet more unknowing seems to physically pain me.

The door clicks open. I look up, expecting Brandon, but the usher is back, bringing with him one final member of the public.

When the usher steps aside, revealing the identity of the person behind him, it takes all my effort not to gasp.

Chapter Nineteen

It's not Marty. It's not Mam or Step-Nan. It's not either of my flatmates. It's not Employer #1 and it's not even Stepdad.

The last member of the public who enters the courtroom is The Fake Boyfriend.

I place my hands on either side of my head – partly so that he won't spot me, and partly so that I can mouth 'oh my God' over and over again.

What the actual fuck?

A security guard brings Brandon into the room. They take their position at the back, behind a glass screen, and the formalities of the plea hearing commence, but I can hardly pay attention. I keep shooting glances in the direction of The Fake Boyfriend, who sits at the far end of the row in front of me, and keeps his head tilted in the direction of Brandon.

'What the fuck?' I whisper.

The hearing unfolds and my brain ticks fervently, toying with half a dozen theories, none of which might be accurate. Because, in truth, I know very little about The Fake Boyfriend. I'd never intended to. He was to be a prop, a normaliser, a thing as opposed to a human. I stare at his dark floppy hair, wondering at the secrets which lie within his brain.

Perhaps he really did fall for me in record speed. Perhaps he's secretly tough as nails, good at intimidating people into doing what he wants. He's worked at a café and a shop; I can see how he might know half the town. Maybe he knows people who saw me commit the murders, and decided to step in and save me. Maybe he's not saving me at all, maybe he's lulling me into a false sense of security, setting me up for an even bigger fall.

I chew the inside of my cheek, not feeling entirely happy with any of the conclusions I've come to, but aware that I'm unlikely to land upon anything more concrete as things are – with me hemmed into the corner of the public gallery, unable to move or speak until the plea hearing finishes.

It doesn't last long, mercifully.

Brandon Pearce pleads guilty to one count of murder. A murmur ripples round the courtroom, further dates are announced and everyone is dismissed.

I wait as long as possible before leaving the public gallery, not feeling ready to face The Fake Boyfriend. This works, but I still emerge to something I'd rather have avoided: the journalists, discussing not Janet Braithwaite's death, but Devlin Mackenzie's.

'I don't think they have any leads, not a single one.'

'Nope. I spoke to his neighbours. I spoke to his school. No one I haven't spoken to. A nightmare. He was a nightmare. That's what they say. That's what they all say.'

'Pah! Well, eh, sounds like a near endless list of potential culprits.'

'Oh aye, just need someone at the cemetery to speak, that's the angle I'm taking.'

'Eh-heh, uh-huh, good luck with that, don't think the boss exactly keeps accurate records of who he's employed.'

I pat my fringe all the way across my forehead and pull my hood up, trying to conceal as much of myself as possible as I push through them, keen to escape the courthouse and the crowds of curious people who inhabit it. I dart across town, wanting to hide, to keep a low profile, to . . .

'Shit.'

I round the corner to the flat, ordinarily a peaceful white beacon amidst an ocean of scrap and fireweed – but this afternoon it's different. This afternoon, a police car is parked outside. My first instinct is to run away, but my second is more sensible; the officers are yet to leave their car. I need to get to them before they can speak to Too-Old-For-This-Shit Flatmate.

I up my pace and greet them as they're slamming the car doors shut.

'Hey, hi, can I help you with anything?' I ask. They're both men this time, both middle-aged, one sporting a monobrow, the other thin, groomed brows – the type that were last seen on noughties celebrities. Seeing them rise and fall on the face of an otherwise fairly rough-looking man near two decades later is briefly discombobulating.

'Err yeah, actually. You're Elizabeth Mandeville?' asks Monobrow. The use of a name I haven't gone by for a while briefly throws me.

I scan for handcuffs. I think about lying. I glance back at the flat. She's told them. My flatmate has told them, and they're here to arrest me.

'Yes. I'm Elizabeth.'

They introduce themselves. Ask me to come to the station with them, and when I ask why, they just say that they have some questions for me. A response which summons an acidic, sickly sensation which swells within me, despite the fact that no handcuffs appear, and they don't read out my rights. I keep swallowing, keep forcing the physical manifestation of my terror down deeper within me during the short trip from my flat to the station, and then into the small interview room within. The same room I was asked about Joe in, when I felt my life, already in freefall, sink to desperate depths I'd never previously been able to envision. A blackhole of a room.

The officers sit down at one side of the wooden table, and I sit at the opposite. They faff with tapes and notepads and I try not to let my gaze drift to the grey wall behind them.

'Thank you for your time today, Elizabeth,' says Monobrow. He's not a local, his accent is very middle-of-the-road English, as if he grew up in the Home Counties but doesn't lean into it.

'That's OK.' I'm polite. The opposite to how I was last time I was in this room.

'We wanted to ask you some questions,' says Plucked Brow. He's from the area, but I'd place him in Yarm, or Nunthorpe. Somewhere fancy.

'Yes. Happy to answer.'

'About Devlin Mackenzie, specifically.'

Here it comes. Here comes the tsunami of shit. I brace, waiting for them to tell me that I was spotted on the night he disappeared in the location he was discovered. And I have nothing. I have no way of wriggling out of those accusations.

It's over.

'I'm sure you'll have heard that his body was recently discovered. I imagine you might also be aware that Courtney Teasdale was killed five weeks ago. And – of course – and we're sorry to have to put you through this, but your brother Joseph died in August.'

'Yes.'

Oh my God. They're going to accuse me of Courtney's murder, too. They've realised what I'm doing. Why I'm doing it.

'They were in the same form group. We understand Joseph's death was an accident, but Courtney and Devlin's deaths were different,' Monobrow says.

If the Ella of the past could see me now, she'd be incensed that I don't protest at him calling Joe's death an accident. But my mouth is too dry, as I wait to see where he's going with these statements.

'A man called Jamie Sleight has been arrested for Courtney's death. He was arrested before Devlin disappeared, but we've good reason to think that Courtney and Devlin's – and to some extent, Joe's – deaths are linked. We think it likely that an acquaintance of Jamie's is behind his murder.'

'I . . .' I don't know what to say. I'm overcome with . . . relief, I suppose, but also disbelief. They lapped up Jamie's confession. They're barking up completely the wrong tree. The murderer is sitting opposite them, and they don't have a fucking clue.

'We've reason to believe that Joseph, Courtney and Devlin were in a gang, or linked to a gang of some description. You know about that?' asks Plucked Brow.

I resist the urge to roll my eyes, for surely there's no bigger cliché than the notion of youth being involved in some generic, faceless gang. Truthfully, I don't think any of them were. Or certainly not a gang in the sense that the officers are probably envisioning: a group who fight rivals and deal drugs and terrorise the town. I think they just had friends or people they knew who – like anyone – acted immorally at times. But I can see the opportunity to further distance myself from my crimes, so I take it.

'I knew bits. I obviously didn't get told everything. Not even close. I'd have probably had to undergo some vicious induction to make it into the circle of trust.' I reel myself in, wary of getting carried away and inventing disgusting gang initiations, pushing my tale past the realms of probability. 'But I knew they were attracting the attention of others . . . knew that Courtney, in particular, had felt threatened. I'd never heard names mentioned – not real ones, anyway – but I got the impression that one of the groups, or gangs, was quite a lot older. Which would match Jamie and his acquaintances – from what I've seen in the news, anyway. So, guess you're right, and these are your next port of call.'

They swallow these lies like they're syrup. They go down easily, for the police officers think I'm edging them closer to a neat resolution in their case. A smug smile stretches across their lips; I've made them feel smart. I've stroked the male ego.

Poor Joe. There was never a chance of his death being recorded properly.

'The video on Janet Braithwaite's phone . . .' says Monobrow. These five words are delivered quietly, directed at his fellow police officer instead of me, but I straighten in alarm and strain my ears to hear their whispered exchange.

'Brandon Pearce. Knows Jamie Sleight. Same gang? Targeting a younger gang who all happen to be recorded on Janet Braithwaite's phone? It's linking up. Jigsaw falling into place.'

Brandon knows Jamie. Brandon Pearce knows Jamie Sleight. It's all linked. Not in the way the officers think, of course, but not in the way I think, either. Clearly. Because I don't have a clue.

Monobrow clears his throat and turns back to me.

'Thank you, Elizabeth. You've been very helpful. You're free to go. We've got your contact details if we think you can be of any more help.'

'Of course,' I say, nodding, and still stuck with the names Jamie and Brandon twisting around each other in my mind.

'Oh, actually,' says Plucked Brow, as I'm standing up. 'Elizabeth, where is it you're working?'

I pause. He's looking at me with just the slightest bit more interest than he has all interview. I should be fine. I've come here and ascertained that they're happily meandering down the wrong garden path. Hell, I've held their hands and dragged them further down the wrong path. But, still. The sudden intensity of his gaze makes the hairs on the back of my neck rise.

I was paid cash in hand by Employer #1. Marty does the same. So, I say, 'Just freelance writing. I'm going to Manchester soon. To work in TV production.'

He nods. 'Good luck with that.'

After I've left, I replay the interview in my head, pausing and rewinding the key scenes in my own private, debauched cinema. It went fine. Absolutely fine. Better than I could ever have dreamed it would go. But Plucked Brows' expression at the end stays with me, destroying any capacity I might have had to relax. Instead, I follow each twist and turn in Devlin's tale as closely as I'm able. I find myself craving the announcement that someone has been arrested for it, that someone has confessed. Is this manifestation? That new buzz word. Except, most people seem to use it to reference 'positivity' or 'attracting their crush' rather than praying for a random nutter to inexplicably confess to the murder they recently committed.

Except it's not random, and the people who confess aren't nuts. It's all meticulously planned. I am always ten steps behind. I wonder if The Fake Boyfriend (he must be behind it, he was at Brandon's trial) is blackmailing someone right now, whether a false confession is being formulated this very second.

In a twisted way, I hope so. For there are eyes on me everywhere: Too-Old-For-This-Shit Flatmate within the walls of my home, Marty when I'm at work and the residents of Middlesbrough whenever I venture too close to the town centre. I take to spending long hours in my room, plucking at Joe's guitar, and even longer hours meandering along the outskirts of the industrial estate, 'Reckoner' by Radiohead on loop in my headphones. If I was still with The Ex, I'd send this song to her, tell her to lie still and listen to it in a dark room. If Joe was still alive, I'd send him a similar message. As it is, I share the song with no one. I keep it to myself, tucked beneath a mauve beanie and hoping it warms my icy heart.

Stumbling upon a vigil held for Devlin in Albert Park is what tips me over the edge. I swear every pair of eyes turns on me the minute I breach the gates. And not just the sad eyes, but the curious ones, too. The eyes of people who don't care for Devlin, are present only to feed their own morbid fascination with death. They clutch flowers and candles and I imagine them storming towards me, setting fire to my skirt, burning me like the witch I am.

So I leave for a little while. On Friday evening, I book tickets to Newcastle and board the train the next day, grateful to see Middlesbrough slip away as the train picks up speed. The town's skeleton might be rigid – iron ore and a stiff upper lip, a dark, northern sense of humour – but it's sheathed in a delicate skin. Middlesbrough strikes me as a sad place to be right now, scarred as it is with three recent murders. I'd only pick at the scabs, if I stayed.

There's a boy in the seat across the aisle from me. And you know what I'm going to say, don't you? He's got dark, curly hair and thin lips. He wears a flannel shirt and silver rings on fingers which he often runs through his thick hair. Headphones loop around his ears and he closes his eyes every so often, lost in the music. I stare at this boy, feeling as Devlin must have when he watched his dad's home. I am so close and so far away. My cheeks tingle. I physically ache for him.

Preoccupation with Joe switches to preoccupation with The Ex, as the train arrives in Newcastle, and I alight in the town centre. Ex Friend #1 didn't confirm her presence, but she didn't deny it, either. As I walk to the flat in Jesmond, my heart feels hot and slippy, like melted butter, as if it's dripping down my rib cage and landing in a pool at the bottom of my stomach.

I try four times to ring the bell, always pulling away at the last second. Eventually, I unblock Ex Friend #1 and call her number. She says she'll come down and meet me. This flat used to be my home, I shouldn't be so nervous to return to it. But stepping back into a building which houses memories which now feel as though they belong to a different person makes me want to run as far away as possible. Plotting the murder of my fourth victim is far less daunting than potentially seeing The Ex.

'I'm so bloody glad you could make it,' Ex Friend #1 says to me when she opens the door. She pulls me into a hug and mumbles, 'She's here,' into my jacket.

I stiffen. 'I don't think I can come in.'

'There's lots of people here. You won't have to talk to her. Just come in for one drink. I won't leave your side.'

I disassociate, leaving my body and watching as Ex Friend #1 walks up three flights of stairs. I should have straightened my hair. Worn tights without a hole in. Should have determined an expression to plaster onto my face: a forced smile to convey wellbeing without her, perhaps? Or a look of worry which she might find intriguing? Do I want her attention? How much of her attention do I want?

It's impossible to remain untethered once I enter the flat; the smell of pizza and prosecco is too strong, the heat from other bodies too sticky. I look around the room and wonder whether my anxieties are shared. Whether other people fret so much about who they might bump into, or whether anyone will talk to them. Whether they worry about being too much of something: too shy, too loud, too emotional, too cold. Whether the people I try to impress are trying to impress me too. It seems obscene that we might all go around worrying so much.

I peel off my jacket, and this is when I spot her. She's shaved her head, and she's wearing a purple shirt which has the same sad, lustrous gleam as a black eye. She doesn't acknowledge me, but I imagine each of her arm hairs rising in the way mine have, fine-tuned to every movement the other makes. And then I feel silly for thinking this. After all, The Replacement is by her side. I'd think of her, not me, if I was The Ex. They'd be simpler thoughts, less marred with conflict and unease.

'Elizabeth? Poison of choice?' asks Ex Friend #1, forcing my attention from my past.

'Um . . . I don't . . . whatever's easy.'

'G&T it is, then!'

Once the drink is in my hand, I make to turn back towards The Ex, but am manoeuvred away, towards another ghost from my recent past: Ex Friend #2.

'Alreet, bonny lass! Long time no see, like. Thought you'd sacked us off, didn't I? Thought you a right rude cow until Kayin told us about your loss. And it all made sense. Bit like going through a breakup, I reckon? And I don't much fancy chatting to people during me own breakups.'

The sayer says. I watch her mouth, outlined as it is with deep red lipstick, motor on about Joe, my behaviour, her interpretation of it. Losing your brother slots neatly into the same category as the end of a relationship, she thinks. I count the tiny rouge stains on her teeth; it's preferrable to concentrating on any of the words which get past them.

'Howay now, Elizabeth doesn't want to talk about any of this,' Ex Friend #1 eventually says, giving my arm a conspiratorial squeeze.

'Well we can't just . . . I mean, this is a party. We can't just stand in silence,' says Ex Friend #2, seemingly baffled. Her fingernails are always bitten to the wick and often bleeding. She uses what's left of them now, to tap against her wine glass.

'We can do whatever we like! Silence! Shouting! Take your pick, it's my party, and I say it all goes.'

Ex Friend #2 halts her tapping and turns to me. 'Well, you are a little out the loop with me love life, want to hear about that?'

I nod, signalling my acceptance of a conversation I have limited interest in. I take a drink and shift my body ever so slightly, while she starts speaking.

'Been seeing this canny lad, but ye knaa, reached a stage when I'm just not sure if I fancy him. Get what I'm saying?'

'Uh yeah, yeah I suppose I do,' I reply, taking another step to my right.

'So, the thing is, I reckon if I squinted at him, I'd fancy him. Wey ye knaa what I'm like, picky, aren't I? Got standards.'

'You do have standards,' I say, taking another drink. The gin tickles my throat, and I inch myself that bit further.

'He's a teacher, and I reckon if I was a forty-five-year-old mam with a little bairn, I'd be all over him. Would plaster me face in makeup and count down the days 'til parents' evening, then sit with damp knickers as he tells me my kid is shite at chemistry.'

'Mmm. But you're not a forty-five-year-old with a scientifically challenged kid,' I reply, taking one more step to the right. I can see her. I can finally see her.

'Well aye, but I will be one day. Got to keep these things in mind.'

There's a weird helplessness to watching the girl in the purple shirt now. As if I'm studying an alien, or a canny copy of someone I was once so intimate with. She doesn't make sense to me anymore. We'd so completely misunderstood one another. Affection is a wriggling beast, and I no longer trust it.

As Ex Friend #1 pours fresh drinks and Ex Friend #2 continues to weigh up the pros and cons of a teacher who's only mildly sexy, my eyes linger on The Ex and The Replacement. And they seem happy. They seem really happy. Is this how we were at the beginning? I'm not sure; I think I was too distant, too detached. They're always touching – sitting on one another's laps, trailing a hand over the other, or kissing. I search for signs of boredom or annoyance in the expression of The Ex and find none. I search for evidence that the relationship might be stuttering to a close, but see little to suggest this. The Ex is besotted. I search the pair of them for things to make me feel better and find nothing. They are a better match. I've already been consigned to history.

A tired, damp sensation ebbs over me, a feeling I envision as a similar shade to The Ex's silk shirt: the purple of fat rain clouds, the purple of bruises. I drink as fast as I can, soothing myself with the knowledge that my pillbox is in my bag. Sweet nothingness is just a gulp away.

But I stick the party out for a little longer, attempting to numb myself with as much alcohol as I can get my hands on. At some point between karaoke and a fresh delivery of pizza, I slip out into the corridor and slide down the wall. My cheeks are damp again. I cry as if on autopilot, these days.

Ex Friend #1 who, true to her word, has been by my side for most of the night, finds me within a matter of minutes. She sits beside me and clutches at my hand.

'She hasn't even acknowledged me,' I mumble.

'Think she probably just feels awkward.'

My tears flow that bit faster. 'She hasn't even said anything to me about Joe.'

'I don't think she knows about Joe.'

A great hiccup of sadness escapes me. You'd think emotional instability would tip me further into bloodlust, that my desire to kill would be keener. It does the opposite. I want to put them all back together – Devlin and then Courtney and then Janet and then Joe.

'I know what she did was really shitty, but I don't think she did it to hurt you.'

'I wish she had,' I say.

'Why?'

'Because at least then she'd have been thinking about me a little bit.'

Kayi . . . I mean Kay . . . I mean Ex Friend #1 sighs.

'It's been six months, Els.'

The sentiment of this statement is clear. Get over it. Carry on. There's a time limit to sadness that must be adhered to. Almost six months since things ended with The Ex. Almost three since Joe's death. I take out my phone and click through the news, refreshing it, manifesting a fresh confession. There's every chance it might not come. Every chance that the police might have gotten their hands on an accurate list of who has worked in the cemetery. Every chance I've been captured on CCTV as I walked over. Every chance that Too-Old-For-This Flatmate has finally turned me in.

There is every chance that I will be arrested before avenging Joe. Despite my earlier wish to stick people back together, it's clear I need to keep ripping them apart. I collect my bag, my butterfly onesie and my signed *Twilight* poster, and then I leave, sights set on victim #4.

Chapter Twenty

Despite the fact that I'm nearing the completion of my goal, and despite the fact a sense of urgency is now more important than ever, it's increasingly hard to get up in the mornings. Increasingly hard to drag my body into a cold, grey day and increasingly preferable to keep chasing a dozy, alternate reality behind my eyelids.

When I do get up, more often than not, it's to find that November mist has mixed with the industrial fog of the town, turning each person that rushes between their jobs into an ominous, shadowy figure. Any one of them could arrest me for the murder of Devlin Mackenzie; I feel it in each of my twisted organs, in each of my brittle bones.

I arrive at the betting shop later and later each day, as though daring Marty to say something to me. He doesn't. We float around each other with equal distrust. I often feel his eyes on me and, whenever they're not, mine are on him. The shop is especially busy on Friday, nearly three weeks after the discovery of Devlin's body. There's a big football match on this weekend, and the punters are here, placing their bets, sucking on their gums and putting the world to rights. It's crowded until closing, with one particular guy staying until gone 9pm, agonising over exactly how much money he's going to lose, and exactly how he's going to lose it. His movements are sluggish, as if he has a lamb kebab, a six pack of Stella and half a box of donuts sitting undigested in his colon.

It's an age before he fucks off, and I corner Marty.

'I was wondering . . .' I pause. There's a mop in my hand, and I lean against it, as if for dramatic effect. 'Whether you still had any of the things from back in the day?'

'Whaddaya mean? Like, newspaper articles and that?'

He's a timid creature, these days. A nervous deer trapped in the body of a small, hard man. So different to who he was – sneaky, fearless and ruthless – that sometimes I wonder whether it's all an act.

Regardless, I need to ask my questions carefully.

'No, I mean, like, I don't know, pepper spray? Burner phones?'

Marty looks confused, and I can't say I blame him. I elaborate. 'I'm just missing my dad, you know. Was wondering if you had anything that might make me feel close to him.'

What dark, convoluted bullshit.

'Nah, didn't keep owt. I've gone straight, getting me daughter back, aren't I?'

I nod, trying to read him. He's watched by half a dozen sports posters; jockeys and footballers grin crookedly down at him. Might he have thrown everything out? It's plausible, and yet . . . he's wearing a jumper I recognise from when I was a kid: three shades of thin stripes, red next to yellow, yellow next to black. Marty continues speaking, but it's a while before I listen again, for I find myself lost in memories of cold afternoons with my godfather in the years after my dad died, when he'd take me to Redcar for a lemon top and a go on the arcades. My tongue searches my gums for the taste of all I used to fill them with on these particular afternoons: cotton candy and pennies and the bloody crusts of scabs I had at the time. Even sixteen years later, the back of my mouth still tastes sweet and metallic, and my body still tenses, anticipating a whack from Marty, telling me to get his coins out from between my teeth.

Marty is a magpie; a nest of his worldly possessions lives somewhere.

I turn my attention back to him, just in time to hear him say, 'Yeah, sound as a pound me, these days. Good as gold.'

I interrupt. 'I remember Mitch had this gun. A small, pretty thing. He'd turn the safety on and let me touch it, sometimes. I think . . . and my memory is hazy, but I think it had a sort of snake-print pattern. It was more a piece of art than a weapon. The crime would be throwing something like that away.'

I trust few memories of my dad, for most have been passed on via Callum and, as we all know, Callum's not to be trusted. But I do recall seeing this particular weapon on the windowsill one day, reaching for it with sticky fingers and having Mam snatch it from my hands. I recall the screaming match between her and my dad which ensued, a reaction which only cemented my fascination with the gun in question.

'I've got bits and bobs, I suppose. Just stuff I haven't gotten around to chucking yet. Might have the gun you're on about but, y'know only for self-defence. A betting shop being robbed ain't out of the question.'

'That sounds very sensible to me.'

'Yeah, that's what I thought. Would appreciate you not saying owt to no one, like.'

I nod. 'Yeah, of course. So, I guess you keep it in the shop?'

Marty pats his pocket and glances back towards his office. 'Aye. Would be silly not to, like.'

I've gotten what I need from him. I don't have everything, of course – lord knows I'd love to interrogate him on his relationship with Brandon Pearce – but I know how far to push my luck. I put the mop away, smother myself in my coat and head out into the night.

It's changing, out here. And I don't just mean the weather, drifting into the worst of the winter. I feel the shift of the souls around me, as they slowly succumb to the recession and sink beneath the swell of inflation. The Northeast has the highest suicide rate in England, and everyone who scurries past me on the walk from Grove Hill to the river seems to have long, delicate necks I can imagine choked by a rope, or sad, small eyes I can imagine widening in pain as tens of sleeping tablets take hold.

I shudder, tightening my scarf and thinking of my own pills. I stop looking at their eyes, but the eyes don't stop looking at me. And they're not sad, these eyes, I realise. They're suspicious. I quicken my pace, tug my scarf all the way up to my nose. Pull my beanie from my pocket and drag it over my skull. Take out my phone and try to . . . try to refresh, see if anything else has come from Devlin's murder . . .

The sound of a siren shakes my bones, and I nearly stumble into the road. I recover, dizzy and gasping, blinking around and trying to see the flashing lights. Run? Should I run? Should I be running?

'Hey!'

Two strong hands grab me, and I'm brought to a standstill. My natural instinct is to kick or spit at my captor, for it's surely the police, or Callum, or a relative of Devlin's.

'Hey, Ella?'

It's none of those people. It's The Fake Boyfriend. Of course it's The Fake Boyfriend. He blinks down at me from behind thick glasses, worry etched into his features.

'You were about to walk out into the road, Ella,' he says.

I look at him, paying him increasing attention as the sound of the siren decreases.

'How did you find me?' I ask.

'I didn't find you. I just happened to see you. And a good job too.'

His gaze darts to the right. That means he's lying, doesn't it? Years of listening to my friends psychoanalyse their wayward boyfriends has taught me that he's lying.

'Have you been following me?'

He laughs. 'Are you OK? I like you, but not enough to stalk you, rest assured.'

'Uh . . . uh-huh. OK.'

'Come back with me, yeah? I mean, my mam's in, but she won't care. She'll probably love it, in fact.'

Every fibre in my body tells me that this is a trap. He's inviting me back so that he can confront me about the murders I've committed, about the people he's had to manipulate into covering for me. Or maybe he's in cahoots with the police, and they're waiting in his kitchen, primed to arrest me. I shake my head.

'No. I've got things to get back for.'

'Stargazing? Clubbing? Graveyard browsing?'

He knows far too much about me.

'Something. One of those. Maybe, yeah.'

Did his grip on my wrists just tighten? Each finger seems to have pushed itself that bit harder into the wool of my jacket.

'You're not worried about what happened to Devlin Mackenzie, are you? They caught his killer. It's OK.'

My knees give way, and I nearly collapse back into the road from whence I was just saved.

'You fucking what?' I ask.

The Fake Boyfriend steadies me. 'Yeah, they . . . it was just in the news. Someone . . . I can't remember his name, Gravel or something, confessed to some sort of drug-dealing dispute. He had Devlin's bloody hoody in his bin.'

I shake my head. How the hell did Devlin's hoody get from the bottom of the grave to this man's bin? It's an impossible question, so instead, I say, 'No one is called Gravel.'

'As if that's the least believable part of the story. No one confesses to murders! At least they didn't until a few months ago.'

'You'd know all about that.' I can't help it; the words are out of my lips before I can do anything to stop them.

The Fake Boyfriend goes to reply to me, but seals his mouth shut. I shake my head, feeling as panicked as ever. My dream of recent days has come true and yet the sick feeling in my stomach continues to swirl. It merely changes direction; the paranoia within me simply turns another rosy shade of fucked.

'Come back with me. Please. I'm worried about you,' The Fake Boyfriend finally says.

I'm too dazed to put up an adequate fight, and I find myself being led to The Fake Boyfriend's abode, where the salty smell of Chinese food hangs thick in the air. Perhaps he was right about the drawbacks of the location of the flat, for already the smell has lost its celebratory sheen. His mam clucks over me, bringing me a hot cup of tea and a selection of biscuits. She tells me I have beautiful eyes and not to worry about my hair, that it'll grow out to a nicer length with time.

The news is playing quietly on the television in the corner of the room, and my eyes are drawn to it.

Gregory, not Gravel. Obviously not Gravel. Gregory is the name of the latest confessor. Gregory Macaluf. Forty-seven (why are they all in their late forties?). He looks . . . I don't know, like a thumb?

Everyone looks a bit like a thumb. He is a thumb among thumbs. But why is this thumb confessing to a murder he didn't commit?

Am I sitting beside the answer to my question?

These are thoughts that circle my brain as my tea grows cold and as time marches towards midnight. I'm so lost in thought I barely even hear The Fake Boyfriend when he says, 'I can call a cab back to yours? Or you're welcome to stay over? I can sleep on the sofa?'

I come back to myself, looking around at a living room which seems suddenly empty – the buzz of the television gone, The Fake Boyfriend's mam away to bed. I look at him – all sharp angles which seem soft and lovely in the half light of the cabinet lamp – and I want nothing more than to share a bed with him. I don't want to have sex with him, but I want to share the darkness, want to wrap myself in a duvet with him and feel his long, bony arms around my shoulders.

This is insanity, obviously. Because The Fake Boyfriend is behind the fake confessors, he has to be. But I can't fathom a reality in which his intentions are malicious. Besides, he's the person I've been most intimate with in this fucked-up period of my life, and I'm overcome by the feeling of needing someone. Anyone. Even an enemy.

'I'd like to stay,' I say. 'But there's no need for you to sleep on the sofa. That's just silly.'

'OK. If you're sure.'

When we're in his room, he hands me a t-shirt ('I am going to stand outside, so that if anyone asks, I'm outstanding') and a pair of shorts, and turns away as I change into them. We climb into his bed, him as far left as possible, me as far right. Only with the light off does he edge himself closer. It takes two or three minutes, but eventually his thin limbs wrap themselves around me.

'You feel so tense, Ella.'

'Mmm. Sorry about that.'

'You don't need to apologise.'

'OK. I won't. Sorry.'

There's a pause, and then The Fake Boyfriend says, 'Are you OK?'

'Yeah, I'm alright.'

'You're really affected by all this Devlin stuff, aren't you?'

I inhale, trying desperately to avoid letting paranoia seize my body once more. 'What do you mean?'

'No, nothing . . . Guess just how on edge you are, kind of feels like you know something I don't.'

'I can assure you I don't.'

I hear The Fake Boyfriend's lips peel open and shut half a dozen times, before he whispers, 'Did you know anything about Janet Braithwaite's death?'

Defence. That's all I can think to do: defend, defend, shut down.

'No. What the fuck? Can you stop questioning me, you weirdo?'

At this, The Fake Boyfriend flinches as though I've just slapped him. I feel his muscles tense and cool air occupy the places where his body had pressed against mine. I don't know what to say to rectify the situation, so I allow him to slowly untether himself from me, to drift away. The panicked hum of his brilliant, kind mind fills the emptiness between us, and I imagine it whirling away, analysing our conversation. I analyse in turn, not sure whether I should just bite the bullet and ask him what I need to know. Shy bairns get nowt. But shy bairns also get to stay in the shadows, get to fulfil what they set out to achieve. I've got two more murders and then I'm done. Two more murders and then I don't care what happens to me. I see no point in forcing a confrontation with The Fake Boyfriend when it might prevent me from properly avenging Joe. Again, the fact that I need to move with more urgency strikes me.

We lie in an uncomfortable silence for a few more minutes. It's not right, sharing a bed with someone you've just upset. I recall the various points at which my relationship with The Ex had crumbled, many of them coinciding with the two of us lying between the sheets, and the damp, purple feeling ebbs within me again.

'You're good with technical things, aren't you?' I say, trying to stop The Fake Boyfriend from thinking about Janet and Devlin, and attempting to mop away the morose feeling which threatens to flood me.

'Yeah, I guess,' says The Fake Boyfriend.

'You're being modest.'

'What do you want, Ella?'

I lick my lips, not sure how to ask what I want to know. 'I have

these two . . . well, I wouldn't say friends . . . I know these two
children. Ten-year-old sisters, sweet girls. But they're very curious.
They love asking me questions and, you know, normally I can answer
the questions, but . . .'

'What weird thing have they asked? Totally normal to have infant
friends, by the way.'

'Again, not friends per se.'

'Colleagues?'

In an investigative sort of way, yes. I don't say this, instead, I say,
'Acquaintances.'

'Friends of your niece?' he asks.

'My what? Oh, shit yeah. Yeah, they're friends of my niece.'

The imaginary, environmentally friendly niece, back to trip me up
again. Christ, that lie, one of thousands recently, feels like it slipped
from my lips decades ago.

'But yeah anyway, normally they're pretty sweet but they seem
to be going through a bit of a dark phase. And you know, I feel
like if I'm not open with them, they'll just be more and more
interested and—'

'And end up being something awful, like serial killers?'

I flinch, wondering if he's making a pointed dig. 'Yeah, something
awful like that.'

'OK, well, shoot. What do they want to know?'

'Whether they could re-wire something . . . a television or a toaster
or, I don't know, a fruit machine, so that the next person to use it
would get an electric shock.'

'Those are all very different objects,' says The Fake Boyfriend.

'OK, well, maybe focus on the fruit machine, given they don't
have one in their house and are therefore least likely to use whatever
information I give them to blow up their parents.'

He mulls it over for a minute or so, his body softening in
concentration. 'Fruit machines will probably be double insulated.
So nothing from the outside can touch the inside. I guess the
easiest way to electrocute someone would be to have them touch
metal plates with both hands. One is the chassis of the machine,
and the other is 230 volts. That would do the trick. Although a

modern circuit board would trip before there was enough current to kill a cat.'

'What about really old fruit machines?'

'Yeah? I guess most fruities are pretty old.'

'I don't really understand all this plate and chassis stuff,' I say. 'Could they not just fiddle with the wires? Hypothetically.'

The duvet rises slightly as The Fake Boyfriend shrugs. 'Yeah, maybe. It would be difficult to determine how big a shock any amount of fiddling with the wires would cause. But yeah, take the back panel off, switch or pull out the live and the neutral wires and there'd certainly be a chance of fucking over the next person to root around down there.'

'Remind me of the colours of the wires?'

'You don't know that?'

'No, funnily enough I would struggle to identify the different types of wire.'

'How odd. Well, the live wire is brown, obviously. Neutral is blue, and earth is yellow and green.'

'Thanks,' I mumble, tiredness creeping over me. 'You'll make two little girls very happy.'

'Stop saying things that make me want to report you to the police.'

I laugh. He doesn't know the half of it. Or, of course, maybe he does.

I wake up to find The Fake Boyfriend staring at me. His glasses are off for once, so I have a clearer view of his hazel eyes. If I was doing a better job of pretending to be in love with him, I might say they resembled pools of silky caramel. But I am not in love and as such they're more reminiscent of swamps.

'You snore when you lie on your back, but not when you're lying on your side. And you mumble a little bit, too. Nothing overly coherent. And I did think you stopped breathing for quite a long time at one point, so maybe you should get that checked out,' he says.

'Ahh, just how I like to be woken up: with a thorough analysis of my sleeping habits.'

I clamber from his bed and get changed. I turn down his mam's offer of a bacon butty and escape as soon as I can. Staying over was weak and puts me in a more vulnerable position than necessary; who knows what I was mumbling in my sleep?

My flat is mercifully empty when I return to it. I grab a cereal bar and head to my room, a restless feeling brewing within me. Once I've eaten the cereal bar, I tear the wrapper into shreds. The objects on my windowsill get rearranged: rusty lighter on the far left, then two pinecones and then the broken China doll and then the two other pinecones. Joe's guitar gets disturbed too; I pick it up and play a few tuneless chords.

And then, because I no longer have Joe's phone, and am running out of ways to feel in some way connected to him, I look through his yearbook again.

A smile crosses my face as I thumb through the messages. So many of them. They're kind, funny, silly. They're thoughtful and nice and I'm so, so glad my little brother got to read them before he died. The messages are all bright and brilliant and they all . . . the gradient of the crosses on the 't's are all the same. The curve on the 'c's. The odd swivel on the letter 'g'.

Every message bar the couple from Devlin and Mr Downing has been written by the same person. This realisation seems to push itself into the bruises on my body, and I gasp as if in physical pain.

I slam the yearbook shut. Reach for my pillbox. Take nine white pills.

Try to forget.

Chapter Twenty-One

A silent mind when I wake is not often cause to relax or celebrate. Sometimes the nothingness within me is more dangerous than a cacophony of thoughts. It presents itself as a deep, dark hole that I'm inches away from tripping into and never getting out of. It sets my guts twisting, prompts sweat to form in the creases of my body.

I suffer a morning of this kind four days after returning from The Fake Boyfriend's home. In an attempt to fill my brain, I reach for my phone and begin stalking the confessors: Brandon Pearce and Jamie Sleight and Gregory Macaluf. I no longer care about maintaining a sanitised search history; after all, my crimes are accounted for. Cases closed.

Except they're not.

As I stalk through their social media profiles and any articles I can find online, I start thinking about what categories I could fit them into, if I had all the information available. Tibia length and IQ and condiment preferences. Attachment types and tongue-curling ability. Trying to articulate what makes a human. Trying to figure out how these particular humans have been convinced to confess to murders they haven't committed.

The honking of a car pulls me from my thoughts, but it takes four more long, loud honks until I move over to my window and blink out at my hazy, overgrown surroundings.

Stepdad's car. The black Ford I vomited on months ago. He's in the front seat, Mam's in the passenger and Step-Nan is in the back. They look about frantically, and Stepdad forces another sharp beep from the car.

I pull on socks, jogging bottoms and a jumper and rush from my room. Too-Old-For-This-Shit Flatmate has heard the commotion. She says nothing, instead fixing me with a hard stare that I feel on the back of my neck all the way down the stairs. It's almost a relief to burst into the damp air and shut her behind me.

'What the hell are you doing?' I ask, as I yank open a car door and throw myself into the backseat next to Step-Nan.

'What the hell? What the hell are *we* doing?' Stepdad asks. There's a manic glint in his eye, a shuddering in his shoulders that makes me want to leap from the car and run as far away as possible. He shoves the wrinkled front page of the *Teesside Gazette* into my face. 'What the hell is *this*?'

It's the article detailing Gregory Macaluf's confession, of course. I push it away from me, feeling suddenly as though I'm drowning in ink and mediocre reporting.

'I know. I fucking know. D'you think I don't know?'

'Aye and yet it's the same every murder you commit: someone else confesses to your crimes. What are you playing at? You brought other people in on this without telling us? Who's going to take the fall next, ay? Me? Your mam?'

'Not so long ago, you considered a rogue confession good fucking news,' I retort, pissed off by the accusations flying my way.

'Not three in a row, though. Three in a row, and I smell a rat.'

'Well maybe you should pull your finger out your arse and do some of the dirty work yourself,' I say.

'What dirty work? We were never on board with killing every Tom, Dick and Harry just cos they looked at you the wrong way the night that Joe died.'

'You know I'd never kill people if they didn't truly deserve it,' I say, opening the car door and stepping out.

Stepdad places his palm on the horn and beeps it until I get back into the car. There's twitching behind the kitchen blinds, and I catch a glimpse of my flatmate's sallow, inquisitive face.

'We need to drive away from here,' I say.

He controls himself enough to speed us down the empty, cracked road for a minute or so, parking so that we have a good view of the river and the bastard bridge from which Joe was pushed.

'How do you know where I live, anyway?' I ask, before Stepdad can accuse me of anything else. I've told extraordinarily few people my address; that it's available to three of the people I most want to keep it from fills me with dread.

Mam turns around. She's applied makeup today, but it's all wrong: messy wriggles of eyeliner, clumps of mascara, streaky foundation. Something about this strikes me as heart-breaking, almost like watching a former champion runner struggle to last place.

'Marty. He has your address because you work for him, apparently,' she says.

Paranoia and validation surge through me. Marty. It's always Marty.

'You hate Marty,' I reply.

'Desperate times.' Mam shrugs, taking a shaky puff of her vape and filling the car with a sickly watermelon scent. 'Don't think it's unreasonable to know where my only daughter lives.'

'Two-faced ba—'

Stepdad interrupts me. 'This is all irrelevant. What the hell is going on with your murders?'

I shift against the backseat, feeling claustrophobic. Step-Nan's wrinkled flesh is mere centimetres from me; I don't enjoy being so close to the old bird. Still, looking at the coarse grey roots of her hair is preferrable to looking outside, at twisted steel and unforgiving water.

'I wish I knew,' I say. 'By all accounts, this is a roaring success. Most of the people who fucked over Joe are thoroughly dead, and it doesn't look like I'll ever face the consequences.'

'It's not right though, is it?' Mam says, setting down her vape and chewing at a loose nail. Her eyes shift about, scanning the land outside the car. 'People just confessing to murders they haven't committed. It's not right.'

'I know. But what d'you want me to say? I've tried to figure out why they're doing it. I'm *trying* to figure out why they're doing it.'

My gaze shifts back to the thousands of hairs sprouting from Step-Nan's head as Stepdad starts muttering about the unpredictability of the confessors. The fact we don't know who might be next to take the fall for 'our' (my) murders.

'If you want to guarantee you don't take the fall, why don't you kill victim number four?' I ask. 'Why don't you kill the man with the dog?'

Stepdad turns all the way around in his seat and fixes me with a hard glare. 'That sounds like a threat. That sounds like a threat, to me.'

'Stop it.' Mam puts a hand on his shoulder. It shakes. She turns to me. 'Do we need to kill this man, Ella? Are you sure?'

'Yes. He stopped Joe getting help which could have saved him.'

'So you say, but we don't even know who he is,' says Stepdad.

'I'm working on it.'

'Aye, and you could be doing that forever. I say we move on to Callum.'

A spark of anger ignites within me.

'Do you even give a shit about avenging Joe, or is this just a convoluted means of killing the kid you never wanted?' I snap.

Something shifts within him. I see it in the cold, dead smile that stretches across his face, revealing those strange, small teeth. I brace, waiting for what's to come. And come it does: a sharp slap which catches my nose and scratches at my cheek.

But the slap isn't from Stepdad.

'Don't talk to my son like that,' says Step-Nan. We all turn to face her, and she slowly retreats into herself, lowering her hand and shifting her gaze so that she's looking somewhere beyond Mam's left shoulder.

'Now then, Mam, remember you're ill,' says Stepdad, placing extra emphasis on the final word. Step-Nan mumbles something about the weather reminding her of some obscure relative, but I don't hear the end of her story; I'm out the car and racing down the street before anything else can happen in that hotbox of artificial watermelon and anger.

They don't follow, thank God. I sling on work gear, chew down a slice of bread and stride from the flat, too wound up to care that this is the latest I've ever been for a shift at the betting shop.

Marty nearly says something to me, when I arrive. I see him chomping at his tongue, trying to decide whether to engage in the conflict he tries so hard to avoid. In the end, he doesn't. He leaves me alone with my various sprays and dusters and mops. Today, I decide that the corners of the shop are looking especially dusty, so I pull high tables over and stand on them to reach the areas of concern.

'Just you be careful, Ella. That's a health and safety nightmare, that is,' says Marty when he spots me.

'We can't have dusty ceilings in your betting shop now, can we?' I reply, grinning down at him – fake and hard.

'Uh, no, no. S'pose we can't,' he mumbles, eventually retreating to his office and leaving me alone to stick black tape across his security cameras.

The days here always seem to drag, but this one is particularly guilty of doing so. The twists and turns of my mop grind to a halt, until I'm pressing water over laminate flooring I've already cleaned half a dozen times. I catch myself staring at men who wouldn't ordinarily hold my attention. I don't think anything interesting about them – not how many fights they've been in or how many people they've fucked; my eyes merely get lost in the saggy folds of their jowls, the bristle above their upper lip, the dark moles on their face and forearms. I'm a windup doll, slowly shuddering to a stop.

But as night closes in and the clock ticks closer to finishing time, I come back to life. The last punter exits three minutes before we close, and I meander over to the oldest of the fruit machines. Marty is in his office, where I know he enjoys a snifter of whisky while he finishes his admin. I have minutes. Perhaps ten of them.

So I slip on gloves, push the fruit machine half a metre from the wall and take a screwdriver from my bag. The screws on the back panel are rusty, but eventually they budge, and I have access to the heart of the machine. And what an effective, devastating heart it is. It's held more men in its luminous clutches than most women. Cutting the wiry organism open with plyers brings me no great sadness.

Once done, I push the fruit machine back so it's a palm's width from the wall, and then I call Marty.

'I'm so sorry to bother you, I know how important your admin is,' I say when he emerges. He locks his office door and then turns to face me, sleepy and a little drunk.

'S'OK, Ella, am here to help.'

'I've just . . . I was cleaning near the fruit machines and my ring fell off, behind that one and . . .' I pause, trying to inject some emotion into my voice. 'And my arms aren't long enough to reach. And it's really special to me, so I . . . I . . .'

My voice is thick and syrupy. I gasp and dab at dry eyes.

'Hey, hey. It's alright.' He pats my arm. 'I'm on it.'

He bends down, groaning about his back, and he sticks his hand behind the machine. My breath catches in my throat as I wait for electricity to surge through his body.

It doesn't.

'Can't feel owt, Ella, I must say.'

'It went quite far, I think. And it's really small.'

'Well I'm trying my best, don't you wo—'

There's a bang, and Marty's body is sent flying back, a metre through the air. He lands on the pristine laminate, body spasming. His hair and eyebrows are singed, and spit dribbles from his mouth. Something halfway between a cough and a gurgle escapes him.

I look down, privileged to be witnessing the final minutes of my fourth target. What? I'm not naming unimportant people, remember? Just Joe. The culprits. And the people who steal my murders.

Dropping to my knees gives me a better angle on Marty's throat, which I grab. It's sweaty. He looks up at me with desperate, confused eyes.

Another gurgle escapes him. It's a sore, damp gurgle that's cans of warm Monster and the smog of his hometown. A lifetime of smoking and now the 230 volts which have surged through his body.

I won't have long with him.

'Why didn't you help me?' I ask. My fingers curl, desperate to squeeze his throat. With an effort, I restrain myself.

Marty shakes his head. 'Didn't . . . a . . . didn't . . .'

'That night when Joe fell. You fucking saw us on the shore, me begging you to call an ambulance and you just *watched*.'

Spit rains from my lips, landing on his whiskery cheeks.

'Didn't . . . El . . . please . . .'

I remember his eyes on that night – clear as day, despite the fact that it was dark, I was drunk and he was many metres from me. They were blank, and ruthless, lethal in their emptiness. The same eyes stare up at me now. Red and watery. Emotion finally present. Too fucking late.

'You didn't even acknowledge the fact you'd seen me,' I say, recalling weeks and weeks of waiting for Marty to say something. Waiting for an explanation from him, and becoming increasingly certain there wasn't one.

'Hoped you hadn't recognised me, Eliz . . . hope you . . . hadn't seen . . . hoped you'd forgotten.'

'You're a coward. You let Joe die' I hiss. My fingernails dig a few millimetres into his flesh. I find an artery and push it back and forth, as if plucking a guitar string.

'Please . . . couldn't get involved . . . in owt . . . police see me near a dead body an'. . . they're just looking to charge me . . . had to . . . Lexi. Had to get Lexi back.'

'He wasn't dead at that point.'

'If he was Mitch's . . . if he'd been Mitch's son . . . I'd have helped.'

'You selfish prick.'

I lose control, squeezing his neck until it stops meaning anything, until I'm merely squeezing a thick, damp object that I loathe. In these minutes or seconds, I watch as Marty's many trials dance across his eyes. The fights, the gangs, the drugs and money. Ghosts of a reckless youth that no mild-mannered middle age could rectify. And then his eyes still, coming to a rest under his feeble lids.

'Fuck.'

I release the pressure on Marty's neck.

'Hey,' I say, shaking him. 'Hey, Marty.' Another shake, desperate now. 'How well do you know Brandon Pearce? How did you know him? And you know Jamie Sleight? Gregory Macaluf?'

I set out to kill him and I've only gone and done it. With too much efficiency.

'Marty? Who's making these people confess to my murders? You know. I know you know.'

It's hopeless; his only answer is to turn an increasingly sickly shade of dead.

'Fuck.'

Finally, I release him. I've won the battle but jeopardised the war. I run a gloved hand through my hair, and it sticks up, bought to life by static.

Next job, then. I open up Marty's jacket and rifle through his inside pocket. A wallet, his phone, a stick of gum, his lighter. And, right at the bottom, his office key.

I'm in his office a few seconds later, rifling through drawers and pushing aside folders of paper. A stack of drawings done by his daughter almost makes me pause, but I push past them, as ever unwilling to dwell on the pain I've just passed along. A crime scene is not the time to be slowed by sentiment.

Photographs appear behind the drawings: young Marty at his first wedding, baby Lexi, his dog when it was a puppy, twenty-something year-old Marty and his mates.

'Hang on.'

I'd discarded the picture of Marty and his mates, but something draws me back to it.

'No.'

I blink at the picture, hardly believing my own eyes. They're younger, all of them are twenty years younger, but there's no mistaking the five people in this picture.

Marty Deng. Brandon Pearce. Jamie Sleight. Gregory Macaluf. And my dad.

'Fuck.'

They all knew each other. They all knew each other *well*, if the relaxed body language in the picture is anything to go by.

I want to stare at the picture forever, I want to get lost in all the possibilities it's just presented, but I know I need to be quick. Reluctantly, I stuff the picture in my pocket and continue rifling through Marty's drawers.

I find knives, a taser and knuckledusters, but none of these will do. I'm fully aware that killing Callum is going to be the most difficult. He'll know it's coming, for one. And he's a strong, manipulative bastard for another. When I face him, I'll need the lethal certainty of a gun in my hand.

My fingers close on something cold and smooth at the bottom of a filing cabinet. I pull it out, shaking. The object in my hand is snake print and nostalgia. Danger and defence, all wrapped into one weapon. I check for bullets before flipping on the safety and placing the gun in my bag.

And then I'm out. Scarf pulled up to my nose, beanie securely on my head and a last goodbye to Marty's limp body.

I shut the betting-shop door and think about smashing a window, staging this as a break-in. I toy with the idea for a couple of seconds, before deciding against making any noise which might alert locals to sinister activity. I turn away, deciding to let the street linger in a deceptive silence.

One step and then another. I walk myself further and further from victim #4.

There's a click from behind me.

Nothing, probably. A tiny, inconsequential noise. I shouldn't look. And yet . . . I find myself turning around, looking back at the betting shop which has been a second home to me recently.

It's dark, hard to make out much. But a shadow shifts by the entrance.

Somebody enters the crime scene.

Chapter Twenty-Two

I have a gun in my bag. The person who has just entered the betting shop is either onto me, or they're completely innocent and just about to find a dead body.

Neither of these possibilities is good.

My hand reaches down and into my bag, rifling past my purse, a spare jumper and a Tupperware box before closing on the small, cool gun. I've never fired one, but it can't be that hard, can it?

Point and pull the trigger. Stride into the shop, raise the gun and shoot whoever is standing there. The Fake Boyfriend? If it's The Fake Boyfriend, will I be able to kill him? What about Too-Old-For-This-Shit Flatmate? Yes? No? Maybe? Easy, it should be easy. Except it's not. Try as I might, I can't move forward. My feet seem glued to the pavement, rendering progress impossible.

Eventually, I'm able to turn around and wade back to the flat, feeling I'm sinking further into my own demise with every step taken. No one is in the kitchen, and there's no light streaming from under my flatmates' doors. I press my ear against the wood, but hear nothing.

I just walked away from my best opportunity to find out who has been meddling in my murders. I'm struck by a pang of regret, but also a pang of relief. Coward. Cowardly.

The only response that makes sense is to complete my plan as quickly as possible. I'm going to be fucked, I just need to ensure that Joe has been avenged by the time it happens.

Once in my room, I drag my chair over to the door and wedge it shut. I make sure my windows are shut and locked, before taking a last suspicious glance at the barren world outside and pulling the curtains closed.

My list gets an aggressive update:

```
                                    FADE IN:
                                           1
INT. ELLA'S BEDROOM - EVENING
  WE OPEN with Ella, as she inches closer to
righting the wrongs surrounding Joe's death.
  Target #1 - JANET BRAITHWAITE
  Target #2 - COURTNEY TEASDALE
  Target #3 - DEVLIN MACKENZIE
  Target #4 - MARTY DENG
  Target #5 - CALLUM MANDEVILLE
```

Callum. Callum Thomas Mandeville. I'm under no illusion that he's going to be nigh on impossible to find, never mind to kill. I pile what little hair I have into an attempt at a bun, and force myself to think where he might be, what he might be doing. What do I know of him, post his leaving home? A new piece of paper is stuffed into my typewriter, and a fresh list begins.

```
                                    FADE IN:
                                           1
INT. ELLA'S BEDROOM - EVENING
  WE OPEN with ELLA, probably days or hours
from being screwed in multiple unimaginable
ways. She needs to find CALLUM (25) as soon as
possible. After he left home, Ella has seen
him in only four places:
  1. The Keys, in South Shields. The evening
of seven shots, a brief hug and a mumble of
'sorry'.
  2. Redcar beach, one unusually cold June
day. He'd been with a red-headed girl. Ella
hadn't wanted to disturb them, she'd merely
watched the jutting outline of his chin and
wondered if he looked at this girl in the same
```

way as he did everyone else: a vacant stare
that left you feeling lonelier with him than
without.

3. Newcastle Quayside. Ella had spent the
evening drinking herself silly after THE EX'S
first indiscretion, and had thought she'd
seen him by the water as the sun rose. She'd
chased but never caught him, couldn't even
be sure it was him she was chasing, but for
the smell that seemed to linger in the man's
wake: the fresh scent of hair gel and the slow
declining scent of nicotine.

4. The night of Joe's death.

The only thing this list really tells me is that he's likely still in
the Northeast. It wouldn't surprise me; he had a passion for our
particular corner of the country that used to burn hot as the ends
of his cigarettes. But what's he doing? He was a practical boy and
it's easy to envision him turning into a practical man: bricklaying
or plumbing or plastering.

I groan – even if I did know his vocation, what would I do with
this information? Wander around every building site in the north
looking for him, gun ready just in case?

'Stupid, stupid,' I mumble.

I shift back over to my window, nudge the curtains apart and take a
cautious glance into the dark, half-expecting to see the town advancing
with pitchforks and a desire to avenge Marty. This doesn't happen, of
course. But the distant sound of a siren sends a shiver down my spine.

I press the curtains closed as best as I can, before sending a text to
The Fake Boyfriend asking whether he's free tomorrow. And then my
standard night-time routine follows: a slow brushing of thirty-two
small white objects I care little about, and the fast swallowing of ten
small white objects which are increasingly becoming all-important.

The Fake Boyfriend has a car – a perk I hadn't even considered but
which instantly strikes me as incredibly useful. As he gets out of it,

he yawns, takes off his glasses and rubs his eyes. My mind jumps to the conclusion that he was up late last night with Marty Deng's dead body. But why hasn't he said anything? Is he going to say something today? Am I?

I repress these thoughts and convince him to drive us up to South Shields with my usual bullshit. (He'll get to see Souter Lighthouse – the first in the world powered by electricity. The townspeople are sometimes referred to as Sandancers – doesn't he want to find out why? Plus, we'll visit a restaurant that does really good chicken burgers.)

The restaurant is, of course, The Keys nightclub, and The Fake Boyfriend groans as we walk through the door.

'Thought we weren't doing any more nightclubs,' he says.

'It's only a nightclub at night,' I counter. 'In the daytime, it serves food.'

A stretch, admittedly. The décor is dark and seedy, the kind of leather-bound establishment Gordon Ramsay would litter with swear words and despair. The food menu is printed on laminated pieces of stained paper, and each of the few food options is inspired by a cocktail.

'Strawberry Woo Woo chicken burger is not what I envisaged when you said we were going somewhere cheap but gourmet,' continues The Fake Boyfriend.

'Cheap but gourmet doesn't exist. You shouldn't be so gullible,' I say, and immediately regret doing so, for the corners of his mouth droop, as if a not insignificant portion of the trust he had in me was holding them up and has just disappeared.

'I'm sorry, OK' I say. 'I'm not going to make you dance to shitty pop songs. I'll get you something good to eat, and then we'll go see the lighthouse.'

'I'm not eight, you can't buy my affection with a banana milkshake and a trip to the beach.'

'I can try.'

The Fake Boyfriend sits himself sullenly on a black couch and I head to the bar. There's a pretty, auburn-haired woman drying glasses at the far end, and a large, bald man chopping up limes closer to me.

Hair loss looks good on him, highlighting his strong jaw and blue eyes. I approach him.

'Can I get a Strawberry Woo Woo chicken burger and a Sex on the Beef bun please?' I ask. 'And two vanilla milkshakes.'

'Course you can,' he replies, moving a card reader in front of me.

I pay and look about the bar, plucking up the courage to ask what I really want to know. The news is playing on a small television behind the man's gleaming skull, a story about rising food prices.

'I was, um . . . was wondering,' I begin. I fish my phone from my pocket and scroll to a screenshot of Callum. It took hours of stalking to find a recent picture of my brother, but eventually one emerged: from two years ago, deep within an Instagram account of someone I remembered being his friend at school. It's a photo of a polaroid picture, making Callum's milky skin and angular features all the more striking. He's by the window of a tower block, with all of Newcastle bathed in dawn or dusk behind him. I've messaged the friend, of course. *Not seen Callum since that party, mate. If you find him, tell him he owes us £38*, came the reply from @jasperoshea97.

So I'm here, instead. Sniffing around an even more tenuous lead.

'I was wondering,' I say again. The news story on the television switches: an image of police tape and vans outside Marty's betting shop. My heart thumps. 'I was wondering if you could turn the TV off, please.'

My voice is high-pitched and mousy with alarm and fear. Still, the bartender moves in the direction of the television. But he's not quick enough to prevent me from hearing a reporter say, 'Teessider Marty Deng was discovered early this morning in the betting shop he's run on Grove Hill for the past five years. He was found to have suffered electrocution, asphyxiation and a stab wound.'

'Hey, woah, sorry, leave it on!' I shout at the bartender. *A stab wound*?

'Turn it off, turn it on, this isn't the hokey-cokey,' he mumbles, returning to his limes.

They don't go into more details in respect of the stab wound. Instead, they confirm his death, and segue into who might have caused it. I hold out the picture of Callum and start talking, hoping to drown out any details I don't want to hear from the television.

'Do you know this man?' I ask the bartender.

He fixes the picture of Callum with a half-arsed gaze. 'Uh. Not personally.'

'. . . Police are gathering eyewitness reports and checking CCTV . . .'

I speak louder. 'But you've seen him? You know of him?'

'I'd struggle to say for certain.'

'. . . recent spate of killings in Middlesbrough, but police would like to reassure . . .'

'He's called Callum Mandeville,' I say, my voice rising in both pitch and volume. 'He used to drink here.'

The bartender shrugs. 'Thousands of kids drink here.'

'. . . Marty's killer will be found and will face justice . . .'

I blanche and turn away from the bar, staggering back to The Fake Boyfriend and the dark booths that surround him. The minutes between sitting down and receiving our milkshakes are filled with random questions that I bark out in his direction: how much do you think the moon weighs? Was Britpop overrated? Have you ever stolen? What's your favourite meat? Would you like to be able to fly? He answers each gamely, though I forget his answers as soon as I hear them.

When our milkshakes arrive, I slurp noisily. When my burger arrives, I chew with as much conviction as I can muster, wishing for once in my life there was more crunchy lettuce sandwiched between the buns.

None of it's enough. I'm incapable of drowning out the news report, and I'm incapable of silencing my own wicked thoughts. I'm never going to find Callum. I'm going to be arrested for Marty Deng's death. Someone's following me. Someone is interfering. I'm on the back foot.

I've driven myself near delirious by the time I swallow my final chip. I'm certain that the bartender is looking at me with fresh interest, and I'm certain he mumbles a threat when he collects our plates. The dark, sticky nature of the bar becomes unbearable; I'm positive that shapes are looming from the shadows, positive I'm going to get trapped against the leather seats, a sitting duck.

'Let's get out of here,' I say to The Fake Boyfriend. He nods. We pull on our coats and I follow a few paces behind him, towards the door. I'm just passing into the chilly air when a hand squeezes my shoulder. This is it. This is finally it. This is me getting caught.

I spin around, muscles tensed, as if I'm ready for a fight. But I find the pretty, auburn-haired woman, rather than the bald man, looking at me. Relief is my first emotion, swiftly followed by apprehension. There's something about the shape of her face and the deep blue of her eyes that I recognise.

'Hey, sorry to bother you. Just heard you mention Callum Mandeville earlier,' she says.

'Oh. Oh, yeah I did.'

'Are you looking for him?'

'Sort of. Yeah, guess I am. Do you know him?'

'Used to, a little bit,' she says. 'He's in a relationship with my sister.'

My heart rate quickens. In my excitement, I almost miss the return of The Fake Boyfriend, back from the car to listen in. His gangly body does a semi-decent job of blocking the chill from the outside.

'Oh, Christ. Well, yeah, anything you could tell me that might lead to him would be so helpful,' I say.

The woman shakes her head. 'They used to live in Gateshead, but they moved away last year. I wasn't sure about him, but she was besotted – he sort of had this, this thing about him. Like hypnotic, almost.'

'But you don't know where he is now?' I press.

The woman, bless her, looks genuinely sorry as she says, 'No. I didn't like her dating him and we fell out. I'm not sure where they went. He was always hard to pin down.'

I nod – a Callum trait I can agree on.

'But in the area, right? He didn't move abroad or down south or anything?' I say, trying to rinse all the information I can from her.

'Don't think so. He always liked it round here.'

'Can I . . . could I have your sister's number?'

The woman chews her lip. 'Err, yep. Yeah, suppose you can. Don't tell her I gave it to you though, please. Would like to be friends with her again one day.'

I nod, grateful as she reads out the phone number.

'Thank you,' I say, turning to leave.

She grabs my hand before I go. 'I think you're better off not finding him. I think he's someone it's best to avoid.'

Chapter Twenty-Three

Her warning joins the cacophony of other shit on loop in my mind as The Fake Boyfriend and I brace against the cold and wind our way over the dunes. I dial the number as soon as we make it onto Sandhaven beach. It rings five times, and then, predictably, it goes to answerphone.

'Hiya, you've reached Rose, please leave a message,' she says. A strange pang of familiarity hits me, before I realise she probably just sounds like her sister. I decide against leaving a message, figuring I'll just keep dialling her number, and she'll eventually pick up.

The Fake Boyfriend's long legs have transported him a number of metres from me, so I put my phone away, zip my coat up and jog to catch him up. He turns as I arrive and tells me I look cute, like a penguin. He tells me about longshore drift, and he tries to teach me to skim pebbles. After a couple of failed attempts, he picks up a fresh stone, but pauses before handing it to me.

'This one sort of looks like your eyes, Ella,' he says. 'It's pretty. You should keep it.'

He passes me the smooth, speckled pebble and my heart sinks. Because my fake boyfriend should be someone else's real boyfriend. He'd be really good at it.

I feel, in that moment – with the wind whipping my cheeks raw and the ocean crashing to my left – deeply lonely. Not just for myself, but for The Fake Boyfriend, too. I don't want to trick him into loving me.

'You've killed people,' I whisper to myself. 'You're going to kill more people. You need to toughen up.'

Still, guilt sits in my stomach for the remainder of our beach walk and the duration of the drive back to Middlesbrough. And then, as we're driving through the town and The Fake Boyfriend's smiles seem that bit more stretched and fake, my feelings begin to turn. He looks right at a junction, and I find myself staring at his floppy hair, pulled back in time to watching him at Brandon Pearce's hearing.

I open my mouth, suddenly overcome by the urge to ask him why he was there. I lick my lips, take a deep breath, but then he turns back to face me, and I lose my nerve.

Manbaby Flatmate is in the kitchen when we return, and this is almost a relief, for his inane chatter distracts me from less pleasant thoughts.

The Fake Boyfriend feigns interest in Manbaby Flatmate's latest boozy story, while I fish out teabags from the stash in the cupboard. All too soon, Manbaby Flatmate leaves, saying he's got a kill streak to maintain, and he's replaced by Too-Old-For-This-Shit Flatmate. I sneak a glance at her and almost gasp in concern. She looks terrible: her eyes watery and her pasty skin the colour of a poorly resurrected corpse. And she stares straight at me.

Fortunately, The Fake Boyfriend starts talking to her before any sort of interaction can happen between the two of us. I turn my back on the pair of them and concentrate on pouring boiling water into my two mugs.

They talk about the cost of living and then my flatmate whispers something. I don't catch what. I picture them behind me, sidling up to one another, The Fake Boyfriend stooping over and putting his head against hers. Black hair next to blonde, united in sharing information about me.

My flatmate's phone is by the chopping board. I imagine her short fingers tapping 999 into the keypad. The curl of her lip as she tells the officer on the other end that she has information in respect of Devlin Mackenzie's death. The pulsation of her tongue as she tells them that Gregory Macaluf is innocent. That, instead, she saw one Ella Mandeville standing by the spot that Devlin's body was later discovered. That the air on that fateful night was thick with the coppery smell of blood, that Ella's damp forehead was illuminated by the moon.

In this kitchen is a kettle, a bottle of prosecco, a stone fruit bowl and a selection of knives. Any of these objects would make an effective murder weapon. It's amazing how sinister so many things become if you shift your perspective just a little.

My hand shakes, and water splashes onto the countertop. More chatter from The Fake Boyfriend and Too-Old-For-This-Shit Flatmate. Was that my name? Did The Fake Boyfriend just say my name?

'Yeah it's . . . with everything going on.'

'You saw the news?'

And then again, a sentence I don't catch. The Fake Boyfriend knows too much. My docile beta prop is anything but. He's shrouded in his own layers of mystery, with thoughts, emotions and secrets I can't keep track of never mind control.

More water splashes onto the countertop as I slam the kettle down. I hurry into my room and dig my pillbox out from underneath a pillow. How many? Eight? Twelve? The whole box? I shake them out into my clammy hand and raise it to my mouth.

'No!'

The Fake Boyfriend charges into my room and knocks the pills from my hand. I watch them scatter across my carpet, some rolling under my bed, others coming to a stop against the desk.

'Jesus Christ, Ella.'

I don't reply, am able to do little more than observe the mess of pills and toy with the idea of picking them all back up. My gaze shifts to my desk, and the turned-over list of targets which sits atop it. My palm itches, but I resist the temptation to grab the list and hide it.

'Were you going to overdose?' asks The Fake Boyfriend.

It takes me a while to come back to him, but eventually I do. I shake my head, clear my throat and say, 'They're not pills. They're Tic Tacs. I've been trying to use the . . . the placebo effect thing with them since my brother died.'

'Really?'

'Yeah. I know that's weird.'

'Your brother died?'

Shit. I've opened a can of worms.

'Mmm. I don't really like talking about it.'

'No. No, of course not,' The Fake Boyfriend says. 'Are they . . . ? They're really . . . ?'

'Try one,' I say, taking one of the few remaining little white oblongs from my box and handing it over to him. He accepts it cautiously, as if I've just passed over an unexploded bomb.

'Oh, yeah. Just a Tic Tac,' he says as he sucks it. The worry still hasn't left his face, though. 'Are you OK, Ella?'

No. No. I'm so aggressively un-OK I'm not even sure how or where to begin. In the end, I say, 'Pretty much.'

'Talk to me if you're hurting. Please.'

'Uh-huh.'

He must be annoyed by my half-answers, in the same way I would get annoyed by The Ex's half-answers. By the way she never let me know her, not completely. And now I'm not letting The Fake Boyfriend know me, partly because of her, partly because I'm on a murderous killing spree, and – most of all – because I don't even know myself.

There's movement from the corridor. The faint smell of citrus perfume I recognise as belonging to Too-Old-For-This-Shit Flatmate. Her presence focuses me. I shut my bedroom door and then turn to The Fake Boyfriend.

'You went to Brandon Pearce's hearing,' I say plainly.

The Fake Boyfriend adjusts his glasses and then says, 'Yeah. I did. How do you know?'

A fair question. Luckily, I've become somewhat skilled in the art of quick-fire lies.

'I've started reporting on local court cases. A sort of extension of my degree.'

'Thought you studied film?'

The problem with my quick-fire lies is, of course, that they're often shit. I say, 'Journalism. Film. It's all media, isn't it? Anyway, why were you there?'

There's a pause, and in this pause my mind fills with all the revelations I anticipate might tumble from The Fake Boyfriend's lips.

I'm not met with anything I was expecting. Instead, The Fake Boyfriend says, 'Brandon Pearce is my dad.'

'What?'

'Yeah. He's . . . he's my dad.'

'Oh.'

'Yeah. I'm not proud of it, especially. He was awful to me and my mam. Had a lot of drug debts too, so even when he wasn't harassing us, someone he owed money to would be. But he . . . he's not a murderer. He didn't kill Janet Braithwaite.'

I shake my head, I can't help it. Because The Fake Boyfriend is right. Brandon Pearce didn't kill her.

'So why did he confess to killing her?' I ask.

'That's . . . sort of what I've been meaning to ask you for the past few months.'

Fuck. Here it is. Here it comes. I brace myself, ready for him to tell me that he knows I killed Janet Braithwaite. That he knows I killed Courtney Teasdale and Devlin Mackenzie and Marty Deng. That he knows I'm going to kill Callum, that he intends to stop me.

'What do you mean?' I choke out.

'I heard about Janet's death in the news and didn't think much of it. A couple of days later, my dad stays out late, really late. Can't say I thought much of that, either. But when he came back, he just sat in the living room, with his head in his hands, and he said the same thing over and over.'

'What did he say?'

'He said that he knew his time with Mitch Mandeville would catch up with him.'

I think back to the picture I found in Marty's office. The five of them together: Mitch, Brandon, Jamie, Gregory, Marty.

The Fake Boyfriend continues, 'The next day he told the police he'd killed Janet Braithwaite. And what do you know, a little later on that day, the gang he owed money to told my mam all his debts had been paid. I asked them who by, but they didn't know or wouldn't say. All I had was that name. Mitch Mandeville. Can't say I especially want my dad out of jail, but I was so curious as to why he'd put himself in there. I *am* so curious.'

I nod. Because I am too.

'And then . . .'

'And then, what are the chances, but you come into Bedford Street Coffee the following day. And as I bring your espresso to you, you answer your phone, and you say your name's Ella Mandeville. It's not a very common surname.'

'No.'

'I don't really have any other leads, and it's not . . . this investigation stuff doesn't come naturally to me. So I figure I'll hang out with you and maybe I'll find out about Mitch.'

A whoosh of air escapes my lips, half sigh, half hopeless laugh. 'And what you learned from me is that Mitch Mandeville is dead.'

The Fake Boyfriend nods. And then he shakes his head. 'But is he . . . is he really?'

'Dead? Yeah. Of course he's dead,' I reply, incredulous.

'You don't think . . . because he knew people . . . and he had, you know, reasons to disappear . . . you don't think he faked his own death?'

I'm smiling, I can feel the corners of my mouth press themselves into my cheeks, as this hard, hysterical emotion seizes my face.

'No,' I say. 'I don't.'

'Why would my dad mention him now then?'

I want to tell The Fake Boyfriend that his dad is insane. But he's not, and Jamie Sleight wasn't insane, either.

'I don't know, but my dad has been dead for two decades.'

'Did you ever see his body?'

I laugh again, brisk and cold. 'What sort of ridiculous question is that? No, I didn't. I was three years old.'

The Fake Boyfriend nods. He doesn't speak for a long time, and then he says, 'I think Mitch Mandeville is still alive.'

This statement leaves me gulping, like a fish out of water. A creaking coming from the stairs outside my room is what eventually forces me into saying, 'Please leave.'

The Fake Boyfriend looks down at the pills on my carpet. He removes his glasses and puts them back on again. He sighs. And then he nods, opens my door and leaves. I hear the pad of his trainers against the staircase carpet. The quiet click of the front door as he opens and then closes it.

I'm shaking. I wrap my arms around my body.

Shock surges through me, and it's not long before a strange sense of loneliness is also twisting its way through my bloodstream. I've just dismissed the person I've leaned on most in the past few months. I've chosen loneliness. My abject isolation is an achievement. And yet I feel such a failure.

I hug myself harder, attempting to squeeze some sort of hope back into my body.

There's a cough from outside my bedroom door, and I'm reminded of the fact that I'm not alone, after all. Too-Old-For-This-Shit Flatmate is just around the corner.

This thought is not a comforting one.

Slowly, I step towards the corridor. Her eyes are on me as soon as I exit my room. We open our mouths at the same time, but neither of us says anything. The skin at the edges of her nails is bitten and a raw, pink colour.

My mouth is suddenly dry beyond what I previously thought to be possible. I swallow, but no extra liquid seems to materialise.

Too-Old-For-This-Shit Flatmate opens her mouth again. She inhales, and I brace, waiting for her to tell me she knows what I've done. That The Fake Boyfriend might not have realised, but that she knows I killed Devlin. That she suspects I killed Courtney and Janet and Marty, too. That she knows I'm going to kill Callum.

She doesn't. Her dry lips close, and she returns to her bedroom, leaving a trail of unspoken words in her wake.

Chapter Twenty-Four

It's been a while since I slept soundly, and tonight proves to be especially problematic. I lie in the darkness with my feelings, turning them over in my mind.

The confrontation with The Fake Boyfriend has dredged up memories of the end of my relationship with The Ex. But, to my surprise, it's almost as if these feelings dull to something manageable. The scar which forms over a once throbbing wound. A lump of pain, but one I have to go looking for, merely a reminder of something which was once agonising and has slowly ceased to be so.

I turn my bedside lamp on, push myself out of bed and walk over to Joe's guitar. It's imperfect, I've always known that much. I run a hand over the sleek wood, anticipating the chip on the head. But as I look closer, I can see that paint is rubbing off the body. There are scratches up and down the wood. One of the tuning keys is wonky, and three of the strings are frayed. My heart sinks and I flush with a mixture of embarrassment and guilt. Have I done this? Did I damage Joe's guitar while moving it?

I squeeze the neck until the veins in my left hand rise, a throbbing blue beneath my milky skin. I place my other hand on the body of the guitar, and I press harder and harder, memories of Joe playing the object with sadness in his eyes filling my skull. There's a sickening splintering sound as the neck of the guitar breaks off from the body. I pause and stare at the object in horror. And then, as if on autopilot, I apply more pressure, until the break in the wood is clean. I pull the strings out, hurting my fingertips and caring little. I'm panting by the time the guitar has been decapitated. I stare at it, expecting to feel happy, but I'm horrified.

I want the broken object as far from me as possible. I squeeze it under my desk and then I slide down the wall, not understanding the person I was a minute ago. And though the guitar is broken, and Joe is broken too, it's as though I can still hear his solemn tunes, living within the splintered wood.

'No. No.'

A memory I try my best to suppress is beating at me, trying to wriggle up and into my consciousness. I shake my head, but it persists and I'm . . . I'm back in my final year of school. It's a cold spring morning, one in which the light is particularly intense. Blinding, even. My back is sore, and I haven't seen Joe yet, and both of these things make me tetchy. I recall picking at a loose button on my blouse and letting myself into Joe's room. He'd been sitting on his bed, guitar on his lap, shirt sleeves rolled up to his elbows.

He'd rolled them down as soon as I entered. And I knew. In that instance, I knew. I hadn't been able to stop myself from asking, as we'd walked along Haverton Hill Road. He'd been evasive, un-cooperative, until I'd had no choice but to grab his wrist and roll the sleeve up myself. His forearm had been criss-crossed with cuts.

He'd shaken me loose and mumbled something about it not being fair that Callum and I were the only ones who suffered. I'd been horrified, glued to the spot, helpless to do anything other than watch him walk on ahead of me, ascending the hill and heading up, into the blinding light.

Self-harm in solidarity. It had made my insides taste rotten, made me want to claw down my throat and drag them up and out of me.

And, despite the fact that Joe was clearly crumbling, I put myself ahead of him. I left home, soon after. It had seemed inevitable that Stepdad's violence would escalate. I sacrificed Joe in the same way that Callum had sacrificed me.

I killed Joe.

'No . . . Callum . . . Callum pushed . . . Callum pushed Joe.'

There are tears in my eyes, but they don't stop me crawling about my floor, collecting the little white oblongs scattered across it. I press a couple into my mouth. They taste of mint and of fluff. They're sweets, just sweets. They were never going to make me feel better. They never will.

'Fuck.'

I paw my cheeks dry and run wet fingers through my greasy hair. I've got to keep moving. I've just . . . I've got to keep moving.

I pile on a scarf and jacket and slip Mam's old Ugg boots onto my feet. It's still dark out, but I'm clearly incapable of sleep, so I decide to continue my search for Callum. I cross the river and skirt around the industrial estate, staring through wire fences into the places we used to play. The wind whispers the stories that Callum would tell Joe and me. He had a gift for bringing corrugated metal and slabs of concrete to life. They're resurrected with the sunrise: all shrouded in an amber glow, all the old scrap gleaming. I press my fingers through the fence, wanting to insert myself into the scene. Wanting to climb in and inhale it.

My fingers wrap themselves around the chain-link metal, as though I'm one of the weeds, slowly merging with the industrial estate. The flesh on my hands is so white it's almost translucent, stretched thin and dry across bones which seem to protrude more harshly than I remember. It's quite a contrast from my blackened fingernails, stained by a filth I can't identify. It's as though I've attempted to resurrect Joe not by murdering others but by clawing his coffin from the ground. I stretch out my ghostly fingers. Months of preoccupation with death seems to have half tugged me into the underworld.

Unsurprisingly I don't see Callum. I see the distant shapes of men who would be about his height. Sometimes I think I can smell ash, and sometimes a bodyless laugh or whisper drifts past me. But in reality, I'm back on the Quayside, this time sober rather than smashed, but still chasing the same shadow. I dial his girlfriend's number a dozen more times, but she doesn't answer. There's something to her voice, though. It's different to her sister's ever so slightly. And I'm sure I've heard it before.

I find myself drifting to Linthorpe Cemetery, to one grave I seldom visit, and one I never have. My dad's is in the centre of the graveyard, beneath a bare oak tree. I stare at the ground in front of his headstone, trying to envisage the body six feet under.

'There is a body,' I whisper. 'And it's my dad's.'

The Fake Boyfriend's parting words echo in my head. But he's wrong, he's all wrong. Mitch Mandeville died twenty years ago. He's not the one pulling the strings. He can't be.

I find Joe's grave among the newer headstones, where the names are still crisp and shiny and depressingly readable. A marker of death, in high definition. Maybe my grief will run in tandem with the state of his headstone, and I won't feel the sting of it quite so hot once his headstone is moss covered and weather battered.

For a second, I think I might wrap my arms around the cold, hard slab, but this urge doesn't overcome me. I stand a few metres away, looking but not absorbing.

The weather takes a cliched turn; the clear sky clouds over and rain starts falling, first a cool splattering and then a Baltic downpour. I turn away from Joe and scuttle back to my flat.

Something's not right. I can sense it as soon as I enter.

The air in the corridor tastes different, as if someone who hasn't ever set foot here has recently entered. There's a staleness, an uncanny stillness, and I suddenly find breathing difficult.

I force myself to take a deep, shuddering breath. Try not to gag. And then I hang up my wet coat and place one foot on the first step.

Pause.

I strain my ears, trying to listen for noises that don't belong. For once, I don't hear the rumble of Manbaby Flatmate's crisp packets, or agitated muttering from Too-Old-For-This-Shit Flatmate. Only one sound fills the flat: the hammering of rain against the windows.

The gun is under my bed, a whole staircase away from me. So I pick up an umbrella and slowly ascend, trying to keep as quiet as possible. When I finally reach the landing, everything looks in order: the kitchen the cleanest it's been in a while, the doors to the bedrooms of my flatmates tightly shut.

But my bedroom door is open. My stomach drops, and I pick up speed. Stupid, I know, but I'm entirely focused on a scrap of paper lying on my desk. I drop the umbrella and pick the paper up, hands shaking.

It's my list of victims. But – in spikey red handwriting – amendments have been made.

```
                                    FADE IN:
                                          1
INT. ELLA'S BEDROOM - EVENING
  WE OPEN with Ella, as she inches closer to
righting the wrongs surrounding Joe's death.
  Target #1 - JANET BRAITHWAITE
  Target #2 - COURTNEY TEASDALE
  Target #3 - DEVLIN MACKENZIE
  Target #4 - MARTY DENG
  Target #5 - CALLUM MANDEVILLE
```

*Target #6 – Elizabeth Mandeville. If you don't meet me.
8pm. Tonight. The old incinerator.*

And p.s. you're a fucking idiot for keeping a list.

Chapter Twenty-Five

My immediate response is to check that the gun is still where I hid it. It is, thank God; I pluck the cool metal from the folds of an old flannel shirt. I keep the gun gripped tight in my sweaty palm as I stalk around the rest of the flat. The doors of my flatmates get hammered on, but neither of them answer. It's noon on . . . fuck knows what day. I recently murdered my boss; my need to time keep has disappeared. Regardless, they're both out, and I find no trace of anyone else in the flat.

When I've done four or five laps of the place, I move on to my third instinct: to contact Mam and Stepdad. I key their home number into my phone, but stop before pressing dial. There's a . . . there's . . . there's a feeling in my gut that's telling me not to call them. So I sink onto my bed and succumb to my final response: staring at the ceiling and waiting for evening to creep up on me.

An alright plan, bar the fact that my room now feels contaminated. But Christ, everywhere now feels contaminated: the riverbed, the industrial estate, even the leafy outskirts of the town. I scratch my arm and listen as the rain slows.

I feel an urge I can't shake, to plot, but there's no need, for my plan is simple. My plan is the gun and a short, clean death. I turn it over in my hands, wondering whether my dad ever shot anyone with it. Whether he attempted to on the night of his death. Whether he was more successful than I've been led to believe.

I'm going to use his gun tonight. This is probably the closest I've ever felt to him.

My body grows itchy as the day wears on, and I leave early. The sun sinks as I walk, dipping below factories. The rain has stopped, but vast puddles have made the ground slick and reflective, creating watery images of the smoggy sunset above. I splash through them, wanting to cause carnage.

The sound of the town changes with every step taken. The cawing of sky rats, the steady flow of the river and distant rumble of cars, the shouts and cries which echo as day turns to dusk seem to slow and merge, as if an illusion, as if Middlesbrough is merely a tape recording which is spluttering into something indecipherable and unreal. And, eventually, white noise. A gushing from the furnaces which drowns out all else.

I stand on the edge of the chain-link fence and watch as artificial clouds are pumped into the sky, emerging as ethereal entrails against the inky black of the night. My nose fills with the rich, intoxicating smell of adventure and danger, and once again I wrap ghostly fingers through the fence.

It's time to go in.

It doesn't take me long to find a rip in the fence. I yank it up and then squeeze under, surprised by how simultaneously familiar and unfamiliar the sensation is. My body has changed, but my brain remembers.

Directly in front of me are concrete towers and a twisted rig of pumps and pistols. But I'm headed beyond this, to a large brown building which slopes down on either side of its centre like a giant silo. We called this building The Woodlouse on account of its resemblance to the creature, and the most revered challenge any one of us could face would be to slide down the outside. Just looking at the gradient had made mine and Joe's stomachs turn. Callum insisted he'd slid down when he was younger, but neither of us quite believed him.

I wrap a hand around the cool metal ladder which runs up the outside of the building, bracing myself for the climb.

I expect the wind to pick up as I climb, but it's an eerily still night, and if the smoke behind me wasn't drifting north, I'd say there wasn't even a gasp of motion in the air. I make it all the way to the top of the building with relative ease, stopping just before I reach the final rung and have to clamber up onto the ridge, exposing myself.

I take a breath. I glance down at the forty- or fifty-metre drop to the ground, where the shifting smoke moves in an almost human fashion. But there's no one below. Just me, clutching on to the ladder, and the person who waits for me at the top of the building. The person who broke into my room and summoned me here.

I'm shaking, but there's no need. I'm on home turf, in familiar territory, and there's a gun in my pocket.

'OK. OK,' I say.

Another breath. A deep one, this time. And then I haul myself up and onto the ridge.

As I suspected, I've got company, at the far end of the building. But a jolt of panic shudders through my body.

Because two people, rather than one, are silhouetted against the night sky. I take my gun from my pocket and stride towards them, heart beating so hard I fear it might escape me. My eyes are agonisingly slow to pick out details of the people ahead.

But eventually I'm close enough to see who they are.

A man and a woman. One is a surprise, and the other is the person I knew was waiting for me.

I tighten my grip on the gun.

Chapter Twenty-Six

'You've brought a gun to a family reunion? Not very friendly,' says Callum, clocking the weapon at my side and letting this slick, teasing grin spread across his face.

I'm ten feet away from him, and my heart pounds. The urge to reach out and touch him is – no matter how dangerous – agonisingly tempting. Callum has always seemed like an illusion; it's difficult to believe I'm really so close.

'She's not family,' I say, nodding in the direction of Too-Old-For-This-Shit Flatmate, who stands beside Callum. She looks worse than ever, her blonde hair matted, her lips chapped and purple in colour. Callum doesn't look much better – perhaps I'm seeing things in the near dark, but his skin seems to have taken on an ashy hue, as if the smog of our hometown has visibly polluted him, or as if he's suffering from the same ailment as I am: an unsettling acquaintance with death.

If I were to edge myself closer to him, I'm certain my hand would go through his body and out the other side.

'Now then, Elizabeth, don't be rude,' Callum says. 'Cos this guest is an important one.'

I don't reply. My gaze flickers between Callum and Too-Old-For-This-Shit Flatmate, trying to figure out how on earth they know each other.

'Marty Deng's real murderer,' Callum continues, gesturing at me, 'meet Marty Deng's pretend murderer,' he finishes, gesturing at my flatmate.

It takes a second for cogs to turn in my brain.

'What do you mean?' I ask.

'I mean I've sourced the next person who's going to confess to your heinous and – quite frankly shite – crimes.'

'Shite?'

Callum nods. 'You're really bad at killing people.'

Despite myself, I'm offended. 'Oh, I thought I was—'

'No, you're really fucking bad. I mean, for the love of God, if you are going to kill me, at least do a decent job of it. I don't want to slowly bleed out through a leg you've not quite managed to hack off.'

I bristle. Callum talking about murder when we're minutes from where he pushed Joe to his death is too much.

'Oh, don't worry. I'd never want to steal the title of "best killer" from you,' I say, lips curling into a hateful snarl.

For a second, Callum seems to lose his cool, as confusion flashes across his face. But he composes himself quickly and says, 'Credit where it's due, your murders were at least fairly creative. But you were sloppy enough that the police would have found you, had other people not confessed.'

I nod, pressing my teeth into my bottom lip. I shift my gaze away from Callum, needing a break from his intense eyes. Middlesbrough stretches out below us, distant and alive. Looking at it makes me feel tiny, and somewhat hopeless; it was always impossible to know all of its secrets, always impossible to know who was watching me, and when. I've more questions than I can see chimneys and I turn back to Callum, not knowing which to ask first.

'How did you know it was me?' is what I settle on.

He shrugs. 'Always kept a pretty close eye on you, but especially after Joe died. Thought it a bit strange that you seemed to have taken up permanent residence in a contractors' hotel in the middle of the industrial estate. Know we've not known each other for a while, but didn't have that on me bingo card of what you might end up doing.'

'No. We've not known each other for a while,' I say. Mention of Joe has put fresh ice back into my voice.

'Divvin be like that,' Callum says. He grins, and I note that he still has slightly crooked teeth. 'Was me leaving home really so bad? You finally got your own room.'

I shrug, not knowing what to say. Callum's departure had torn me apart, but what rips into your soul at fourteen is often repaired with a haphazard cast of metaphorical plasters by the time you reach twenty-three. I've learned to live without him.

I look at my flatmate, whose silence strikes me as ominous, much like Step-Nan's. She doesn't meet my eyes. She's looking past me, as though she's left mine and Callum's conversation to follow her own thoughts through the plumes of smoke and up into the night.

I turn back to Callum. 'So, you suspected I killed Janet?'

'Didn't suspect you'd killed Janet, knew you had. Saw you go into her house and dash out, looking panicked, ten minutes later. So I went in the way you'd exited and found the mess you'd made.'

'So it was you? You framed someone else?'

'Aye. Wouldn't say I framed someone, would say I offered them a lucrative opportunity and they gratefully accepted.'

I recall what The Fake Boyfriend said about his dad's debts being paid off.

'Brandon Pearce. You offered him money. But . . .' I shake my head. 'I know his son. The night before Brandon confessed, he said that his time with Mitch Mandeville had finally caught up with him. *Mitch*. Not Callum.'

'Well, aye. In a way. When I left home, I thought – who better to find than Dad's old mates? Marty Deng, Brandon Pearce, Jamie Sleight and Gregory Macaluf. Except they weren't Dad's mates, not really. Turned out they betrayed him, set him up in an awry drug deal. They hung him out to dry, he lost his life. Course, I couldn't do anything at the time, was barely a man at that point, but I kept a candle burning for all four. Wanted to get them behind bars in the fullness of time. You murdered Janet and I knew the police would investigate properly if a lamb wasn't offered up for slaughter. So I found Brandon – all bald and angry. No hair but a lot of debt. A lot of scary men in his face, in the faces of his wife and son . . .'

'Fucking hell,' I say, suddenly feeling dizzy. The world below me seems to shake, and I steady myself, not wanting to fall to my death. 'So you used . . . ?'

'My inheritance. Yeah, not all of it, like. But a decent chunk, alongside a bit of intimidation. Helps that I look like Mitch. Helps that he was a ruthless bastard, that they were all terrified of him. Had to make sure Brandon would stick to his word.'

'And then?'

'And then I thought, oh fuck me, Elizabeth's on a madden. She's a woman possessed. She's cut up about Joe and maybe Liev's in her head and she's off to kill everyone who was there that night.'

'Liev didn't get in my head,' I say.

'You sure about that?'

I'm about to bite back, but my mind is flooded with images of my stepdad's broad shoulders, his cold eyes, his small teeth and the words which passed through them. I shake my head.

'They've been nice to me, actually. Nice-ish.'

'Oh aye, and pigs can fly.'

'What would you know, you left us all?'

Callum shakes his head. He runs a hand through his dark, tousled hair. 'I've always been with you, Elizabeth. Was there at the nightclub, when you murdered Courtney. I made sure she stayed shut in that toilet cubicle, made sure she couldn't run out screaming your name. There wasn't CCTV in the staff bathroom, but I wiped the CCTV in the upstairs corridor. And the next day, I found Jamie, begging by the beach. Took him back to me girlfriend's place, was able to tell him all the details necessary to convince the police he'd done it: method of murder. Time of murder. What Courtney had been wearing. I'd taken a couple of her things. You know, to really convince the police they'd caught the killer. Thought I'd better land it in their laps, make sure there was no way for them to fuck up. Did the same with Janet, too.'

I nod, remembering what Jamie had said about a ghost from his past. I'd thought of my dad, or Marty, but if Callum had gone to Dad's old mates when he left home, Jamie would have known Callum as well. And then there's my Redcar door knocking. The girl with thick, red hair. Rose. That's where I recognised her voice from. I recall the way she'd reacted to mention of Jamie. She'd been Callum's girlfriend.

'And then, of course,' Callum continues, 'I watched the night you killed Devlin. I watched one of your flatmates' – he points to his right – 'as she saw you kill him.'

My stomach turns. In my gut, I've always known that she saw me kill Devlin. But to have it confirmed makes my skin crawl. I look at Too-Old-For-This-Shit Flatmate, but she's still lost in her own thoughts.

'Course, after I'd grabbed something from Devlin to give to the next confessor, I was right on her case,' continues Callum. 'Couldn't have her telling the police about you, could I? And luckily for me, she's dating a man whose cancer treatment isn't covered by the NHS. Has been easy enough to buy her silence, hasn't it now?'

He gives my flatmate a small shake, and she nods.

'Fuck. I'm . . .' I'm what? Am I sorry? Confused? Angry? Grateful? I'm a mess, that's the only certainty. Ten steps behind everyone else.

'Found Gregory Macaluf, poor lad, with a right fuck-off gambling addiction, banned from the town centre these days and all. He just wanted a bit of peace and quiet, really. Gave his daughter some money and he happily confessed to Devlin's murder. Off to jail for three square meals a day and his daughter's doing better than ever, so I hear.'

I laugh. 'Oh, Patron Saint Callum Thomas Mandeville. You think you're hero of the poor. But you're just a psychopath.'

Callum's ever-present smile stretches wider. 'Takes one to know one.'

'I'm not a psychopath,' I say, surprised by how defensive I feel about this.

'You bludgeoned a teenager to death. You electrocuted your godfather. You poisoned a girl on her birthday. You used two children as pawns in your plans. You still don't have gravy on your Sunday roasts. That last point alone generally qualifies someone as being a psychopath.'

Despite the cold, I feel my cheeks flush. 'I literally met the two children as they were dissecting a dead mouse. They were hardly innocence personified.'

'I'm only pulling your leg, like. Your methods have been sloppy, but your heart's in the right place. Janet, Courtney, Devlin, Marty. They all sort of deserved it. And Brandon, Jamie and Gregory belong behind bars.'

'But why . . . It's so much effort. So much money and effort,' I say. 'Why are you doing this? Why make other people take the fall for me?'

For the second time tonight, Callum looks confused.

'I'm your big brother,' he says simply. 'I protect you, no matter what.'

A burning sensation rises up from my toes, getting hotter and hotter as it moves up my body, until it fills my mind with molten rage. It takes all my restraint to not throw myself towards him, punch his hard, angular face, his pretentious leather jacket, his smarmy smile. Spewing all this shit when he murdered Joe. He fucking murdered Joe. My lip curls once more.

Callum continues talking. I quiet the rage in my mind enough to listen, but tighten my grip on the gun.

'And finally you knocked off Marty, didn't you? Or at least you tried to. He wasn't quite dead, like, had to go in and finish the silly bugger off meself.'

The shadow who slunk into the betting shop after me. Of course it was Callum.

'And now she's going to take the fall for his murder, is she?' I ask, controlling my shaking body enough to point in Too-Old-For-This-Shit Flatmate's direction.

'Aye,' says Callum. He turns to look at her. 'No more of Mitch's old crew left. But what do we think a hundred thousand pounds will get us? Three years of treatment for your boyfriend? Maybe four?'

'Four years, two months,' says my flatmate. It's the first time I've heard her speak for ages. But her voice isn't hoarse. She projects a surprising amount of power from behind her chapped purple lips.

For a couple of seconds, no one speaks. The sound of smoke being pushed out of the chimneys behind us fills the air, and I cough. This, combined with a quick glance down at the ground, summons butterflies to my stomach. I've been up here for far too long. I've been wasting time. Clean. Quick. That was my plan. I lift the gun an inch upwards.

'Now, there's just one thing I don't understand,' says Callum, filling the space between us with his crass chat once more. 'When your lovely flatmate let me in, and I went up to your room and found your list of targets – mental that, by the way, just asking for jail – what I don't understand is . . . why was I on it too?'

I'd kept the anger inside me under some sort of control. But no longer. I'm burning. I am burning with rage.

'Are you taking the piss?'

'Nah. Nah, I'm not.'

'You murdered our brother.'

The smirk disappears from Callum's face. Finally gone for good, I suspect.

'Are *you* taking the piss?' he asks.

'I watched you push Joe off,' I say.

'Never.'

Enough. I raise the gun and point it at Callum. He lifts his arms and turns his pale palms towards me.

'Woah. Woah. You've got it wrong.'

I shake my head. The sequence that I'm haunted by plays in reverse in my head. Joe's body hitting the water. Joe's body hurtling through the air. Joe and Callum at the top of the bridge, Callum with his hands on Joe's back.

'I know what I saw,' I say.

'He jumped, Elizabeth. I was trying to stop him.'

I shake my head, my vision blurs. At first, I think I'm dizzy again, but I realise I'm crying. Always, always crying. I use my free hand to paw away the tears.

'Joe would never have jumped.'

The corners of Callum's mouth droop. His dark eyes meet mine with such intensity it's as if I'm being held hostage, incapable of looking away from him.

'How many times did you meet Joe in the last few years of his life?' Callum asks.

'Loads. I phoned him loads. I FaceTimed him loads. I've lost count,' I say.

'No. How many times did you physically meet Joe in the last few years of his life? Howay. Cos he was still twelve, in your head, wasn't he? You infantilised him. You had this simplified, polished view of him, and I get that, I really fucking get that, and I wish that was the case, but it wasn't. It really fucking wasn't.'

I open and close my mouth, not trusting myself to answer. A

sick, sullen feeling spreads through me, starting in my heart and surging to each cell in my body. My hand shakes so much that the gun twitches in the direction of my flatmate. She's still out of it, she barely even reacts. I take a deep breath and re-focus the gun on Callum's chest.

'Elizabeth. How many times did you physically meet Joe in the last few years of his life?' repeats Callum.

Heat floods me once more. But this time it's the heat of embarrassment, rather than anger.

'Only a handful of times. I hadn't seen him for a year before he . . . before he died. I hated going back there,' I eventually say.

Callum nods. He looks neither smug nor chuffed with this information, and for some reason this makes what I've just admitted to feel worse.

'I met him every week. Every single week,' says Callum. 'But I know. I understand you not wanting to go back. I've not seen Liev in years. I'd hate to see him.'

There's a question that's had me in a chokehold since I was a teenager. Now isn't the time, but I can't help it; fourteen-year-old Elizabeth needs to know.

'Why did you keep in touch with Joe and not me?'

Callum shakes his head. 'You didn't want to keep in touch with me. I called you. Messaged you. You'd reply telling me to leave you alone. I wanted to respect that.'

My torso contracts as I'm dealt an emotional gut punch. All the time I didn't have a phone. It was a favourite punishment, even when my only crime had been not shutting a window, or leaving water marks on the kitchen counter. I try to stand tall, even as it feels like my grip on reality is crumbling.

'You didn't help me pull Joe from the river. You didn't see if he was OK. You didn't even go to his funeral.' This squeaks out of me, wet and hopeless sounding.

Callum shrugs. 'I called the ambulance. By the time I made it down, it had arrived, along with Liev and Mam. I'd done all I could do. I hadn't been near Liev for almost a decade. My arrival wouldn't have helped. Same with the funeral. Wanted to grieve Joe me own way.'

I shake my head. Because as much as I want to believe that Callum hasn't spoken to Stepdad for years, that Callum's absences are justifiable and that he wanted a relationship with me, it would mean accepting that the worst thing possible had happened.

'Joe didn't kill himself,' I choke out.

'I'm sorry. I loved that kid. I would never have harmed him.'

The weight of the gun becomes unbearable. My arm is no longer capable of holding it up, and it sags down to my side, defeated. But it's not heavy enough, the gun. I want it to be so heavy that it drags me through the building and through the crust of the earth and into the depths of hell.

'Please. Joe didn't kill himself,' I say.

'It breaks me too, Elizabeth.'

I shake my head. Because I saw . . . I saw . . . but I saw . . . I know what I saw. I know what I saw . . . Callum, with his hands on Joe's back . . . and Callum . . . my two brothers . . . all the way up, high, away from me . . . and Joe's body plunging through the night . . .

I want to believe Callum. I want to believe Callum because I loved him, too.

But the image of the pair of them. Callum with his hands on Joe. It's too much. It's all I've thought about for the past three and a half months.

'I'm sorry, Callum,' I say.

'You're trusting the wrong people. Please, you're trusting the wrong people.'

I shake my head.

'I saw you push Joe.'

I raise the gun.

Chapter Twenty-Seven

I call Kim and Liev's house as I walk back to the flat. They answer on the third ring.

'He's dead,' I say simply, and then I hang up.

My response comes a couple of minutes later, a text message from Liev. It says:

Celebratory dinner at ours tomorrow night.

I have a lot to do before then.

Once back in my flat, I discover that there's been a surprising but helpful development in Marty's murder inquest. The police are spluttering to the same conclusion they arrived at in respect of Mitch Mandeville, twenty years ago. That Marty was a marked man, and that any number of people might have murdered him. The list of culprits is too high, the list of motivations too numerous for the crime to ever be solvable. They compare Marty to Mitch, draw parallels between the two deaths and scratch their heads in a way which must infuriate anyone who isn't me.

Twenty years ago, Brandon, Jamie, Gregory and Marty benefited from this incompetence. Today, it's me. For once, I'm grateful to Mitch. It's about the most use he's ever been.

I tell Lauren that this means she doesn't have to confess to the murder. I agree to keep paying for her boyfriend's cancer treatment, provided she takes what she knows about me to the grave.

She nods, and a little life and clarity seems to worm its way back into her eyes. Her chapped lips almost stretch themselves into a smile.

I do other things with my inheritance, too, working through the night and into the following day. Spending it after so long makes me feel anxious initially. After all, I'm touching something which

I've always kept myself removed from. But eventually, I get into the swing of things. I buy Ben a pair of flamingo slippers, which he accepts with a mixture of confusion and delight, promising to wear them around the flat at all times. And then I divvy the remainder of my inheritance up between three charities: Young Minds, North East Homeless and Addictions North East.

I feel lighter, when it's gone, as if I've unshackled myself from money which should never have been mine, and sure as hell should never have been Mitch's. I feel lighter, too, when I strip myself of Kim's leopard-print jumper, her sequin leggings and her Ugg boots. I replace mauve eyeshadow with lashings of black kohl, and I smear red lipstick across my lips. The foundation behind my ear gets removed, and a satisfied smile shapes my blood-red lips as I trail a finger across the snake which has been hidden for too long. I unclip my hair, releasing it in all its short, curly glory. And then I pull my old clothes out from under my bed and put them on: corduroy dungarees and a brown flannel shirt. Black boots and my own pretentious leather jacket. The clothes smell a bit stale, but I don't care. Putting them back on is like slipping back into my skin after months away from it.

I take out my phone and text Phil, thanking him for the way he's treated me over the past couple of months. I promise to tell him why his dad confessed to a crime he didn't commit. I end the message by saying that we don't have a romantic future, but that I hope we can be friends. I include a tick at the end of my message.

Kayin gets a message too. I thank her for not giving up on me and promise to see her in the new year.

And then I type a final scene out on my typewriter, tear it off and pack it into my bag, alongside Joe's yearbook and my list of victims.

It's dark out, once more, and I barely even acknowledged the daylight.

That means it's time for me to leave.

I retrace the familiar route back to the house I grew up in. It's almost December, and the Christmas lights are just appearing. I smile at them, trying to anticipate the food awaiting me. My money would be on a parmo, if they didn't prefer the takeaway version from down the road. A pie, perhaps? Lasagne?

My question is answered as I approach their house, and the rich, meaty smell of bangers and mash fills the air. I inhale greedily, looking forward to my first good meal in a few days.

Knocking at their door would have once made me apprehensive, but tonight I'm filled with certainty and confidence. I'm greeted in a similarly positive way: Liev pats my shoulder and Kim pulls me into a tight hug. Even Valeriya seems to have a smile twitching about on her thin lips.

'Well done, Ella, well done,' says Kim as she leads me through the hallway and into the kitchen at the back of the house, where the smell of her cooking is even stronger, and seems to fill the room with a salty, viscous liquid it feels possible to wade through.

'I'm Elizabeth again,' I tell her.

'Oh. Of course. Back to formalities, your majesty,' she says, as she adds a splash of milk and knob of butter to the potatoes, currently softening on the hob.

'Shall we have a drink in the front room?' Liev asks me. 'Leave your mam to get on with the cooking?'

'Sure,' I say. The thought of resting my tired arse in the crushed velvet armchair is a pleasant one.

Valeriya and Kim stay in the kitchen, while I follow Liev into the living room. He pours me a glass of wine and sits opposite me. Just the two of us in one room. For so long, the mere thought of this would have terrified me. But a sense of calm washes through me now, and I spend a few seconds looking at the man who loomed so large over my childhood. His hair is now more grey than brown, and I think – finally – it's retreated back far enough that he should shave it off. There are bags the colour of cigar-ash under his small green eyes.

His eyes meet mine.

'Well. Cheers, Elizabeth,' he says. 'Mission complete.'

'Cheers.'

I lean across the coffee table and clink my glass against Liev's. His eyes track my glass as I raise it to my lips. The cool rim comes to rest against my bottom lip, and I tilt the liquid towards me.

'Tea's ready!' shouts Kim from the kitchen.

I move the glass away from my lips without drinking. I set it down and smile at Liev. He smiles back, a straight line across his face, no teeth on show this time.

When I return to the kitchen, it's apparent that Kim's gone to town, bless her. The cutlery glistens, there are fresh napkins laid out and she's bothered to get placemats out. Four piping-hot plates of bangers and mash occupy the small wooden table, alongside four glasses of a fizzy liquid I assume is prosecco. Three sausages each, a generous serving by anyone's standards, but especially by Kim's.

'Wow. It smells amazing,' I say, pulling a chair out and making to sit down.

Kim stops me, laying a gentle hand on my shoulder.

'Oh, no, Elizabeth, you're in that seat.'

'Sure.'

I smile and move one seat to the right. Liev sits down opposite me. Kim sits to my right, and Valeriya struggles into the chair on my left.

'A full family meal,' I say, picking up my glass. 'What a rare treat.'

'Well, it's a very special occasion,' says Kim. She joins me in picking up her own glass.

We look to Liev, anticipating a satisfied toast. He opens his mouth.

'It's not been eas—'

WEEE – OOOH – WEEE – OOOH

The sound of a siren interrupts him, and I jump an inch out of my chair. My reaction is matched by my family who set down their glasses and look about in alarm and confusion.

'Nay bother, we hear sirens all the time. Howay, come on, what's the marra with you, Kim?' says Liev, trying in earnest to regain his composure.

He tries to re-start his speech, but the sound of the siren grows louder and louder.

'Fuck,' I say. I look to Kim. Her eyes are big, round, watery. 'Do you think . . . ? D'you think they know?'

'They know nothing,' Liev growls.

But the sound of the siren increases, until it seems to be coming from right outside the front door.

'I'm just . . . oh God.' Kim dashes from the kitchen.

240

Annoyed, Liev shoves his chair back and follows her out into the hallway. Even Valeriya can't resist a glimpse at what's going on; with more power than I've seen present in her body for a long time, she too leaves the kitchen. There's a click as the front door opens.

I need to be quick.

I swap each of my sausages for one from Kim, Liev and Valeriya's plates respectively. I section my mash into thirds, and scoop a third onto each of their plates, before wiping my plate clean and replacing mine with their original mash. I wipe my cutlery clean and place it back down next to my plate. And then I pour out some of their drinks before topping them up with liquid from my own glass. I rinse and refill my glass with water, hoping no one will notice that it no longer contains bubbles.

I'm just sitting back down when the three of them return to the kitchen.

'Was it the police?' I ask, clutching my glass in my hand in an attempt to conceal the liquid within, and looking up at them with what I hope is wide-eyed innocence.

'Couldn't see owt,' grumbles Liev.

'Doesn't matter, sounds like it's moving away from us,' says Kim.

She's right; the sound of the siren grows quieter until it's no longer audible. Kim exhales.

'It's alright. You know what it's like around here, all the little shits,' says Liev. He taps her hand before picking up his drink. 'Anyway, where were we?'

'We were about to make a toast,' I say.

'Of course,' says Liev. A wide grin stretches across his face, and I count his visible tombstone teeth. All nine of the little buggers. 'To successfully avenging Joe's death.'

'To successfully avenging Joe's death,' I repeat, before taking a generous gulp of my drink. All eyes are on me, and I swear I see a glint of happiness in Liev's as he watches. He takes a big gulp of his own drink, and then we all tuck into our dinners.

It takes seconds. Mere seconds. I don't know what the fuck they used, but it's a matter of seconds before all three start spluttering.

Liev's eyes, so victorious just moments ago, bulge in shock and horror. He dry heaves. Kim retches. Valeriya makes a gargling noise, as if she's drowning on land. All three of their faces turn a delightful puce colour.

'You fucking . . . you fucking little shit,' says Liev. He tries to haul himself up but he's incapable. A thick foam emerges from the corner of his lips, and sweat drips from his brow.

I watch the chaos ensuing before me, keeping my face as neutral as possible.

You don't think I ever really trusted them, do you? I wanted to. Oh God, I wanted to. I ached to trust Kim. But I know them. And people don't change. That's why everyone who contributed to Joe's death needs to go.

And the answer to death isn't more death, I know that much. But I want them gone from the earth. I want their evil exorcised from this town.

'You fucking horrible . . . you horrible girl,' chokes out Kim. She claws at the table, leaving bloody scratch marks across the wood.

'I told you . . . I told you not to trust her,' says Valeriya. Despite choking, her voice is clearer than I've heard it in months, all signs of the dementia Liev told her to fake when he first thought his plan might be possible, gone.

There's a loud bang as Kim's head smashes into the table and she finally stops choking.

'You FUCK!' This from Liev, who reaches across the table for me, before convulsing.

'There's no money left, by the way,' I say. 'I know that's all you ever really wanted. But Callum's is all gone. And mine is all gone, too.'

Liev shakes his thick, purple neck. He has more to say (the man has always had so much to say) but no longer any ability to speak. It's strange, seeing him like this. So human. So vulnerable. For so long, I saw him as a sort of god, someone who had singlehandedly banished the gangs which used to congregate near our house, someone who had ended the spate of vandalism and threats which used to plague us, someone who protected Kim from the terrifying men who would follow her through town. We could overlook the fact that he spent all her money on himself. That he pushed Kim if she said something he didn't agree with. That he'd strike Callum and me with his belt for no reason at all. We turned a blind eye until he became insidious. Evil no longer lurked outside the house. We'd invited it in.

He polluted the bricks and mortar, but also my mind. I blamed Callum's ghost for the abuse I suffered, rather than the monster in front of me.

He gags a couple more times and then he slumps, lifeless, into his poisoned mash.

Valeriya, battle-hardened old bird that she is, clings on the longest. But eventually she too surrenders to death, and falls sideways onto the floor with a satisfying thunk.

After all the noise of earlier – the siren and the shouting, the gagging and choking and swearing – the complete silence which now falls over the kitchen almost unnerves me. I look from Kim to Liev to Valeriya, and exhale. I stab a sausage with my fork and pop it into my mouth, chewing and settling into the peace.

There's a knock at the front door.

I take my time getting up to answer, swallowing the last morsel of meat, taking a drink of water and letting my eyes linger on my three dead relatives. And then I scrape my chair back, stand up and move from the kitchen into the hallway.

A single silhouette is visible through the frosted glass.

I open the door to him, and over the threshold he steps, eyes glinting, a smile twitching at his lips.

'Welcome home,' I say.

'Good to be back,' he replies, nodding his head. 'It is fucking good to be back.'

I follow him down the hallway and into the kitchen. Watch as he shoves Liev from the broken chair and takes his place at the head of the table. I grab fresh glasses from the cabinet and crack open a sealed can of cider from the fridge. I set one glass down in front of him, before sitting in my original seat opposite.

'Nice job with the siren, by the way,' I say.

'Aye, I nicked it a while ago. Dead effective. Sounds like the real thing. Never know when you'll need it. Got lucky with the timing too – kitchen window's at a funny angle, I could see when the plates were put down, but not when you all started eating. Didn't want to leave it too late, like.' He pauses to glance at the three dead bodies who occupy the kitchen with us. 'What are you going to do about them?'

'Kim's fingerprints are on all the cooking utensils. The poison too, wherever that is. Plus she kept diaries hidden away, I found them once when I was a kid. There was never much in them, think she was scared of Liev finding them. But you know – "rib cracked. He pushed me down the stairs again" – that sort of thing.'

'I always thought she was in complete denial. Maybe recording it was her way of proving it was really happening.'

I look at Kim's lifeless body and sigh. 'Who knows? I'm going to leave a couple of her diaries lying around. Frame it like "beaten wife finally has her revenge", you know. I know that isn't what happened. But it's what I'd have liked to happen. And I think, deep down, Kim would have too.'

'Wonder how the hell they thought they were going to get away with it. Killing you and then getting your inheritance, like.'

I shrug. 'Don't think anyone ever said no to Liev. I'm sure he imagined his side of the story would be believed. Besides, I think this has always been Liev's plan. Just something that was destined to go right for him.'

Not wanting to waste any more of my breath on Liev, I turn my attention elsewhere, pushing my plate away and setting three things out on the table in front of me. One is my list of victims, with the warning scribbled on in pointy red handwriting. I open up another of the objects – Joe's yearbook – and flick through to the pages and pages of funny, supportive messages, all written in the same sharp scrawl. 'You wrote all of these, didn't you?' I ask.

A nod is my answer.

'Did Joe see them?'

Another nod. I trail a finger over the messages.

And then I turn to a scrap of paper. It's what happened on the day Joe died. And it's finally correct.

```
                                    FADE IN:
                                    1
INT. TRAIN CARRIAGE - AFTERNOON
  WE OPEN in carriage E of the train from
Edinburgh to London, as it travels between
Newcastle and Darlington. The weather is mild.
ELIZABETH (22) opens a can of cider. She's
drinking too much because she's yet to get over
something that everyone else has already moved
on from. She meets JOE (18) for his birthday
celebration on the banks of the Tees. COURTNEY
(18), DEVLIN (18) and CALLUM (24) are also
in attendance. Courtney and Devlin bully Joe
throughout, finally telling him to climb to
the top of the Transporter Bridge. He does
so, and Callum climbs up after him. Callum
tries and fails to stop Joe from jumping to
his death. Courtney and Devlin run away. JANET
(56) films Joe's death. Marty (47) ignores
Elizabeth's cries for help. Elizabeth tries
in vain to save Joe. And then she tries to
forget.
```

No more forgetting. No more pretending that things were one way when they were another entirely. No more sugar coating. No more lying to other people. No more lying to myself.

'You should write in it.'

'In what?' I ask, refocusing my attention on the present rather than the past.

'In Joe's yearbook.'

There's a pen in my pocket, which I take out now. I remove the lid and bring the book closer to me. I open to a fresh blank page and bring the tip of the pen towards the paper.

I pause. Turn and look at the back door, where I can all too clearly imagine Joe emerging, fresh from an adventure, a curious stone clutched in his hands. He smiles at me, and I try really hard to smile back. I imagine a life in which he didn't have to go hungry for being incapable of meeting Liev's impossible standards. A life in which he moved happily through school, knowing exactly who he would sit next to at lunch. A life in which he was loved plainly, without manipulation or expectation. I imagine a life in which neither of his siblings left him. I imagine Joe as a man: tall and shy and interesting and interested and flawed and sad sometimes and brilliant. I see myself. How lucky I'd have been to know the man. How lucky I was to have known the boy.

I put pen to paper and write thirteen words:

I love you. I miss you. I'm proud of you. I'm sorry. Elizabeth.

A warm, firm hand is placed on top of mine. I look up, tears in my eyes. Flip my palm around and squeeze tight, as tight as I can.

I use my other hand to raise my glass.

'To Joe,' I say.

'To Joe,' repeats my brother.

Acknowledgements

This book is ultimately about siblings, and I'm lucky to have two of the best. Harry and Matthew, I'm grateful for you every day.

I'm grateful too for the rest of my family. My dad, who reads approximately one book a year while eating his breakfast (almost always a book about sheds or a UFC autobiography) but cleared space to read the first draft of this novel – getting it laminated and ring bound and hitting a key twist while waiting at the barbers. Trying to explain to them that he was really enjoying the scruffy looking document in his hands, and probably sounding mad in the process. My mum, who reads considerably more books ('but she doesn't read every word!' I'm sure my dad would say, if allowed to infiltrate this acknowledgement) and whose feedback influenced the ending of this particular tale. My gran, who has read everything I've ever written, and would really, really like it if I wrote something nice for once. Alas.

James, thank you for letting me borrow your name. Hope you enjoyed being a 'bad guy'. The rest of the Sleights, thank you for being fun and supportive relatives.

I'm lucky to have amazing friends who promoted and supported the release of my first book. Your presence and enthusiasm meant a lot to me. Special thanks to Angie, who cast her critical eye over an early copy of this book, and Pippa for sharing her police procedure knowledge.

Paul Telfer – my sixth-form English teacher, who I credit with inspiring a passion for writing which has added so much to my life.

I've spent two decades in Middlesbrough, and it's a place which is incredibly special to me. I wanted to bring it to life in an accurate but heartfelt manner – highlighting the good, but not shying away from the town troubles. Hopefully my fellow Teessiders consider this a job decently done.

Thank you to my agent Amy St Johnston and editor Cara Chimirri, and the wider teams at Embla Books and Aitken Alexander. I still can't believe I actually *have* an agent – especially one as supportive and creative as Amy. And Cara, whose ideas and vision really elevated this book. You deserve all the credit possible.

Finally, thank you to the readers who have taken a punt on either of my books.

About the Author

Charlotte grew up in Middlesbrough, before migrating to London for a more tropical climate, and to work as a terrorism insurance broker. When not telling anyone who will listen how warm it is, or the correct way to pronounce 'bath', she enjoys zhuzhing up the more mundane aspects of being a twenty-something-year-old by putting a fictitious, killer spin on them. Her first book, *It's Not Me It's You*, is available in paperback, audiobook and ebook.

She can be found on Instagram @biglandbooks

About Embla Books

Embla Books is a digital-first publisher of standout commercial adult fiction. Passionate about storytelling, the team at Embla publish books that will make you 'laugh, love, look over your shoulder and lose sleep'. Launched by Bonnier Books UK in 2021, the imprint is named after the first woman from the creation myth in Norse mythology, who was carved by the gods from a tree trunk found on the seashore – an image of the kind of creative work and crafting that writers do, and a symbol of how stories shape our lives.

Find out about some of our other books and stay in touch:

Twitter, Facebook, Instagram: @emblabooks
Newsletter: https://bit.ly/emblanewsletter